BOOK ONE IN THE FIRST EARTH SERIES

THE WHITELIGHT OF TOMORROW

D. PIERCE WILLIAMS

ACKNOWLEDGEMENTS

The White Light of Tomorrow is dedicated to the
memory of Brian E. Palmertree.

I'd never have started this without the support of my parents, John and Betty Williams. Along with them, I am in debt to a number of other people for inspiration, motivation, and support: Sabrina "Sabine" England and Shawn "Cowboy" Heidingsfelder, Jim "Doctor Solar" Kinney, Todd "Mustafa" Boaz, Thomas "How does this spear gun work?" Ayles, and Rita "Sack Full of Pain" Connally. Finally, my friend Jane Ryder provided invaluable mental-health support as well as technical and literary advice of the finest quality.

"*Malice is the universal language. The victorious speak fluently, with confidence, impassioned. The vanquished are shouted down and silenced.*"

—Holy Roman Empress Sophia I

CHAPTER 01

The cagey little girl aimed to kill him.

Good. Death to the nonbeliever.

The dawn's light flickered and sparked on clashing sword blades. Adrian of Tarsus matched his daughter's pace, blocking and parrying beat for beat as she struggled to land a blow. The longer he held her at bay, the angrier and more frustrated she became.

He grinned.

Mariel met his eyes and came at him hard, as though she meant to do real harm. Her blade traced a bright arc, right to left, across his stomach.

A few centimeters short of the mark.

The mighty swing was reckless—an impulse, not a tactic. She lost balance. Lost her guard. Only for a second...

Adrian thrust for her heart, straight and true.

Mariel tried to parry—blade whipping up to meet his—too late.

His sword hovered over her chest, the tip tickling her linen blouse. "You're a girl," he said. "You don't have the reach for that."

Father and daughter. Knight and squire. Teacher and student? Sometimes, when it suited her to listen. They stared at one another atop a seaside ridge, under tiny flakes of snow that swirled in an unsteady breeze. Away down the hillside, slate-grey waves hammered a murky shore of coarse black sand and rock while above them the planet's thin silver ring, just visible through broken clouds, cut the sky in half. Beyond this, past the frontier of Christian space, there was nothing.

Mariel shifted from foot to foot, her body tense. A bead of sweat ran down her brow and reddened cheek to drip from her chin and spatter on the frozen ground. Many men would have seen a victim in waiting.

She narrowed her eyes.

Good girl. Never accept defeat.

"I'm not a girl!" she shouted.

His brow furrowed. His thoughts stumbled.

Her counter-attack came between heartbeats.

She blossomed into a pirouette, knocked his threatening arm aside with the flat of her blade, and spun inside. Her empty hand plucked an unseen stiletto from the crimson sash hugging her waist. Instantly, she poised the assassin's tool beneath his lowest rib and held it one short stroke from his death.

"I'm a woman." She set her jaw with grim determination, grinding her teeth, but her face was lit with pride.

Beautiful. Fast and confident, like a warrior. Despite his long experience, her quickness always surprised him. If she would only develop some accuracy to go with it—*what did she say?*

"A woman?" He asked. "When did this happen?"

"Really, Adrian?" She reproached him with a shake of her head. "A man ought to be able to tell the difference between a girl and a woman. I'm fourteen years old."

"You don't know that. Hell, even I don't know how old you really are."

"Being an orphan has nothing to do with it. Things happen when a woman becomes a woman." She held her head up, chin forward as he'd taught her, though with a slight tremble. "Must I elaborate?"

He looked into her brown eyes. Took in her face. Then stepped back and regarded her, forcing himself to see beyond the child. Yes, there was something different. Something in the way she held herself. Something in the way she looked back at him. "If you're going to lecture on anatomy, do it in Latin. You need the practice."

"Ugh! You can be a right fatherless bastard, sometimes."

"Fatherless, motherless, and penniless by the grace of God." He raised his sword in salute, conceding the match, then sheathed the rapier and pulled a heavy cloak of coarse wool around his shoulders against the damp, saturating cold.

A woman. If only that were the extent of the danger she faced. Maybe it was time to tell her? As an adult she should know what she was up against, no matter how grim. "Mariel…"

She waited for him, cocking her head to one side, then the other. "Adrian…"

"Let's get a Goddamned move on, girl." He picked up his satchel and set off walking. It wasn't the right time, and besides, he might save her today and moot the damn thing. Would save her today. Never accept defeat, remember?

She grabbed her little coat and hat and scrambled behind him as he strode down the hillside. "Add heartless and faithless to your list of faults!" she called out. "Aren't Knights of the Military and Hospitaler Order of Saint John of Jerusalem and Rhodes and Malta and Valetta supposed to be compassionate and full of sympathy?" She chanted the Order's ponderous name in a choirboy's treble singsong.

"You benefit from my compassion and sympathy each time I refrain from boxing your ears. 'Whosoever shall receive one of such children in my name receiveth me, and whosoever shall receive me, receiveth not me but him that sent me.'"

"So, I'm just your means of making friendly with God."

"Don't be silly, love. God doesn't make friendly."

She followed along behind him.

He could feel her thinking about it, contriving to continue their sparring by other means. She was always thinking, dissecting everything he said, pouncing on and slaughtering his sacred cows with girlish mania.

"You're wrong, Adrian. God made the snow, and the stars, and the ocean. He wouldn't have done that if He didn't love us. It's people who are unfriendly."

"Because God loves you doesn't mean He's your friend."

"That's...that's rot. That doesn't even make sense."

"God made the ocean because He loves you, but He'll let you drown in it without so much as lifting a finger."

"Did someone piss in your porridge this morning or are you just turning into a cynical old ba—"

"Look," he cut her off short, desperate to avoid a row, or worse, an early-morning theological debate. "As a woman, you'll require more privacy than our cabin affords, curtain or no." They shared a space aboard the ship barely four meters square with only a peculiar melon-colored damask curtain to separate them. "I'll see if Mustafa will give you Bryan's cabin now that he's gone."

"Oh!" She ran to his side. "Would you do that? I'd be the Lady of the Manor in my own room."

"Indeed, but outside of your room you're still a squire, agreed?"

"Agreed!"

He looked down at her face and saw it return to its normal, creamy complexion despite the icy wind. Mutual smiles sealed their amended compact, and they walked on, silent, while the dirt and clay under their feet gave way to cobblestones.

He'd know soon enough whether he'd succeeded, or failed her again.

As knight and squire approached the ramshackle town grown up around the port, the fresh smell of the sea disappeared, replaced by the seamy tang of animals and compost.

The town of Saint Anthony boasted the tallest church in the struggling little Barony, its steeple visible to travelers kilometers away. It wasn't a true cathedral, but neither was the town truly cosmopolitan—the immovable stone walls, towering spire, and sparkling stained glass windows were more than enough to impress the glory of God on the locals.

"How can you and Mustafa be friends?" Mariel asked, seemingly out of the blue and true to form. There'd be some reason she asked that particular question, perhaps in response to something he said that morning, or last week.

"What do you mean?" Mustafa Ali Pasha was the owner of the *Miranda*, the ship they traveled on, and while a bit odd, and maybe a bit pompous, he was far from unfriendly.

"You two sit up drinking and smoking until late—"

"Wine is restorative, and tobacco palliative."

"You spend hours at chess wearing very serious faces though neither of you is any good at it—"

"Chess or wearing serious faces?"

"And you, Mustafa, and the whole crew tell filthy jokes to each other when you think I can't hear."

"Does that trouble you?"

"Of course not." She rolled her eyes. "What I mean is, how can he tolerate you at all, much less be your friend, when your job is to take his gold for a church that hates him?"

Damn. The day had only just begun and they were already exploring inter-faith politics. What would the conversation over dinner be like? "Mustafa knows that I don't make the law."

"If you did make the law, would you change it?"

"No."

Adrian and his inquisitive squire arrived at the Office of the Assessor of Tithes, a squat brick building with heavy oaken door and narrow windows barred with iron.

He pulled the door open and followed her in, where a wood-fired stove brought the temperature up to something more civilized. How many squires of the Order had doors opened for them by their knights? Only one.

The clerk manning the office looked haggard. "What the hell do you want?" he asked in a dry, scratching voice.

"I'm paying tithe for the *Miranda*." Adrian lifted the flap of his satchel and removed a ledger and a small bag that clinked when he tossed it on the desk. He opened the book to the current date, and turned it to face the clerk.

The Church found it expedient after the last war to put a *Militium Publicanus*—military tax-collector—aboard each large merchant vessel operating in its territory to enforce payment of trade tithes, and the Order of Saint John was tapped to provide trustworthy men. They never retired the practice, such was its efficacy.

Adrian had held the post aboard *Miranda* for nearly four years, and the rare mobility it afforded was his only hope to save Mariel.

"Let's see." The clerk ran a bony finger down the page, his bloodshot eyes telling of a long sleepless night, the liquor still on his breath telling why. "Four of gold and twenty of silver to be paid on two-dozen bolts of silk, two tonnes of fruit...and three-thousand liters of Genovese spirits. Lovely. Who has that?"

"Hadley, I think."

"Old George will have to give some of it up. Taxes, you know."

"Of course." Thieving prick.

"But this *is* the tax," Mariel said.

The clerk raised an eyebrow. "To every thing there is a levy, young lady. And a tithe to every purpose under heaven."

She stepped up to the desk, striking a righteous pose, head held high. "Every man should enjoy the good of all his labor."

The clerk looked over her, to Adrian. "She knows her scripture, at least. Better than I do. Still, that'll be four and twenty from *Miranda*. Say, isn't that the ship run by that sodding Turk?"

"Mustafa Ali Pasha," Adrian said.

"Mustafa Ali Kinderficker, more like. I hope you squeezed him hard."

"He squealed when I showed him the assessment," Adrian lied. Weasels like this clerk were quick to disparage the Saracens because they'd never fought the blackguards. Men who'd held the crumbling walls of a breached fortress against waves of Janissaries tempered their hate with grudging respect.

The clerk put a hairy hand on the bag and pulled it closer. He counted out four gold and twenty silver, then noted the transaction in his own ledger. He dropped the money into a strongbox beside the desk and stamped Adrian's receipt.

They left the office for the center of the grungy town. Adrian strode purposefully, while Mariel jumped and dodged slushy puddles behind him.

What mischief now?

Mustafa's round head, capped with a brazen red fez, was visible from blocks away and as Adrian drew closer he saw that the *Miranda's* cherubic owner and master was dressed up in a purple robe with gold embroidery and a pair of dainty slippers with tassels and curled toes.

Koray Kemal, Mustafa's manservant and purser, accompanied him. A short, skinny stalk with a dried apricot for a head, his black eyes squinted and he scowled in a way that made him appear permanently constipated. He was an unexpected sight, as he rarely left the ship, and was wholly useless.

The Turks stood in the road engaged in a fierce argument. Mustafa pounded a finger into his palm and unleashed a torrent of foreign bluster while Koray shook his head, arms folded on his chest, chin up in defiance.

"What are they fighting about?" Mariel asked.

"Who knows?"

"And why are they all dressed up?"

"Maybe it's a Muslim holy day."

"It isn't."

He stopped and produced a silver quattro from his purse and started to break it in two, then relented and handed the whole coin to her. "Buy yourself something, but be back aboard the ship in an hour. And no more damned holographic butterflies and ladybirds—your menagerie is full." With a pat on the back, he scooted her off to shopping.

His eyes returned to Mustafa who by now had seen him and was gesturing to gain his attention, along with that of everyone else in the street. Adrian skirted the half-frozen mud to meet them by a shabby-looking pub whose shingle promoted it as The Sprung Bung.

"Brother Adrian," Mustafa said, raising his arms in greeting, "how good of you to arrive at just the right time. Do you remember William Easley?"

"The crook who sold you a thousand liters of vinegar?" Adrian's mouth puckered at the thought of the terrible, bitter wine Mustafa once bought from the liar and third-rate middleman William Easley.

"It was Riesling, Adrian, and he's in the dry goods business now. I had a message from him, and it seems that he's brokering something unusual and wants me to take a look."

"I pray that 'unusual' means profitable." He laid on some scorn, enough to appear suitably reluctant.

"Heaven smiled upon me when it provided a tax man with an appetite for graft. If we're lucky, it'll be a relic."

"Not this again." He looked down on Mustafa.

"Adrian my dear, don't worry. I'm not going to buy *Machina Infernus* and get us all, but especially myself, burned at the stake. You keep ledgers. You know what I made off that damned fruit—I was lucky to break even, and that's down to the liquor. I don't want to think about that wasted trip to Rota. A relic will easily put me back in the black, and line your purse as well, eh?"

"Do you really think something valuable will turn up here, in this sewer?" Adrian pointed to a pile of frost-covered horse dung in the road.

"I'd tell you to have some faith, but the irony would start me laughing. Ha!"

Mustafa's dream of getting rich off the black-market relic trade irritated Adrian's conscience at the same time it served his increasingly desperate purpose.

"Is he here?" Adrian jabbed his thumb at the pub's door.

"No. Come with me to his shop, will you?"

"Afraid to wade through the sea of pork by yourselves?"

"Doing so could undermine my plan to enter Paradise."

"Right." Adrian shook his head. "After four days in this town I'm tempted to adopt the Muslim view of pigs."

"I'll convert you eventually, if only because our Empire smells better than Christendom." Mustafa prodded the group into moving. "Cross the market, that way." The Turk pointed Adrian in the general direction of Easley's shop.

"Christ would have my bollocks if I converted to your heathen ways."

"Is that what your Bible promises to apostates?" Mustafa nearly slipped in the muck.

"The line for confession would be longer if it did." Adrian held up a hand and mimicked a pair of shears with his fingers, aware that Mustafa, following behind, couldn't see his facetious grin.

"An appeal to the prurient interest is a far better motivator, Adrian. The Heaven that awaits me is filled with plump virgins who'll rub me down with olive oil and feed me figs." The crowd grew thicker, and Mustafa stayed close behind Adrian's shoulders.

"I thought you fancied young Greek boys?"

"Who do you think the plump virgins are, my dear? But I resent your implication—if a boy be hung well enough for me, he's as good as a man." The Turk sniffed. "Truly, though, I fancy everyone. I will only enjoy this life's pleasures once, so I will enjoy them all in equal measure."

"I suppose I lack your capacity to generalize. I'll have to make do with women, wine, and an occasional brawl over their ownership."

"Adrian, someday I want to know the real story of how you wound up in the cloth. I know shit when I hear it and your talk of faith and duty is just that."

Adrian hesitated to offer a riposte. A few years ago he'd have met such an impertinent comment with anger. Now, though? "Hmm. The truth is a tale replete with perverse sex and bloody violence. You'd love it, but I shan't say more as the thought of arousing you leaves me uneasy in the stomach."

The stalls of the open-air market overflowed with farmers and butchers selling everything from Berkshires by the hundred-head to spicy pig's-ear sandwiches. Mingling with the bacon, merchants peddling an array of oddments competed for loose coin. Leather goods, a brazier's wares, and produce of questionable freshness were all for sale. An ancient woman peddled caramel-dipped apples for one copper bit each next to a Catalan potter with a selection of *caganer* among his wares.

"There, the shop just past that tanner." Mustafa pointed.

W. Easley & Co. Hardware, the sign above the door announced, with a hammer painted below for the illiterate.

They wove their way through the throng of people, Mustafa deftly avoiding stray lumps of trimmed fat that had fallen into the street while Adrian kept women selling links of raw, ferociously spiced sausage at arm's length.

The front room of the dry-goods shop was packed with items for the local laborer, from awls to wheelbarrows, and there was barely enough room to walk between the rows of precariously stacked stuff. An aroma of builder's lime and cedar wafted over everything, but missing was one William Easley.

The floor creaked with each step as Adrian ducked under low ceiling beams and walked to the back of the long room, to a door standing ajar.

"Easley." Adrian called the name with military force, turning it into a summons. When no one answered, he pushed the door open and stepped through.

A few well-used boxes and barrels. A feeble oil lamp. Dirt floor. A stock room.

Two shady men stood in front of a scarred old crate. Both were young, with ruddy skin and long black hair pulled back in braids. Adrian guessed they were Bulgars, though their clothes were plain, cut in the style of Imperial merchants. Small-swords hung from their belts. The type of light blade was favored for dueling and self-defense in areas more urban than this. Most important, though, the Bulgars stood flat on their feet, unprepared.

The crate itself was rather larger than Adrian had expected. A strange thought, it occurred to him, as he had only the vaguest idea of the contents.

Still, everything confirmed the rumor he'd picked up on Acre: a pair of Easterners with an Apex relic carefully avoiding the larger cities where Papal law was more strictly enforced. Problem was, few people out on the fringe could afford a true relic and Gereon was scraping the bottom of the barrel. But they were here, and in the box might be—*would* be—another box, ancient, with five letters machined into its metallic top: ASCNT. The letters had been in Adrian's head every day for the past decade, since the day he'd found Mariel, and he still didn't know what they meant.

He heard Mustafa's slipper-clad feet enter behind him. He stood close to the strangers, close enough to draw and strike either in one motion and likely have time to kill the other before any defense could be mounted. He made a note to mind the ceiling if it came to that—low lines of attack would be necessary.

"*Merhaba*, gentlemen," Mustafa said, smiling.

The first Bulgar looked at Mustafa, then Adrian, seemingly perplexed by the unlikely pairing.

"I am Mustafa." The Turk strode up to the strangers, arms held in front with palms opened as if to show he had nothing up his sleeves.

Adrian felt the first icy tickle of adrenaline. All Mustafa had to do was make the deal. Don't bugger it up.

"Easley said to meet here." The shorter Bulgar spoke, his accent thick. "He said he found the buyer. Are you the buyer?"

"How awkward," Mustafa said. "Buyers and sellers present but no broker to smooth the way. When I find Easley, we'll have a talk about the etiquette of business. How may I address you?"

"I am Gavril," the Bulgar said. He nodded at his partner. "And he is Mladen."

Adrian silently willed Mustafa to get down to business, when a new voice broke in.

Strident.

Behind them.

"If his name is Gavril, mine is Saint Cecilia!"

Armed men swept into the room.

Four.

Swords at the ready.

Adrian recognized them as *Landsknecht*. Expensive, battle-hardened mercenaries from the Holy Roman Empire rarely seen in fiefs, such as Gereon, held in escheat by the Pope. They moved quietly in soft boots and light leather armor, deploying without speaking. Unlike the Bulgars, the Landser were taut and ready to act. The state of their gear told of frequent use and careful repair.

Damn it. Adrian turned his body slightly—geometry was crucial to swordplay. His reflexive movement created the best angles possible against the mercenaries.

A little goat of a man followed the Landser. Comically short, he carried himself with the gravity of a titan and dressed like a rake in tight black breeches and Spanish doublet of gold brocade. He looked Adrian and Mustafa over. "Why am I not surprised to see a Saracen and a Templar huddling together in a dark room?"

Templar. Only the Inquisition referred to the Knights Hospitaler as Templars, an insult from the early days of the Church and a sign of the intense rivalry between the two devout groups. This little ass looked more like a dainty altar boy than an Inquisitor, but the agents of the Holy Office were many and varied. Still, they'd never hire *Landsknecht*—the German mercenaries were too closely associated with the Roman Emperor to be considered reliable.

Mustafa covered his anxiety with a smile. "Well then, are you here to bid on the item as well? May we know your name?"

"You can call me Girard." The little man nodded at one of the Landser, who dumped the contents of a burlap sack onto the floor. A round object hit the ground with a sick thunk, and wobbled between Adrian and Mustafa before coming to a lazy stop. A face looked up at the men with cloudy eyes in battered orbits. Its smashed mouth hung half open and a trickle of blood seeped from the roughly hewn neck to drip from dangling bits of spine and throat.

"Easley." Mustafa croaked. He rubbed his hands and stared at the head.

Adrian blinked. In the years he'd spent fighting in the last war he'd seen atrocities, but this was the first time he'd seen one so completely...ludicrous, and without context. Girard was insane, or worse, a true Inquisitor.

Adrian focused on the mercenary nearest him, playing out the next few seconds in his head.

Girard looked at the crate. "I'm taking that, and I'm afraid there can be no witnesses."

"Surely we can come to more equitable terms?" Mustafa asked. He held up a finger. "For example, we could just leave and forget about all this."

Adrian clenched his fist. Like hell they would. The only way he was leaving was with the crate. Seizing the initiative would even the odds a bit.

Girard cocked his head and stared at Mustafa. "You don't know what's in there, do you?"

"In truth, no." Mustafa shrugged.

Girard laughed. "You poor sods. You picked the worst possible day to stick your noses in here."

The Landser were sprung as tight as bear traps—each kept one eye on Girard, anticipating a signal.

The Bulgars inched toward the back door while Koray stood resolute by Mustafa.

A sharp rasp and Adrian's rapier cleared the scabbard.

Cut an arc through space.

The point aligned with the nearest Landser's heart.

With a powerful lunge, Adrian thrust the tip deep into the mercenary's chest. He pushed several centimeters of red steel through the man's back, stopping just as Girard gave his signal to attack.

He wrenched his rapier out of the Landser's chest. The last beats of his victim's bisected heart pumped a sputtering jet of blood into the air.

Steel flashed in at him from the left. Failing to heed the low ceiling, the swordsman aimed at the junction of Adrian's neck and shoulder. His blade hit a beam, lodging itself deep in the wood.

Adrian gutted him, and a dark, pungent mix of liquids spilled out onto the floor.

A man screamed somewhere to his right, but Adrian couldn't spare the time to look. High-pitched. Koray or Mustafa?

A strong odor of rusting iron reached his nose.

Girard pressed an attack straight in, aiming for the center of Adrian's chest.

Parry or die.

Adrian thrust his sword arm up across his body with all his strength. The combat almost ended there.

Swords chimed on contact.

With a tremendous effort, he forced Girard's shining point up away from his heart and over his shoulder. Not quite enough. The sword penetrated flesh and lit him up with searing pain. Enraged, he shoved Girard back bodily.

The smaller man could do nothing but backpedal against Adrian's arm. Girard stumbled over Easley's blood-slicked head and fell to the floor.

Adrian stood over Girard like a falcon looking down on a rabbit, but he couldn't complete the kill before another mercenary charged. He sprang back to avoid the rush, put his boot out and tripped the man, who sailed by and landed flat on his chest.

Girard was back on his feet quickly.

Snapping back to guard, Adrian and Girard presented blades simultaneously. A series of expert attacks, parries and ripostes allowed Adrian crucial time to learn his rival: fine technique, and fast, but a slave to cadence. Girard wanted to play at a strict *vivace* pace, and each time he was parried he offered the same predictable, frustrated riposte.

Another attack threatened. Adrian sensed that the Landser he'd tripped was back up, maneuvering behind him.

Girard smirked.

Attacks would come from two sides at once.

The pincers moved to strike. Adrian turned his body to present the thinnest profile. He parried Girard's weapon to one side, leaning into it as the point passed. He sucked in his stomach to allow the mercenary's sharp edge to pass on the other side, scraping his leather jerkin as it slid by.

From between the two swords Adrian swung his arm around, slamming the pommel of his rapier into the Landser's forehead, cracking his skull.

Adrian and Girard took up guard against each other yet again, and Girard attacked quickly and eagerly. This time, instead of offering the expected parry, Adrian dropped his blade under and around Girard's, and with a semicircular turn of his wrist, pointed the opposing weapon harmlessly away. Seizing control of the inside line, he set up a counter attack. He forced his blade straight down the length of Girard's, metal rasping on metal, until the tip pointed obliquely at the little man's right breast. A powerful thrust backed by a shout and the killing point struck a rib bone, cracking it audibly, before penetrating several centimeters into Girard's lung and glancing off his spine.

Never linger over a kill. The temptation was always to savor the victory, an indulgence that often proved fatal. Adrian turned and took up a new guard, but faced only silence.

He looked around and took in the grisly scene. Seven men lay on the rough wood floorboards. He saw a skinny body slumped over a dead mercenary.

Koray.

One of the Bulgars lay dead nearby, but the shop's back door was open and it seemed that the second had escaped. The crate remained.

"Koray?" Mustafa stood and steadied himself.

Adrian walked over to the body, face down in a nasty pool of fluids, and turned it over. The acidic smell of escaped gastric juice was nauseating. He turned to Mustafa and shook his head.

The Turk stared.

Adrian read confusion on his face, then detached curiosity that quickly crumbled into revulsion.

While Mustafa recovered, Adrian stood over Girard's body.

Son of a bitch. Hot anger finally overcame the cold adrenaline of the fight. He drove his boot into the corpse's gut.

Then again.

Adrian retrieved his cloak from the floor and wrapped it around himself. "Wipe your face off and turn your robe inside out. We don't want to look as if we've walked out of a slaughterhouse."

Adrian and Mustafa carried the crate down a wide, crowded street at a brisk pace.

"Don't run," Mustafa said.

"I'm not running."

"You're walking so fast that *I* have to run. It looks suspicious." The tassel hanging from the Turk's fez slapped him on the side of his round head.

"You always look suspicious. Especially in that damned hat." They each grasped the crate by a rope handle, and Mustafa was indeed jogging to match his stride. Adrian's body was electrified in the wake of the adrenaline storm he'd just experienced. He forced his legs to slow to an easy walk as they pushed through the crowd near the landing.

The mass of dock hands and lumpers parted, allowing the two men to pass through their ranks and into the shadow of the *Miranda*. The ancient transport, thick and curvaceous, sat in a clearing with her loading ramp hanging open underneath, looking like the mouth of a bottom-feeding fish.

Lars Thoresson, the boatswain, stood on the ramp smoking his characteristic meerschaum pipe. He shouted at his mate, Gilly Preston, and pointed at a set of small, muddy footprints that tracked up the otherwise spotless steel and into the ship.

A sure sign Mariel was aboard.

Adrian and Mustafa hauled their cargo up the ramp, the surprised boatswain and his mate following close behind them.

Mustafa pounded his fist on the red button that raised the ramp and staggered, sucking for breath, to an intercom box on the wall.

"Nezumi!" he shouted into the box.

"Here, chief," a voice said, buzzing out of the intercom.

"Take off at once."

"Where to, chief?"

"Orbit!"

The ramp slammed shut with a boom that reverberated around the cargo bay. A green light blinked on above the actuator, confirming the door closed and the pressure seal engaged. Mustafa slumped to the floor.

"Aye, liftoff in five," came the calm reply.

Adrian turned to the boatswain. "Lars, is Mariel on board?"

"Yes. Everyone but Koray is. Are we not waiting for him?"

The *Miranda* shuddered under the power of her main engines. The ship vibrated, roughly at first, but the grind smoothed out as the temperature of the thrusters rose. A pulsing tone played over the intercom, warning all aboard that liftoff was imminent.

"Koray's dead. Let's get Mustafa to the flight deck," Adrian said.

Mustafa gasped. He was too winded to move.

They each threw one of his arms over their shoulders and manhandled him forward, through the galley and along the gangway that led to the flight deck. Together they shoved him into a chair and pulled the five-point harness tight around his shoulders and waist, then strapped into their own seats. Liftoff and ascent were often rough. Best to be cinched down tightly or one risked a dangerous toss about the ship.

Nezumi, the diminutive Oryantal pilot, sat at the controls with the engineer, Bernt, at his station behind, studying the ship's status displays.

"Nav is okay, engine *ein* okay, engine *zwei*...fucked." The Bavarian engineer had a binary personality for which everything existed in one of two states: okay or fucked. "A cold start on two, hold ten percent throttle until intercooler temperature is two-five-zero, okay, okay she will fly."

"Lifting off," Nezumi said. The thrust vector set at 80 degrees and the automatic stability control slaved to the delicate gyros of the inertial navigation platform, she would jump into the air with a rate of ascent of five meters per second and enough forward speed to clear the landing field crisply before turning out over the sea. He advanced the throttle, and with an awful groan swallowed whole by the wail of the engines, the *Miranda* took flight.

Adrian watched Gereon fall away below them before the ship's nose pitched up and they rocketed skyward.

CHAPTER 02

Damn these shoes.

Sabine Adler worked her way down the narrow back staircase from her apartment on the third floor to her pub's kitchen at street level. The hard leather of her new shoes dug into her feet, pinching and scraping. She winced with every step.

The damn things were fit only for princesses who never had to stand, much less walk.

Making things worse, the smells of savory roast beef and ham filled the air and set her stomach grumbling.

Ruth, her plump, grey-haired cook, stood over a cast iron pot full of bubbling gravy.

"Are we ready for evening meal?" Sabine asked. She hardly needed to—her ladies were hard-working and mostly trustworthy.

"Sure as sunshine, Miss," Ruth replied in her heavy brogue.

The cook's two assistants worked on peeling an enormous pile of potatoes, preparing to roast them.

Sabine inspected the ingredients: garlic, rosemary, olive oil. "Don't skimp on the garlic." She smiled at Lara, a young girl recently hired, and gave her a playful elbow in the side. "Serve our hungry family food with plenty of flavor."

"Yes, Miss. Pile in the garlic."

Sabine's stomach growled loud enough to be heard over the kitchen noise.

"Let me make you a sandwich to take along," Ruth said.

"No. I'm already late, and there'll be so much food at Lucas' party that I'll likely gain a stone before midnight."

"You could use a stone, maybe two." Ruth slapped herself on the rear. "Men want women they can take hold of."

The assistant cooks giggled.

Sabine looked down at herself. Nonsense. Her figure was curvy enough for a woman who barely reached one hundred sixty centimeters, and that standing on her toes. "Don't start, Ruth. Not tonight."

"Then come here, Miss Blue-Eyes, and let me have a look at you." Ruth waved her over.

"Do I look all right?" Sabine turned once around. She wore a pale pink dress with lace sleeves, white stockings, and little white shoes with a raised heel playing the devil with her balance. She'd twirled her rich blonde hair up into a bun on the back of her head, and her face was dusted ever-so-lightly with a fine white powder.

"I wish you'd let that golden hair down on your shoulders, Miss, you'd look like an angel. And it's a Goddamned shame you're going out for business and not to capture a man and drag him back here."

"I said not tonight."

The cook shook her head. "If not tonight, when?"

Ruth wasn't a subtle woman, and lately had taken to reminding her employer that she was thirty years old and unwed. That the Bee's Knees pub made Sabine a living without the bother of a man never entered into it.

Sabine took a bottle of clear liquor from a cabinet. She sat on a stool and kicked off her infernal shoes, poured alcohol into both of them, sloshed it around, and put them back on.

The cooks stared.

"It makes the leather stretch," Sabine said. She bounced up and down on her toes to force the issue.

Before walking out into the dark-paneled dining room, she checked the large kegs sitting on wooden trestles near the door. There were three choices: red ale bursting with hops, a cloudy, lightly sweet *hefeweizen*, and a thick dark lager whose hint of chocolate was agreed by most to be very satisfactory.

She took a pewter mug from a rack and held it under the tap, filling it halfway with cool ale. The acerbic smell of the double-hopped brew tweaked her nose before she tilted her head back and drank it down.

Her feet felt better already.

Out in the pub, the softly-lit main room was beginning to fill with locals eager to wet their tongues and fill their bellies.

The Bee occupied two floors on the corner of an old timber-framed complex with charming Tudor jetties and a lush courtyard nearly invisible to the casual passersby. Her patrons treated the venerable establishment as a second home. They took care of it, and regulars were quick to encourage drunks and troublemakers to take their problems elsewhere.

She looked around the room, proud. When she moved from the Imperial world of Frisia six years earlier, she carried her whole fortune in one small purse. Now, she had something of value. Not the building, but the people—friends, many of whom returned every night.

She greeted a few of her regulars on the way out, then passed through the pale yellow doors, propped open to welcome the late-summer breeze. At the street corner she raised a white-gloved hand to hail a two-wheeled black carriage.

The coachman reined in his horse, jumped down to the street, and held the door for her, but she refused his offered hand and climbed inside on her own.

"Via Veneto, please, at Sebastian Square," she said.

"Aye, Miss." The crack of the whip launched them eastward toward the heart of the city.

Civitate Dei. Four-hundred thousand faithful Christians, thirty-five live births a day, thirteen natural deaths, one God.

Christendom's largest city crowned a high plateau. Backed by an idyllic blue-green mountain range to the north, the city overlooked a broad coastal plain that rolled out like a carpet down to a distant ocean.

Looking out the carriage window, Sabine could see the ground rise up. On top of the plateau, surrounded by the great metropolis but standing apart and above, was the walled district known as the Old City. Once the seat of the colonial government overseeing the planet now called Bethany, the Old City was the corrugated alloy heart of the human apparatus that terraformed the planet. At the center, visible for miles around, the shining spire of Saint Mary's Cathedral stood like a blade held aloft.

Enveloping the central citadel in a vast stone and timber ring was the New City. Chaotic, organic, it housed the inns and taverns, shops and brothels that served the needs of the clergy and their attendants. Beyond that whitewashed ring, the many neighborhoods of the laity. Some of these precincts were affluent, most were poor, and each operated like a little outpost on its own secluded island.

The carriage rolled into a large square. Lost in her thoughts, Sabine had failed to tell the driver to go around.

Damn.

The people called this Heretic's Square. Officially, it was Saint George's.

In the evening light Sabine could see the long wooden scaffold erected atop a stone foundation. Built to stand the test of time, as many as ten people could hang at once. Today was Monday, the day when sentences on the condemned were traditionally carried out, and the scaffold wasn't empty.

Three bodies swayed at the end of taut ropes, flies swarming. Black sacks covered the heads of the executed, but Sabine could tell that two men and a woman had met their ends here earlier. They might have been murderers or thieves, but odds were even they were heretics, convicted by the Inquisitorial Court of crimes against the faith.

Anger welled up in her heart. What did these wretches do? Were they caught with some forbidden scrap of technology? Did the wrong person overhear a critical word about the Holy See? Or were they just common criminals after all?

At least it was a hanging, and not a burning.

Sabine's driver reined in his horse and brought the carriage to an easy stop at Via Veneto, where the street began across from Sebastian Square in the city's wealthiest neighborhood. She opened the door and jumped out before he could climb down and help her, then handed him a pair of silver quattros. He tipped his hat and set off to circle the square looking for a new passenger.

It was early in the evening, the sun still well above the horizon. The sound of a lively quartet in E-flat major wafted down the street. She knew the piece. Composed before the Advent, it was called *The Joke* because its playful stops and starts tricked the audience into applauding several times before the real ending came.

She waved her hand in time. As she approached the house, first one, then another false ending was played. There was silence while the audience hesitated, expecting another trick, before breaking into applause and laughter.

She stared up at the mansion, taking in its huge dimensions, the sand-colored stucco and the red clay roof tiles. The architecture was splendid, the proportions perfect. It could house a hundred people in luxury with plenty of room for all.

Lucas was a trader, a go-between with his fingers in many pies. Among his holdings were several breweries that supplied the Bee, so no one found it unusual for Miss Adler to attend his parties. She climbed the steps to the waiting doorman.

"Good evening, Juan," she said to the muscular man at the door.

"Good evening, Miss. Nice to see you again." He waved a wand-like threat detector in front of her with a quick swipe. The tip of the tool lit up green, and he opened the door. "Enjoy the party."

The quartet struck up a new tune as she entered, and the parquet dance floor filled with couples eager to do the *volta*. The athletic dance called for men to lift their ladies into the air as they spun around, and was best done early, before the wine decanters were drained.

She drifted around the edge of the floor, mingling with Lucas' other guests, many of whom she knew and exchanged pleasantries with, while looking for the host.

Sir Reymont Lucas was one of her best customers. Like many of the wealthy—including many of the clergy—he coveted relics of ancient technology and competed with his peers in secret to build the most impressive collection.

As a broker of such illicit goods, she was only too happy to enable his hoarding.

A flash of crimson caught her eye, and she found him. His partner in the *volta* was a fetching young brunette who turned, stepped, and jumped effortlessly in time with the music. The woman couldn't have been more than twenty, her charms fixed on Lucas, who was a widower at least thirty years her senior. Sabine felt oddly embarrassed watching the stranger press close against him during the three-quarter turn, and rub his face with her breasts when he boosted her into the air on the third beat.

Sabine didn't know the woman, which was strange in itself. She studied people with money and power in the city, and this newcomer was a mystery. More puzzling was that her appearance gave no clue where she came from. Without any notable heredi-tary traits, she was attractive in the sense that, from her tapered waist to the flowing scroll of her neckline, everything about her was correct. The state of perfect balance carried to her face, where her delicate features combined to form the most properly aligned of all possible visages. And yet, she fell just short of beautiful.

Lucas looked funny next to her. Silesian, and a little short of height, he was stocky, built thick but powerful. Sabine had always thought that he looked like an Imperial *Jaeger*, and indeed horse-back riding and hunting were among his passions.

The music ended, the dancers bowed and curtsied, and the young lady gave Lucas a deep, long, open-mouthed kiss that lin-gered for far too long. Taking him by the arm, she led him to the side, took a cup of wine from a serving tray and handed it to him.

He swallowed it in one gulp.

Sabine approached the pair. Lucas' face was flushed, and a little sweat ran down his brow. His companion had certainly worked him up.

"Sabine. I'm happy you came," Lucas said.

"Thank you for inviting me."

"It wouldn't be a party without you. Sabine Adler, meet Lady Alisa Conti, the charming niece of Archbishop Conti of Levant."

"My lady." Sabine curtsied and received a hazy stare in return. Lady Conti had the most perfect skin she had ever seen. Without a hint of powder or paint, she showed not the slightest blemish. Her smile was broad and inviting, but her eyes were lifeless, like colored glass.

"Miss Adler, it's a pleasure to meet another friend of Reymont's," the young woman said. "I myself have only known him a short time, but we have become very attached to one another."

"He's quite an endearing character." Sabine looked at Lucas sideways. She needed to pry him away and into his private office before sunset. "Sir Reymont, could I impose on you for just a moment, to discuss a special delivery?"

"Of course."

Sabine turned to Lady Conti. "I'm so sorry to interrupt, my lady, but I need something special for a wedding party tomorrow."

"Alisa, will you excuse us for a few moments to talk a little business?"

"Of course, Reymont. Here." She took his cup and refilled it from a decanter. "Take some wine with you."

"Thank you, my dear." He drained half of it immediately.

"Don't make me wait long," she said.

Lucas followed Sabine through a gilded door into a side chamber with a vast desk and plush chairs. One of his men,

Lorenzo Bruno, followed them in and shut the door, muffling the noise of the party outside.

Lucas held a chair for her, then sat down behind the desk. "I don't know who Archbishop Conti is, but I thank him for sending that ripe young lady to visit the City of God."

"You know she's after something." Sabine shook her finger at him.

"Yes, she's already let slip her interest in what she called archaeology. I'm enjoying her attentions, though, so I'll play coy for a while."

"Is she buying or selling?"

He chuckled. "Are you worried about her encroaching on your territory?"

"From what I just saw, I'd say she's staking a claim on *someone's* territory."

"I wouldn't mind that at all."

"Reymont, are you ill?" He looked pained. Her concern was genuine. After she had made it clear that roaming hands and lecherous advances would not be tolerated they had become friends, sharing interests in music, wine, and banned technology.

"No, no. It's just a bit warm out there." He wiped his forehead with his sleeve. "What have you brought me?"

She stuck her fingers in the small purse she carried and withdrew a silver rectangle only two centimeters long and very thin. Unknown to Lucas or his man, she also withdrew a little disc, a few millimeters wide, which stuck to her finger.

She slid the silver object across the desk to Lucas, and while both men were distracted, pressed the bug under the edge of the desk.

"I have DNA drives already. Why do I want this one?"

"You'll like what's on it."

Taking a key from his waistcoat pocket, he opened a desk drawer and removed a razor-thin translucent screen and held it close to the little aluminum ingot. It lit up, displaying the data stored on the nucleotide chains inside the drive. "Hmm."

"Over one-thousand," she said, "all in English. Some have translations in Spanish, French, or German."

"*The Tempest.*"

"Among others. I enjoyed *At the Mountains of Madness.*"

"You made a copy?" He raised an eyebrow.

"No, it would dilute the value. This is one of a kind. I'll admit that I read several of them."

"Price?"

"Ten of gold."

"Far too high." He laughed and pushed the drive back across the desk.

"Tomorrow it'll be fifteen, and I'll sell it before sunset. The checksums will show that these were downloaded from the World Library. They're complete, original texts. Ten or you lose them."

"Eight."

"Ten."

He tapped his finger and looked at the device. "You win." He threw his hands up and went back into the desk drawer, rummaging. He took out an ingot and pushed it to her.

"A pleasure doing business with you, Sir Reymont." The gold secured, she stood, straightened her dress, and walked to the door where Juan let her back out into the party. Lady Conti was waiting with another cup of wine in her hand for Lucas.

"May I have my Reymont back now?" the young lady asked with a wide smile.

"As you wish, my lady."

Her business finished, Sabine wandered to a serving tray, took a cup for herself and watched the salacious couple on the floor. Reymont was slowing down as the evening went on. The poor man's body would pay for this for days to come.

Her gaze wandered around the room, focusing here and there on people that she knew. Sitting in a deeply padded chair watching the dancers was crusty old Archbishop Maturin. The arch-fornicator was Metropolitan of the local diocese and administrator of the City of God. Also present were Lord and Lady Huygens, a rich, pretty couple who were popular among the young genteels. Their secret—that they were brother and sister—had not yet been revealed publicly and was a potentially productive bit of intelligence that Sabine held close.

She sipped her wine and skirted the dance floor. The white wine was chilled, with hints of pear and apple but a little over-dry for her taste. As she sorted out the flavors, she saw the man she had come to observe.

Selim Bey was the Ottoman Ambassador to the Holy See. The last war between Christians and Muslims lasted forty years, and ended only eight years ago with a treaty that did little more than suspend hostilities, allowing Christian armies to regroup and replace heavy losses while the Ottomans turned their full might to repelling a fierce invasion from the Golden Khanate. The treaty called for an exchange of ambassadors so each side could more effectively spy on the other, and the urbane Selim Bey had held the office for a year, appointed by the new Sultan, Osman VI.

He appeared just when Sabine expected him, about half an hour past sunset, after evening prayers in the Muslim enclave. Two attendants, his Janissary bodyguards, followed him. They were not large men and so didn't draw attention, but they would be experts with the *jambiyas*—made with blades of bone to evade threat detectors—hidden in their robes. She recognized one of the men as the captain of the guard himself, the loathsome Serhan Kaş.

The Ambassador was tall and dark, with a meticulously groomed mustache and deep eyes that penetrated everything they fell on. He wore a dark green robe, quite elegant, trimmed with just a splash of gold and tailored to accentuate his athletic body. Atop his head was the traditional fez, with a starburst insignia in gold signifying his status as a member of the *Divan*, the elite council of advisors closest to the Sultan.

She held back, hoping she wouldn't catch his eye.

Lucas was with Lady Conti on the floor, and one of his men walked up and whispered in his ear. He excused himself and met the Ambassador with warm smiles and handshakes.

Very friendly. But who held the winning hand in this game?

Sabine watched them enter Lucas' office, then she took a seat in a darker alcove that was almost quiet. A man in a sky blue doublet sat nearby, head down. At first she thought he might be dead, but his chest moved slowly up and down. Red stains in his white beard gave away the cause of his slumber. She took a little object from inside her glove and put it in her ear, where it disappeared against her delicate pink skin.

There was a bit of electrical static and some muffled noise as the men sat down and the door closed behind them. Designed to enhance sound in the vocal range while filtering background noise, the device was adaptive and took a moment to stabilize.

"His Majesty grows impatient for a response to the generous offer he has extended," the Ambassador said.

Yes. Lucas was heavily invested in the Ottoman trade routes, but what was his relationship with the Sultan?

"I don't wish to keep the Sultan waiting, but I cannot agree to the proposal as it stands." There was a short silence, and Lucas continued. "I'll pay the agreed five thousand in gold for exclusive access to the ports, but I must have five years of exemption from all fees and tariffs. I want to *own* those ports for five years."

Sabine's hand gripped the arm of her chair. Five thousand in gold. A massive sum, a large part of Lucas' fortune, and an influx that could tip the balance of the war with the Khanate if it ever wound up in Osman's treasury. It couldn't be allowed to happen.

"You walk a dangerous path, Sir Reymont Lucas. His Majesty might consider your conditions an insult, an affront to his generosity."

"Not at all Ambassador," Lucas said smoothly. "This is business. I have something the Sultan needs, but in exchange he can only offer something that I want. In these circumstances it's inevitable that I'll get the better end of the bargain, but does that really matter?"

"Am I to understand that if we agree to five years' exemption, this business will be concluded?"

"Yes," Lucas said without hesitation.

Damn. Five thousand set to be dumped into the Sultan's war chest. Was it too late to stop?

"Very well. You'll have an answer within the month, but I suggest you prepare the gold for shipment."

"Wonderful, Ambassador. Truly wonderful."

There was a ripple of sound in her ear as the men stood. She looked across the room, saw the office door open, and noted that Lady Conti was waiting nearby. The Ambassador and his men exited, followed by Lucas, whom the lady handed a cup of wine. Could she be any more obvious?

With them outside the office, the transmitter could only just pick up their conversation.

"Alisa, I regret that I may not be able to dance again. I feel rather poor."

"Nonsense, Reymont, one more dance and then I'll put you down for the night." She pressed her open mouth to his again.

Naive. Whatever reputation this Conti woman possessed wouldn't last long. If she believed that what happened on Bethany wouldn't find its way back to Levant, she was mistaken.

"I suppose I have another in me," Lucas said.

Lady Conti took his arm and led him back to the floor.

Sabine watched. Lucas was slow, almost stumbling, and unable to keep time with the music. Lady Conti didn't seem to care as she pushed him around the floor.

Something was wrong. Sabine started to push through the crowd towards the dancers. Was the Conti girl too stupid to see that he was exhausted, or...?

The music ended. Lucas dropped to his knees, chest heaving, arms reaching out for something to hold. Several guests came to their host's aid, pushing Lady Conti aside.

She didn't resist and fell back into the crowd.

Lucas drew a long, labored breath, then another, then convulsed as his chest made one final, desperate, attempt to pull sustenance into his lungs. He fell over onto his face. Dead.

Sabine stood shocked, searching the crowd for Alisa Conti, but the crimson dress was gone. Then her eyes met those of Selim Bey.

He stared directly at her from the opposite side of the room, cold, judicious, then his lip curled up into a hint of a smile. He nodded at her before he and his men made for the door.

Did he...did he just make her for an assassin?

Bloody hell.

CHAPTER 03

Adrian enjoyed a few seconds of near-weightlessness as the sky darkened and the stars came out. Artificial gravity plates kicked on with a thump and eased up to nine-tenths of standard G. The *Miranda's* flight deck, with its vast expanse of glazing, became a wonderful observatory, a work of art more spectacular than the stained glass of any cathedral.

"Orbit, four thousand kilometers, seven km/s." Nezumi announced their status. He flicked the attitude-hold switch, locking in the computer to maintain their speed and trajectory.

"The board is green. The bitch is okay," Bernt said. The most common problem was leaking pressure seals around the hatches, but the oxygen and nitrogen mix that the crew survived on held steady at 6.34 newtons per square centimeter, a little low but perfectly safe. Ships like the *Miranda* were centuries old, and each had her own quirks and bad habits.

"Now what the hell is going on, chief?" Nezumi unbuckled and turned his chair to face his passengers. An easterner from the Khanate, the pilot had been with Mustafa longer than any other member of the crew.

Adrian watched Mustafa as he looked from his pilot, to his engineer, and finally to Lars before answering. "Koray is dead."

"What is this?" Bernt slammed his fist on the console in a fit of Teutonic belligerence. "Who fucked us?"

"I don't know. The blame lies at my feet. Adrian is gravely wounded and Koray is dead."

Mustafa looked beaten and old. His robes were filthy, marred by stray blood spatter, and he clutched at his sad, flattened fez.

Adrian crossed his arms and shook his head. The Turk didn't deserve to carry the guilt for what had happened. "My injury isn't grave, and we all walked into that shop with our heads up our asses—it was no one's fault."

"If you hadn't appeared on the street when you did, I'd have gone to that meeting with only Koray at my side, and I would surely have perished with him," Mustafa said, his voice weighted with despair.

"That's shit," Adrian said. "Don't worry about what might have happened. Worry about what happens next."

The walls in the crew's shower were a consumptive green. Spider-web cracks in the paint spun out from the corners creating an accidental mosaic, while diodes recessed in the ceiling offered a dead white light so diffuse that it wiped the shadows from the room and with them all contrast.

Stripped to the waist, Adrian closed his eyes and poured grain alcohol from a glass bottle onto his shoulder. The wound screamed an orange lance. He tore off a piece from his ruined shirt's tail, soaked it in more alcohol, and drew it through the gash with gritted teeth to remove the clot. It ran red again, so he held pressure on it and waited.

A light rapping on the door caught his attention.

"Adrian?" Mariel stood in the corridor.

"Come in."

She carried a stack of folded clothes, the Saracen finery Mustafa had insisted that he measure for. "I brought you something to wear."

He dismissed the lapis blue *kaftan* with the wave of a hand. "I'd look like a tart in that." Enhanced by gold embroidery, the long coat was conservative by Mustafa's standards but lavish for Christendom. Why had she dug down to the bottom of the chest to get it? And now, of all times?

Adrian was to have worn the expensive raiment during a visit to the Ottoman home world, but he never had the opportunity. The Sultan died suddenly and Osman, the Grand Vizier who ascended to the throne, hated Mustafa passionately for reasons Adrian never fully understood.

The *Miranda* left in haste, and the outfit had sat in the bottom of his trunk since then.

"You'd look like Grand Master Orsini, leading the Order from ancient Rhodes," she said, running her hand over the fabric. "You have the same dark eyes and martial nose."

"Martial nose? Who in Hell is Grand Master Orsini?"

"He was Grand Master a thousand years before the Second Coming. There's a portrait of him in my history book, wearing a robe like this one when the Knights lived on the island of Rhodes, on Earth."

"Before the Advent, eh? He was a lucky one, then, to live on the First Earth. Sit up here; let me teach you something useful."

She jumped up and sat on the stainless counter.

He peeled the cloth from his shoulder, showing the raw cut running straight across his clavicle. "If I'd been any slower it would have been here." He pointed to his heart.

"It must hurt terribly." Her eyes fixated on the wound. He had trained her in swordsmanship for years, but beyond the occasional, shallow slice she gave him, she'd never seen—or felt—the russet product of the art.

"Yes. It hurts." He grinned. "We'll have to sew it up."

"We will?" she asked with wide eyes.

"You are a squire in the Military and *Hospitaler* Order of Saint John, are you not?"

"I think you and I are more on the military side of affairs."

"Well, every coin has two sides. When I was a squire, they gave me a commendation for cleaning and dressing wounds, suturing, even cutting out gangrenous flesh. I saved a few amputations. Open that." Beside the sink lay a small cordovan leather case with a brass clasp.

She did, revealing a red velvet interior with recesses for curved needles, three rolls of silk thread, and a jar of strange mucous-colored balm. She picked up the jar and studied it.

"It's an ointment called quist butter that numbs pain. Not fully, but some is better than none, take my word. It also works against rot, and staunches bleeding. Scoop some out."

"Oh, this smells worse than that pig-planet." Her nose wrinkled.

"As long as the smell is pungent, the balm retains its potency. Press it into the wound."

She spread some over the gash, not pressing very hard.

"Get it down in the furrow."

It stung, short but sharp, before the numbing effect set in and the burning in his shoulder cooled.

"Don't be timid. You have to get it down inside." He used his own finger to force it into the seeping cut. "Now, take out the second needle from the bottom. The smaller the wound, the smaller the needle. The same applies to the thread. This is silk, but catgut works almost as well. You'll not want to use common thread unless there's nothing else at hand."

"Obviously," she said, clearly more interested in the smell of the quist butter than the needles and thread.

"Show that cheek again at your peril." He cut a length of thread, squinted, and slipped it through the eye of the needle. "This'll need four stitches, placed a little less than a centimeter apart. We'll use what's called a cruciate pattern—little crosses—so the wound will stay closed if one breaks."

He showed her the technique, running one stitch through. Buttered up, the pain was merely annoying. "Tie me a square knot, will you? Don't pull the skin together too tightly—it's going to swell."

She drew the wound together and tied the stitch.

"Well done." He watched her work in the mirror. Again, she showed her gift for tasks requiring dexterity and finesse.

"What happened to Koray?"

Christ. "Watch me put another one in, then you can try." He repeated the process while considering his answer. Adulthood entitled her to the truth, and she'd see through a lie anyway.

She tied off the second stitch as precisely as the first.

"He was killed by men who opposed the business we were conducting."

"Killed by the same men who did this?"

"Yes."

"Did you kill the villains in kind?" she asked, voice flat.

"Yes. Try putting a stitch in by yourself now."

She ran the needle through the edges of the wound.

He felt the need to justify it, somehow. "It wasn't 'in kind.' It wasn't revenge." If killing a man was wrong, it should always be wrong. Why wasn't it?

Her hands were nimble, and she finished the suture easily.

"Not bad for a novice," he said. "Finish up, will you, love? Only one more to go."

"Of course I will, but don't think that I'll mend you like Geoffrey every time you burst and your innards come out."

Geoffrey, the stuffed lion he'd given her many years ago, was no longer her constant companion but still sat by her bed.

"We should have named him Lazarus." He'd sewn Geoffrey back together countless times while she sat at his feet, nervously awaiting the surgery's outcome.

She clipped the thread and tied the fourth suture. "Lazarus only rose from the dead once—hardly noteworthy compared to Geoffrey. Thank you for not lying to me about Koray. I could tell you were deciding what to say."

"As an adult, people will stop lying to protect you and start lying to hurt you, manipulate you, and deceive you into works that are in opposition to your good interest." He paused. "Their intentions will seem divinely pure. They'll use words like *justice* and *fairness* to signal their virtue. They thrive on the power they gain from manipulating people against each other on grounds of high principle. In this, you should not follow my example."

"Your example? Being brave and righteous and fighting for a noble cause is bad?" she asked.

What devil fed her these questions?

"Just don't be fooled into thinking you're anything other than Mariel. Don't be a squire, a woman, or…even a Christian. Mariel is more than all that." Why could he never find good answers?

"Am I not a Christian?"

He took a pull from the liquor bottle. "Perhaps you should pray over the question, and see what comes of it."

She inspected her work. "There, my other fuzzy lion is mended."

"Off with you, then, young physician, so I can shower."

She slipped off the counter.

"Hey." He stopped her. Her color was draining, and it wasn't a trick of the light. He gently brushed her hair back from her brow. "You're looking pale."

"It's my head again. It'll pass."

"Go lie down. I'll look in on you soon."

She scrambled down and out the door.

"Squire!" he called.

"Sir?" came the reply from down the hall.

"Chin up, eyes on tomorrow!"

Adrian admired himself in the mirror and admitted that Grand Master Orsini might have been on to something. The long, exotic coat was comfortable despite fitting close to his body. The short grey hairs slowly invading the side of his head made him look all the more distinguished in the Saracen thread.

Arrogance, now? On top of everything else?

He rechecked the dressing on his shoulder to be sure that nothing would seep out and mar the fine fabric.

Passing through the dark galley, he startled the two young boatswain's mates, Tomas and Gilly. The pair huddled in front of the open refrigerator, Gilly with a thick slice of roast beef in each hand and Tomas frozen in the act of stuffing biscuits into his pockets.

"Oh shi—" Tomas started, dropping a biscuit on the deck before recognizing Adrian. "Brother, you scared the shit out of me. Thought the Turk had caught us again. How's your shoulder?"

"And why are you done up like a Saracen, sir?" Gilly asked.

"The shoulder will be fine. As to the clothes…" Adrian eyed a slice of roast beef. His stomach spoke up, nominating the juicy cut for a late dinner. "Hand me a biscuit will you? And a slice of that."

Sandwiches made, they set about eating when Lars entered.

"What's this, then?" the boatswain asked.

"Roast beef," Adrian said. "Have one."

"I will. Mustafa wants to see you, Brother. He sent me to prod you."

"I know."

There was a long lull. Adrian felt the crews' eyes on him, all asking the same question.

"So…" Lars let the ambiguous query trail off.

"Mustafa was making a deal with a couple of Bulgars when a madman burst in with some hired help. Landser. Wanted to steal the crate and snuff us." Adrian finished the sandwich. "It was a near thing."

Lars nodded. "Good thing you were there."

"A good thing for Mustafa, not so much for Koray. Say, Lars. It's not my place to pry into a man's business, but now that he's dead, why was Koray really onboard?"

"Well, he was the purser and Mustafa's valet. You know that."

"All he ever did was copy *my* ledger, and did you ever see him valeting?"

"No, but that just made him a lazy purser and valet. No doubt hired to complement these two lazy gluttonous asses." Lars jerked his thumb at his mates. "I assume Mustafa had him along for some reason that seemed good to Mustafa. As you said, it's not our place to pry."

Adrian left the galley for the cabin he shared with Mariel. He slid the door open and found her lying face down on her bunk with her pillow over her head.

He sat down on the edge of the bed. Each time he saw this, he felt a deep-rooted, corporal pain, as if he himself were stricken.

"What's wrong, love?" he asked, quiet.

"My head hurts." The pillow muffled her voice.

"Is it just a headache? Any vertigo this time?"

"Just a headache."

"Look at me, will you?"

She came out from under the pillow, hair tousled and eyes red.

"Close your left eye. Now tell me how many fingers I'm holding up."

"Two."

"Switch eyes. Now how many?"

She stared at his unchanged hand blankly for five or six seconds. "Two."

Anomalous PCD resulting in temporal coding jitter. Whatever the hell that meant. The medical records he'd found with her were written in the dead language of Apex technology, and so much ancient knowledge was hidden away, even from a Hospitaler. Heretical. Five letters were the only clue he had: ASCNT. The acronym was found throughout the records, and on nearly every piece of equipment they'd destroyed in the bunker at Golan.

"It's just a headache, Adrian. I can have normal headaches."

Stubborn. No matter how often he told her to drink the tea when the headaches started, she always waited for him to make her.

He took the bottle of black liquid off the shelf and poured her out a small dose of the poppy-seed infusion. If she were lucky, this would be one of the short spells lasting an hour or two. If not...for the past few months the headaches had grown more and more painful, and bouts of vertigo, nausea, and delirium crept up more frequently. At its worst, the only relief came from an injection of opium.

"Drink up, squire."

She swallowed the inky shot.

He brushed back the hair from her brow. "I'll be in Mustafa's cabin if you need me." Before he left the room, he turned the lights off and set the thermostat low.

A few steps down the hall, he knocked on Mustafa's door.

"Come in."

The *Miranda* was built with the most advanced alloys and ceramics produced before the Advent, but entering the Turk's cabin was like stepping into an Anatolian coffee house.

The walls and floor were rosewood polished to an unnaturally high gloss. The ceiling glowed, covered with interlocking brass panels etched with a complex geometric pattern, and unlike the pale white diodes throughout the rest of the ship, these shined a pleasant, creamy yellow. Green and gold carpets lay under the artificial sun while lush red draperies dressed the walls.

The centerpiece was a great hookah sitting on a low table with four snaking tubes, purple and yellow striped, rolled up at its base. On either side were long settees upholstered in green silk and loaded with stacks of pillows so deep one had to dig out a place to sit.

"You look like a proper Janissary now." Mustafa waved Adrian to one of the sofas. "Do sit down."

"Janissaries are slaves, as you well know."

"Ah, sort of. Yes. It's awkward, however you choose to describe it." Mustafa leaned forward and picked up a half-full decanter sitting next to the hookah. "I always said I would convert you, but I didn't expect such progress so soon." He managed a smile and gestured at Adrian's new clothes.

"A woman manipulated me into wearing this." Adrian smoothed the front of the *kaftan*.

"Drink some of this wine with me with me?" An empty cup sat on the table. "It's not half bad."

"Gladly."

Mustafa filled the cup almost to overflowing. "I find it entirely believable that a woman manipulated you, especially a precocious one like Her Ladyship. I trust she's feeling well?"

"She's fighting a migraine right now, but it doesn't seem like a bad one."

"I feel so sorry for her. I have an uncle who gets the most infernal migraines. You know, just the other day I was thinking that the poor girl needs her own room. Why don't we move her into Bryan's?"

"I was going to bring that up this evening, but after what happened…" He waved the thought away with the motion of a hand. "This morning she informed me that she's a woman and wants to be treated as such."

"It had to happen." Mustafa shrugged.

"It feels as though it happened overnight."

"That's why you must live in the moment, Adrian. Enjoy each little slice of life as you cut it from the bone. It's sad to experience something for the first time as a memory."

"Still, it's too soon." Adrian emptied his cup. "She's not ready for what's waiting."

"She's as ready as you've made her, which to my eye is far more prepared than most. You Christians have a rite for this. For becoming an adult."

"Confirmation."

"Well, you must perform it for her. This Sunday. The crew will attend."

"You're certain?" Three religions were represented aboard, and each man typically saw to his own observances privately.

"Of course. I'm the only Muslim on the ship now, and I have no intention of providing the *casus belli* that ignites the next war."

"She'll appreciate your kindness, as do I." Adrian refilled his cup and raised it to Mustafa before drinking.

"Koray was a distant cousin, you know."

"I didn't."

"Yes, my aunt Ferah—aunt once removed—will be quite distraught."

"Being distraught is normal. How do *you* feel?" Adrian took another sip of wine. Deep red, highly tannic, bold.

"Are you attempting to minister to me, my friend?"

"Leave Christ out of it if you like, but anyone with a soul will feel that a piece of himself is gone along with the dead."

Mustafa rubbed his chin and stared at the ceiling. "I was exhilarated until we got back to the ship, and now I'm exhausted. I'm ashamed to say that I haven't been, nor am I now, bereaved to any great degree."

"When a fellow Hospitaler died, it would sometimes be hours or even days before I felt the loss. I expect your thoughts are jumbled from our brush with death."

"Death. Yes. Look, Adrian, you must make me a promise." Mustafa leaned forward.

"What promise?"

"Should the subject ever arise, any time or anywhere, we must never reveal that Koray did not receive a proper burial. He died of natural causes, and was laid to rest following the rules of Islam."

Adrian nodded. Muslim's were no different from Christians in their regard for ceremony. "Fine."

"Good. Now then, I'm dying to know why that fellow killed Easley, and tried to kill us."

Adrian stood. "The answer's in the crate."

Mustafa declined to take on any porcine cargo at St. Anthony, leaving the hold empty save for several shipping containers full of spare parts and the casks making up his wine reserve. Foot-steps echoed on the steel grating that formed the main deck, but were barely audible over the white noise of the ship's systems.

The two men approached the crate. It sat where they had left it, near the cargo ramp, peppered with dried blood-spatter and mud. The box was anonymous: no markings, no seals, and no hint of ownership nor origin.

"An insignificant looking thing, to have cost a life," Mustafa said.

"On the outside." The 'insignificant' thing would only help Mariel, but Adrian had never intended to trade one life for another.

"God's will be done. Would you open it, my dear?"

Adrian retrieved a pry-bar from a scratched and dented yellow wall-locker. Two strokes of the lever and the crate's top was off and set aside. Tightly packed raw cotton filled it to the top— someone had gone to some trouble to protect the contents.

Mustafa removed the clumped material, working like an archaeologist, building a little mountain of cotton on the deck next to him. "Here's something. A box of some sort. Definitely a relic, though. Ancient, and very valuable."

"Sure it is."

Nestled inside was a box some sixty centimeters long and thirty in width. Adrian reached in and lifted it out of the crate, revealing a shallow depth of only ten centimeters. He felt the weight.

"About thirty kilos," he said as he placed the thing on the workbench.

Flat black, the box reflected none of the light shining down on it from the bright overhead diode. A thin crease ran around its sides, and, centered on top, a small, smoky glass window two centimeters square.

Also on the top, in large block letters, the word ASCNT was etched in the material. Beneath it, smaller, the equally mysterious legend: Participant Field Retrofit, 2820-12A.

"Yes," Mustafa said, drawing the word out thoughtfully. The Turk went to the intercom box and keyed the unit on. "Engineer to the cargo hold."

Bernt's acknowledgement came seconds later.

Adrian ran his hand over the box. Cool to the touch, it had the texture of rubber, but was hard like steel. When his finger brushed the little glass window, a red light flashed on, then off. "Hell, I've awakened it."

"Don't worry, Adrian."

"Red lights mean you're buggered."

"That's why brothels hang red lanterns, my dear. It's the universal color for buggery."

Mariel walked into the hold, a little woozy and wide-eyed. "What goes on here?"

"What are you doing on your feet?" Adrian asked.

"It didn't last long, this time."

"I'm glad of it." No use sending her back to bed. The hurt was either on or off. "We're trying to figure out what this is."

She looked at the relic. "It's a black box."

Adrian rubbed his forehead. She had far too much sass in her.

Mustafa laughed. "The young lady is astute."

Mariel crossed her arms and looked at Adrian with a satisfied smile.

Bernt rushed into the bay, wrestling with a half-on shirt. The engineer was stocky and rough, with hairy forearms and stubble on his shaved head. "What is it? Pressure seal?"

"If it were a seal," Adrian said, "half our air would have been gone in the time it took you to get here."

"Fuck you, you fu—"

"Give us your appraisal of this, Bernt," Mustafa said, interrupting and pointing at the relic.

The engineer turned away from Adrian to examine the black box.

"Stop provoking him, will you?" Mustafa whispered to Adrian.

Adrian grinned. Provoking the foul-mouthed, curmudgeonly engineer was his favorite sport.

Bernt looked over the box, running his hand along its beveled edge as if it were the thigh of a beefy Frau. "This is what you picked up planet side?"

"Indeed," Mustafa said.

"She is ancient," Bernt said. "Very advanced, from the Apex."

Apex. The apex of mankind's technological advancement, just before the Advent. The Church frowned on the description.

"She is a secure storage container. We call them Black Boxes, obviously."

Mariel elbowed Adrian in the side.

"Ceramic shell," the engineer said, tapping his finger on the lid. "Very strong and resistant to every fucking thing you can imagine. You would put something inside that you really wanted to protect."

Mustafa's eyes lit up, and he rubbed his hands together.

"I will check the emissions, in case the micro-fusion plant is leaking." Bernt went to the tool box mounted on the bulkhead and removed an ionoscope, then aimed the fragile device at the relic. "Okay. Some gamma, which is expected."

Bernt touched his index finger to the glass window. Just as when Adrian touched it, a red light flashed. "Biometric lock. Fingerprint reader." He turned to his audience with a frown on his face.

"What's wrong?" Mustafa asked.

"She is ballast," Bernt said. "Black Boxes are fucking indestructible, and they cannot be cracked electronically. Without the right fingerprint…" He shrugged.

"Can't you cut it open?" Adrian asked.

"No, I cannot fucking cut it open," Bernt said. "It would take hours to burn through that ceramic coating with the plasma torch, and whatever is inside would be molten by then."

"When you say you can't crack it electronically, what do you mean?" Mustafa asked.

"Inside there will be a security module, with the biometric data—the fingerprints—hard coded. It might be keyed to one print or a hundred. The only certainty is that the owners are all long gone. The problem, of course, is that the only way to get at the module is to open the box."

Adrian looked at Mariel, then Mustafa. Bernt was right about the near-impossibility of cracking a lock like this, but if Adrian's hunch were true the engineer was wrong about the necessary fingerprints being lost.

"I know my finger doesn't work." Adrian touched the scanner, and again the red light flashed. "Mustafa?"

"It can't hurt to try," The Turk said.

"This is idiotic." Bernt shook his head.

Mustafa pressed his finger to the scanner. Red light.

"Can I try?" Mariel asked.

"Of course you can, love." Adrian nodded. "Go ahead."

Bernt exhaled, flaunting his vexation.

Mariel tapped her fingertip on the sensor.

The light blinked green.

She pulled her hand back as a rush of air escaped the box. The lid slowly raised a centimeter.

"Impossible." Bernt stared at Mariel and the box.

"Have some faith," Adrian said.

"Fuck. The odds are impossible. It must be a malfunction. A fortuitous glitch."

Mariel looked at Adrian, her eyes asked whether it were true.

Don't lie. He shook his head.

"Stand back," Mustafa said. He moved in front of the box and carefully lifted the lid off.

Everyone peered in around him.

CHAPTER 04

Sabine threw back the hood of her grey cloak. The foggy morning air was cold and sodden, leaving tiny beads of water on the stonework. The odor of feral cats wafted through the alley on a weak breeze.

Ahead, another figure in grey leaned on a wood post sunk in the ground to no apparent purpose. The tall, lanky shape of Henry Monday smoked a roll of tobacco and watched her approach. He took a drag, then flicked the remains of the fag at a cat that hissed and darted behind a pile of trash.

"You smell like shit, Henry," Sabine said.

"Top o' the morning to you, too." He pushed himself off the post and joined her as she continued down the alley. "I have a lead on those Hansa you've been bitching about."

"Tell me. Those bastards have been upsetting the market for months." Thievery, blackmail, and murder were stock and trade of the Hanseatic League, the only legal mercantile guild. This aggressive new cell scared her clientele, who were skittish at the best of times.

"I finally got eyes on one of them, and followed him through the West Gate where he went into the cistern. Too risky to tail him in there, so I set some men up to watch. It turns out that the cistern is a popular place. We've identified four men coming and going."

"Keep watching them, we'll have to do something soon. Maybe use the *Condottieri* again."

"Guess who's among them."

"No games. Who is it?"

"Martin Dietrich."

"Son of a whore. Listen to me." She held up a finger to accentuate her disgust. "What happened in Merse won't happen here. Not if I have anything to say about it."

"Sabine?" Henry asked.

"What?"

"It can't be a coincidence. This is proof that the Hansa know—"

"No. This proves nothing."

They continued in silence, past the backs of little shops, some starting to show signs of life as the morning came on.

"Reymont Lucas is dead, Henry," she said.

"Dead?" He pulled his hood back, revealing a long, gaunt face and tussle of copper-colored hair.

"Deceased. What do we know about the Conti family?"

"There's an Archbishop Conti on Levant. Beyond that, nothing."

"See what you can dig up on them."

"Wait." He came to an abrupt stop with his arm in front of her. "Did you kill Lucas?"

"Don't be stupid." She shoved his arm aside and continued. "There was a woman named Alisa Conti at the party. She's strange. Suspicious."

He laughed. "A suspicious woman with Reymont Lucas? I'm shocked. You think she killed him?"

"She didn't do much other than lick on him while I was present, but my gut says look into her. Then there's Selim Bey."

"The Ambassador is involved as well?"

"No, but I think he made me for it." Made her for ending a deal worth five thousand of gold. That could have undesirable consequences.

"How does this affect our plans?"

"How do you think?" She looked at him through narrow eyes. "Lucas was golden. He bought nearly everything and hardly negotiated with me. It's a strange thing with men—they'll do anything for a woman who remains distant, and nothing for those who are close."

"Maybe you don't know the right men."

"Believe me, I know."

"This from a woman who had a Knight Hospitaler in her pocket, and let him go."

She laughed, though she wished he hadn't dug that skeleton up. "He was a devout Papist, and he had a child. Poor girl. He's probably dead by now, and she an orphan."

"You rant against muddled men and reject the honest ones."

"Find out about the Conti family, Henry. After I sleep, I'm going back to Lucas' place. His man Lorenzo might work with us. If I'm lucky, I can get a blood sample for Enn."

They reached an intersection, put their grey hoods up, and parted ways, Sabine continuing to the Bee while the sun breached the horizon.

Lucas' grand mansion was as dead as its owner. Sabine tapped her foot, waiting in the kitchen after being let in the back door by a maid.

The enormous fireplace was cold. The marble-topped preparation table in the center of the room was stacked with fancy hors d'oeuvres and food prepared but unserved the night before.

"Miss?" a man asked.

Sabine flinched. She hadn't heard Lorenzo Bruno enter.

There were dark circles under his brown eyes. His head, normally clean shaven, showed a little stubble as did his angular jaw, and his white collar and cuffs were unbuttoned.

She knew from talking to Lucas long ago that Lorenzo had spent some time in the army of the Holy See, and that he was discreet—a characteristic essential in a manservant.

"Miss Adler, what can I do for you?" His face was grim.

"Call me Sabine now. I'd like to talk about Lucas."

He tilted his head slightly to one side and raised an eyebrow.

"We could go to his office," she said.

"Of course." He led her down the hallway and pushed through a swinging door into the cavernous parlor that had been so loud and boisterous just hours ago.

Sabine remembered the many times she'd been a guest at the house and how it was always full to overflowing with Lucas' friends, business associates, and no small number of hangers on. No one would've described Lucas as a good man, or even a benign one, but standing in the desolate house she felt sad for him and his people, who would soon be displaced.

Inside the office Sabine took the same seat she had occupied the night before. Lorenzo's back was to her for a moment as he walked past, and she ran her hand under the edge of the desk feeling for the transmitter.

Gone.

Lorenzo hesitated to sit in Lucas' big leather chair.

"Go ahead, I'm sure he wouldn't mind," Sabine said.

He sat and put his hands in front of him, palms down. "Well then. What can I do for you?"

"I'm going to put my cards on the table, Lorenzo. Is Lucas' body still here?"

"Yes, Miss, we carried it down to the cellar, where it's cool. Why?"

"I'd like to draw some of his blood, and take it to a friend who can tell me whether he was poisoned."

"I swept the food and drink again early this morning, and went over most of the house with a threat detector. The food is clean, all I found was this." He took the little round transmitter out of his pocket and put it on the desk. "I'm not sure how it got in. Any ideas, Miss?" He narrowed his eyes.

Sabine picked up the listening device and pretended to examine it. "There are ways to defeat threat detectors."

The bug was an advanced model, made from a composite that was invisible to scanners as long as the tiny internal battery was empty. The trick was to bring it inside with the battery dead, then let the wireless power resonators that kept all Lucas' other toys charged do the same for the bug.

"Who was he doing business with during the past few days?" she asked. "I should think one of them snuck it in to gain an advantage." She watched his eyes. Who did he distrust more? Her, or the Saracens?

Lorenzo nodded. "I think one of the Turks planted it. They'd been negotiating with Lucas for months over a deal for port access." He waved his hand, dismissing it. "If you think Lucas was poisoned, who do you think did it? That young slut he was with?"

"Lucas was also a terrible slut," she said, bristling at the hypocrisy, "but, putting the question of their virtue aside, it's possible Alisa Conti killed him."

"Well, whoever did it, it puts us both in the same position."

"How do you mean?"

"This gold mine is played out."

"Who will inherit?" Sabine asked.

"No one knows. His wife died years ago, and not long after that his son Marc ran off to who knows where. No one's seen him since. Lucas had attorneys so I suppose they'll take the spoils in the end."

"Speaking of spoils, how have you managed to keep the house from being stripped?"

"I sent most of the help home immediately. Besides Juan and I, the maid Alexis is the only other person who lives in the house. She'd never steal anything."

"It's tragic. I liked Reymont." She looked hard across the desk. "Lorenzo, help me dig into this, and I'll make sure you get at least one more good payment."

He thought for a moment. "Yes. I want to know who killed him. They owe me quite a lot, and I intend to collect."

His voice darkened when he spoke of retribution, his brow furrowing into a brutish ridge. His civilized manner was a veneer.

He stood and walked to the door.

She followed him down into the cellar, where the body was waiting, lying on a wooden table, covered with linen.

✦

Sabine jumped from the carriage before the black-capped driver could bring his horse to a halt. It was a poor, dirty quarter, set near the river and home to some of the city's more notorious dens.

The flowery sweet smell of opium wafted down the street, and she kept her eyes on the windows above—in this part of town, people were liable to dump their garbage and worse from on high.

In front of her, a heavy old door stood strong despite looking as if it'd been beaten, burned, and battered with an axe. She pounded her fist on the door, waited, then knocked again, rapping her knuckles with painful force.

Enndolynn, round face flushed, pulled the door open and threw it wide, her ample chest heaving with deep breaths. Her bodice was cinched tight around her plump belly but mostly open at the top. She stood in the doorway holding a riding crop.

"Cousin?" Sabine asked.

Enndolynn was very short, even more so with her boots off, as they were now, her small toes peeking out from under her skirts. Sabine could look right over the top of her head, and as she did she saw a man, naked except for a four-pointed jester's cap held over his privates.

The imp dug through a pile of clothes on the floor until he found a pair of breeches. He then scurried away, turning his naked buttocks her way, and she saw that they were striped with a dozen or more bright red welts.

She looked down at the riding crop, and then to Enn's face.

"Equestrian vaulting," Enn said, still catching her breath, holding up the crop.

"Who was that fool?"

"My new lover, Raphael. He really is a fool. *And an escape artist who will be punished,*" she shouted over her shoulder. She smiled ear-to-ear and waved Sabine in. Enn had a crooked tooth on the right side of her mouth that made her grin look kinky and devilish. It mirrored her personality.

Sabine tried not to look around. The room was a mess with clothes and strange implements strewn around the floor and furniture. An iron ball with a chain and shackle attached sat on the hearth stones. A strong herbal smell fought with the smoky fireplace to dominate the air.

"Go ahead, let it out," Enn said.

"No, it's your place." Sabine puckered her nose.

"Cleanliness is for the dimwitted, cousin. A mess keeps you on your toes. Literally."

"I suppose you have to grow your mold and fungus somewhere."

"Yes, so try not to trample on my screw-moss. What brings you all the way down here?"

"A mystery." Sabine produced a small glass jar filled with dark red fluid.

"Who did you squeeze this out of?"

"Reymont Lucas."

"Rich blood. What's the matter with him?" Enn asked.

"He's dead."

"That's difficult to cure."

"Can you tell me whether he was poisoned, and with what?"

"Maybe. Tell me what happened. How did he die?" Enn took the jar and walked to the back of the house, Sabine following.

"I don't know. I was at his party for at least two hours before he died. He looked tired, but the girl he was with was pushing him hard. Dancing, drinking. I noticed him sweating, and near the end he was stumbling and seemed very confused."

"It was a party—none of that sounds suspicious. Sometimes people's hearts just give out. One minute they're dancing a jig and the next—croak." Enn stuck her tongue out and rolled her eyes up into her skull.

"I need to be certain."

Sabine followed Enn up a set of creaky stairs into an attic with large dormer windows that let in shafts of bright sunlight.

"Did he eat anything?" Enn asked.

"Not that I saw. He drank a lot of wine. Enn, where did that man go?"

"Raphael? He comes and goes through the bedroom window." Enn sat down at a wooden table covered with instruments. Beakers, flasks, oil-fueled burners and delicate glass pipettes were arranged neatly, in contrast to the rest of the house. There were bottles and jars full of chemicals, powders, and colored liquids.

The smell was a pungent, indecipherable mix of metallic, organic, and caustic. It shocked Sabine's nose, and she sneezed.

"So, we're probably looking for something that kills slowly?" Enn thought aloud.

"Oh, another thing. He seemed to be having trouble breathing right before he died."

"Kills slow and affects the lungs. Hmm. This would be a lot easier if you'd find me a working blood analyzer."

"Right, a man in an alley tried to sell me a biochem analyzer just the other day." Sabine sneezed again.

"I like you when you're cheeky, cousin. I'll run some tests and we'll see what we can find."

The shafts of yellow light entering the windows turned orange and started to fade while Enn ran a series of tests on the blood. She took tiny samples with pipettes and subjected them to a myriad of processes, mixing the blood with powders and liquids, watching the color change in various solutions, heating it over a burner and examining the residue. All the while she recorded the results on a glass datapad.

Sometime in the early evening Sabine nodded off on an old settee, and she slept until after sundown when Enn flipped on the bright overhead diodes.

"Acetonitrile."

"Speak plain," Sabine said as she sat up.

"Methyl cyanide. An interesting choice."

"How so?" Sabine rubbed her eyes and struggled to break out of the fog, her head feeling thick from lack of sleep.

"It isn't the most potent form of cyanide. It's organic, and has to be metabolized into a different form before it kills, slowing it down. That explains the creeping death, but any threat detector should have caught it."

"The wine?" Sabine asked.

"Say it was in the wine. You'd have to be careful to serve the laced wine only to the victim, otherwise you'd kill the whole party." Enn laughed.

"No, I saw him drink from several different decanters. I drank from some of the same ones."

"Really?"

"Yes, why are you looking at me like that?"

"When was this party?"

"Last night."

"Hmm. There may be a chance." Enn went to a cabinet and retrieved an empty syringe. She took a long steel needle out of a jar of alcohol and attached it. "Give me your arm, cousin."

Sabine and Henry stood in the shadowed entrance to an alley. She yawned. It was a day after her visit with Enn, but there had been no time to rest.

They watched the back of the wine-merchant's shop from across the dirt street. It was near sundown, and most of the workers had left for the pubs, but a light burned in the office window and the owner, one Nicholas Kresimir, was still inside.

"This Kresimir is behind it?" Henry asked.

"Lucas bought his wine from Kresimir. A reagent was in the wine."

"Yet Lucas is the only one who died?"

"The reagent was inert, allowing the casks to slip past Lucas' security. The assassin brought in a second component, also undetectable on its own. When combined they created methyl cyanide."

"Tricky."

"Scary. Everyone who drank the wine was half poisoned, including me."

"Tell me your plan?"

"I recruited Lorenzo to talk to Kresimir's workmen. Turns out he sometimes has a lady caller at the warehouse who puts the fear of God into him, and she was there the night before Lucas was killed."

"This Lorenzo learned this by talking?" Henry asked.

"There might have been some coercion—I hear his fist is quite loquacious. That reminds me, keep an eye on him tonight, see what you think. He may be of use to us now that he's unemployed."

Two figures approached from deeper in the alley. Henry started to step in front of her, hand on sword, until she pushed him back. "It's Lorenzo. It looks as though he brought Juan, the valet, too."

Lucas' former servants acknowledged the grey cloaks with a nod. "He's in there alone, Miss Adler," Lorenzo said.

"I think we can forego the 'Miss Adler,' Lorenzo."

"Whatever you say, Miss."

"So, an interrogation?" Henry asked.

"Only if he turns it into one. He can either tell you what he knows, or Lorenzo and Juan can beat it out of him."

Henry turned to the two servants. "You two must really have loved Lucas, to get involved in this."

"We had good reason to be loyal," Juan said, "and besides, you don't know how well he paid us. Even the hired help lived like kings in that palace."

"And now it's dried up," Lorenzo said. "So you're damn right we're going to break whoever killed him."

The group made their way across the empty street as the sun set. The door had a heavy but rudimentary lock, which Henry picked after some fiddling. It swung open smoothly.

They found Kresimir sitting behind an oak desk poring over his ledgers and invoices. He wore a pair of little brass spectacles and worked by the light of a diode lamp with a yellow filter. Middle-aged, average in most respects save for a nose the shape and color of a radish, he had a bit of a paunch and a fleshy neck. Buried in his work, he didn't notice the intruders even as they filled the office doorway.

Lorenzo clenched his fist, and the sound of his knuckles cracking echoed in the silent room.

"Wha—" Kresimir finally noticed them and jumped in his seat. "What is this? We're closed!"

Henry entered first, flanked by Juan on his right and Lorenzo to the left.

"We're not buying," Henry said.

"Oh, breakers then? Well you'll not get anything. The cartage company has already taken the strong box away."

Henry sat down in one of the wood-framed leather chairs in front of the desk. "We're not stealing."

Lorenzo and Juan walked slowly around the desk and took up places on either side of Kresimir, standing tall over him. Henry sat and waited, saying nothing.

Sabine watched from the doorway.

"Nick," Henry said, "you delivered wine to Reymont Lucas two days ago."

"No." Kresimir looked rattled already, he glanced at the two men hovering over him. "Yes."

Henry nodded at Lorenzo.

The big man pulled his arm back and drove his fist into Kresimir's face. The thick, heavy sound it made on impact reminded Sabine of her mother in the kitchen, thinning cuts of veal with a wooden hammer to make schnitzel.

Kresimir's whole body rocked and he nearly fell out of his chair.

"Don't kill him," Sabine said.

Juan slapped the dazed man in the face twice, then grabbed him by the jaw and forced him to look at Henry.

"Nick, you have to tell me the truth, every time, understand?" Henry asked.

Kresimir nodded slowly, blood running from his nose and the corner of his mouth.

"We know Lucas bought the wine from you. Tell me what you put in it."

"It was...Merlot...I...it was two years old, from the Boudinaud estate."

"That's not what I asked, Nick." Henry turned to Lorenzo. "Don't break his jaw, he'll want to talk."

The beating commenced slow and deliberate, a crushing blow from the left, followed a moment later by a bruising hook from the right. As the back-and-forth continued, Henry turned to Sabine. "He won't hold out long. Are you sure you want to watch?"

"Just make sure they don't kill him before he talks." Kresimir was a dead man—she had promised Lorenzo that he could do with him as he pleased after the interview—but he had to be kept alive long enough to talk.

The blows to Kresimir's face soon became sickly wet smacks as his blood ran. It was painful to watch, painful to listen to, but the gold they had made from selling to Lucas was important to the cause. She needed answers.

Kresimir screamed something unintelligible.

Henry waved the bruisers off and took a good look at the pummeled head in front of him. "Let's try again, Nick. What did you put in the wine?"

They had done a fine job of smashing him without breaking any pieces, probably saving the worst for later. Still, he bled a river from the nose and mouth, and there was already swelling around his eyes.

Kresimir sputtered and red drool dripped from his mouth onto his chest. "She..."

"What did you put in the wine?" Henry repeated, monotone.

Sabine stepped into the room. "Who is 'she?' Alisa Conti?"

"I don't know any Conti." He took a heavy breath. "She's... sister..."

Lorenzo pulled Kresimir's head back by the hair and raised his fist.

"Wait," Sabine said. She looked the beaten man in the eyes. "Your sister?"

"No...a sister, a Dominican...I think...she brings the poison... makes me..."

"A nun made you put poison in Lucas' wine?" she asked.

"This is shit, Miss, let me—" Lorenzo started.

"I said to wait." She held her finger up, and he lowered his fist. "Kresimir, a nun brought the poison you put in Lucas' wine?"

"Yes."

"Why?"

"I don't know. When she comes, I do what she says. Three, maybe four times now."

"She pays you to do this?"

"Yes, but…"

Sabine could see that he wanted to talk. There was something holding him back. Fear, and not fear of another beating. "But what?"

"I have to do it. They have my daughter." He slumped back in his chair, as if having told someone relieved him.

"I don't understand."

"My daughter joined the convent when she was fifteen. She was so happy. Then, about two years ago, this Sister came with poison for one of my customers…if I don't do what she says, they'll…"

"I see. And you know this Sister's name?"

"No."

Sabine looked at him. There was no fight in him. He was telling the truth.

"We're finished, for now. Henry, help Kresimir to a carriage—"

"Goddamn it, Miss. You said he was ours when you finished asking questions," Lorenzo said.

"I've paid you. He lives until I've finished with him. Besides, he's small." She waited, the room quiet. Would they back down and see that Kresimir was a pawn?

Lorenzo straightened. "Right, Miss. We want the big fish."

"Henry, get him to a carriage and send him home." Sabine took a last hard look at the beaten man, then turned and left the room.

CHAPTER 05

Shimmering white silk wrapped Sister Mary Frances' coifed head, melted around her shoulders and flowed down her body in a rippling current that clung to her curves. She wore her veil of white velvet up, while at her side hung a lustrous silver rosary. She fancied there was more of Venus about her than the Virgin when she entered the Palace of the Holy Office of the Universal Inquisition.

A palace in more than name, the building's bright, arched Romanesque facade defied the popular image of the Holy Office. The interior's warm hues of cream and orange with gilded accents welcomed visitors with open arms. Beautiful sculptures, exalting paintings, and a magnificent fountain lent an air of serenity and safety—there were simply no shadows for evil to lurk in.

She stopped at her favorite image, a painting of a young shepherdess. The girl, in a blue dress and red scarf, stood with her flock on rough grass scattered with dandelion seedheads. At her side, a black sheepdog kept her company. Mary Frances reached out and nudged the frame until it hung exactly level. A docile flock, grazing as one, with simple, supreme trust in their protector. Perfection.

Up the wide stairs to the third floor. She entered a quiet ante-chamber attended by a sleepy young monk. He saw her and stared, then quickly turned his eyes away from her lithe body.

"Tell the Cardinal I'm here."

"Yes, Sister." He quietly let himself into the private office, returning a moment later to hold the door open for her.

The Grand Inquisitor, Cardinal Grégoire Duval, stood tall in front of his desk, red silk robes trimmed with gold wrapping his lean body. He might have been posing for another portrait, but, as she entered his glossed and polished office, Mary Frances sensed the presence of another.

Duval waved her in, flashing his signature smile, broad, jubilant, painted with baroque detail on a gentle face. Whenever he assumed that manner, his eyes narrowed, sharpening the pattern of venous, somehow scaly wrinkles surrounding them. He became to Mary Frances an old, dry reptile.

"Do come in, Sister," Duval said. "Allow me to introduce you to His Holiness, Pope Alexander the Twelfth."

She stopped short. Resting in a leather chair opposite Duval was the most important man alive. Close-cropped grey hair, prominent jowls, and wrinkles at the corners of his mouth from years and years of joy in God's close proximity. He seemed a cheeky little grey squirrel next to Duval's serpent.

"Holy Father." She fell to her knees. She'd seen him many times, but always from afar.

The Pope stood, a small man, but as he reached his feet his personage grew larger. He walked to her in his snow-white robes and held out a hand.

She placed her lips on the gold and ruby Piscatory Ring and kissed, playing her tongue lightly over its jewel.

"Sister Mary Frances," he said, enunciating as if he were reciting poetry. "We've heard much about you."

"Surely there's little to hear, Holiness." She stood slowly. The Holy Father had spoken to her, directly, causing her to tremble, arousing her, stroking her with invisible fingers.

"Posh! We have it on good authority," he said, nodding at Duval, "that you are an exceptionally devoted and skilled servant of our mother Church."

"Thank you, Holiness." She bowed.

"Exceptional men and women will rise within our Church, we assure you. And we cannot allow Cardinal Duval to monopolize your talents, can we, eh?" The Pope smiled at Duval with palpable deliberation.

"Of course not, your Holiness," Duval said.

"We shall take our leave now, Cardinal."

Duval bowed. "Holiness."

"And you, Sister. Do not be surprised if we call upon you." The Holy Father strode out, smiling even broader than before. Not a squirrel but a mongoose, Mary Frances decided.

"I thought the Holy Father liked to keep us at arm's length," she said when the door was closed.

"Yes, he wants us to do the dirty work so he can keep his hands clean, as if our work were somehow distasteful. Someday it will not be so. The Inquisition will be the Church."

"When you are Pope?"

"God willing, yes. Now tell me about Lucas. You've done as I told you?"

"He's dead, Father."

He tightened his fist in triumph. "How?"

"The binary poison again. It's almost too easy."

"His last moments?" Duval asked.

"Pitiful. His last sound was a little toad-croak as he struggled to breathe, on his knees, gawked at by hundreds."

"Did you see anything else of interest at this party? Surely it was a hotbed of sin."

"The ambassador of the heathens was there, father. I don't know what his business was, but I suppose it's stymied now. There were one or two others who deserve scrutiny."

"Good, good—another obstacle out my way. Lucas' money will no longer back the Pope's cabal."

"You work against the Holy Father so directly?" she asked.

"Do as you're told and let me worry about the details. As I rise, so do you."

"Of course, Father." Bastard.

He cocked an eyebrow, and she could swear he felt her anger. "You are a most special arrow in my quiver, Mary Frances. Unique, as I've often told you, but still *my* arrow to aim. Never forget that."

She bowed her head.

"Come, I want to reward you for dealing with Lucas so efficiently."

"No, Father, I want for nothing." She pushed away from him.

"It's only right to recognize the good you do, and my gift isn't a material thing, but an opportunity." He walked to his mahogany bookshelf and removed the copy of the second volume of *De Doctrina Christiana* that served as a lock. The shelf rolled easily to the side, revealing a small chamber. Pressing a button on the wall, white diodes lit up an old emergency stairwell.

Far beneath the surface, in caverns carved from the bedrock, human colonists built their first habitats on the planet. The underground bunkers no longer controlled the great terraforming engines, which had long since gone silent. Now, they housed prisoners of the Inquisition in dark recesses from which neither they nor their cries could escape.

Duval escorted Mary Frances to one particular cell. One anonymous hole in a line of many. Inside was a thin man, on his knees, facing away from door. He wore only a rough burlap shirt stained with sweat and blood. Mary Frances' keen ears picked up a faint murmur, a low chant, the words of the Apostle's Creed. He whispered the verses with a sandy rasp in his throat.

"This man is convicted of preaching against the supremacy of the Holy Father. He asserts that men can have a personal relationship with God outside the hierarchy established by Saint Peter. What do you think of that?"

She couldn't answer. The words personal relationship had little meaning with respect to God or anyone else. "What should I think about it, father?"

"God is supreme. The Pope, as head of His Church is infallible— *ex cathedra*, of course. Happiness, prosperity, pain, and suffering, he receives all these things and more from God and distributes them to the faithful according to their need and their desert."

She nodded eagerly. "The Holy Father is the embodiment of order, and fairness. Everyone gets just a little. A tiny, little bit of the good, and as much of the bad as their sins warrant."

"Yes."

"To deny the Holy Father and reach out to God as an individual is to deny one's appointed place in the order of things," she said. "Followers are born to follow, they will never lead."

"The truth is in your heart, I hardly have to guide you." Duval smiled at her. "Mary Frances, we are a vanguard. The Inquisition. You and I. We will put men back in their places, and in doing so, re-forge the covenant broken so long ago."

"Has he not recanted?" She asked, turning back to the prisoner.

"No, despite our gentle persuasion he remains committed to his blasphemies. So, onto your reward. How should we punish our brother, here?" Duval crossed his arms on his chest and waited.

"For preaching heresy, remove his tongue with the dragon's tongs. For rejecting the Holy Father, seven days of fire, that he may reflect on the basic element of Creation. Then, crucify him."

"Very good." He placed his hands firmly on her shoulders. "It will be done exactly as you say."

CHAPTER 06

Aglass data pad sat nestled inside. A common enough item—a thin sheet of hard, transparent glass twenty by ten centimeters. Their integrated, practically invisible molecular computers made the things handy for a range of tasks. Why did they pack this one so securely?

"This is interesting." Bernt took the glass pad out.

"A glass?" Mustafa said, slamming his fist on the workbench. "All this for a damned glass pad? Koray died for a sodding glass pad? *God and His Prophet shit on me in turns!*"

"Patience," Bernt said.

"Patience my brown ass! There are thousands of glass pads. They're worthless—your Inquisition doesn't look twice at them."

"Look here." Bernt pointed to a brushed aluminum module that ran down one side of the glass.

"So what?" Adrian asked.

Bernt frowned. "I have never seen a compute module like this attached to a glass before. I have never seen a compute module like this at all."

"That bodes well for its market value, I should think?" Mustafa asked.

"Yes," Bernt said. "The League itself might want it, if it really is uncatalogued. I believe…yes, the top of the module is a composite material, a transmitter, if I do not mistake. Short range, but high energy. Good for sending a large burst of data a short distance."

"Turn it on," Mustafa said, reaching for the glass.

Bernt brushed his hand aside. "It will not work."

"Why not?"

"No power."

"Use our resonator, then."

"Ha!" Bernt laughed. "I wager this glass is hardened, including the charging system. There will be an encrypted carrier wave, and without the key our wireless resonator will ignore it."

"Try it anyway," Adrian said. He forced his anger down. At least he had the bloody thing, and over the years he'd picked up some of Job's patience. If Bernt couldn't make it work, there was someone who could.

"Fine." Bernt went to a control panel and pulled up the resonator status screen. "Look. It is just as I said. No encryption key, no connection, no power."

Mustafa frowned and tapped his slippered foot on the deck. "See what you can do with it, Bernt. Carefully. Adrian? Let's talk."

The planet Gereon filled the windows on the *Miranda's* flight deck with nasty shades of brown and olive. Adrian slumped in an anti-G chair and watched the muddy ball.

"We need a specialist," Mustafa said. He held up his hand before Adrian could reply. "I know, I know, we don't want Bernt to think we've lost confidence in him, but I doubt he can crack the encryption on that thing."

"You're right. We need someone who really knows *Machina*." To Hell with Bernt's feelings. Mustafa wasn't showing any curiosity about Mariel's magic finger, so the job now was to keep the Turk focused on activating the glass pad.

And that's where the whole endeavor became dangerous.

In the wake of the Advent, with the colonies cut off from Earth, religion returned from a long exile to fill the vacuum of power and structure. As the Church grew more powerful, it built a doctrine around the belief that man, in his quest to create and manipulate life, angered God and broke the Covenant.

The resurgent Church strove to end the use of the technology and unleashed the Inquisition to enforce what became known as the Doctrine of Reconciliation, a set of laws that made most tech, called *Machina* in the Church's Latin, illegal.

They failed. The allure of *Machina* was so strong that even the fear of immolation wasn't an effective deterrent.

Pope Paschal III convened an ecumenical council some two hundred years ago, and, after months of debate, the theologians presented a scheme that divided technology into three categories.

Machina Vulgaris. Simple, common tech and personal baubles that kept the people happy and docile.

Machina Suspicax. Implements seen as potentially threatening. Ships, communications gear, the few weapons surviving from the Apex. Ownership and use of such devices were lawful only at the pleasure of the Church or an allied secular authority. Indulgences were available, but expensive.

Machina Infernus. True heresies. Devices for biological or genetic manipulation, computers designed to mimic human thought, and a catch-all category of 'tools, instruments, and machines that deface the human soul or depreciate the work of a man.' Mere proximity to such a heresy could bring a death sentence.

The innocuous-sounding 'field retrofit' was certainly *Infernus.* Everything surrounding ASCNT was.

"I thought we might go to old James Collum on Rimini," Mustafa said.

"You know where this is going to end up."

The Turk huffed and snorted. "Yes, but—"

"But what?" Was Mustafa easy to manipulate, or did he want to be manipulated?

"She's so far away. We'll be twelve days in the bubble and I really don't want to go there, Adrian. I really don't."

"She's the best."

"That's true." Mustafa nodded from side to side as he thought.

"And there's more demand for relics at Civitate Dei than anywhere else." An appeal to greed was always efficacious.

"Bah! You make too good a case."

"Then we're agreed." Adrian ended Mustafa's equivocating. "We're taking it to Sabine."

Sabine Adler.

Adrian's heart quickened.

Sabine.

Two years now?

On a muggy summer evening, he and Mustafa had visited her pub after a rain shower had broken and the water was steaming up off hot cobblestones.

She was the first thing he saw when he walked through the door, and the last. He couldn't remember anything else from that night except her, in a long black skirt and a white blouse darkened with perspiration around her neck and down her back. She'd worn her blonde hair up that night, tied with a ribbon of green silk. She fluttered in and out of the crowd, sweeping mugs off tables with the grace of an angel and a smile so sincere that he mistook her for the universe's loveliest barmaid. As he soon learned, she was the universe's loveliest bar *owner*.

"Adrian? Are you listening?" Mustafa asked.

"What? No. I wasn't." The picture vanished and he was dimly aware that Mustafa had been rambling.

"I was asking you what the authorities will do. How much time do we have? In our haste we left Koray's body behind. They'll follow the trail back to the *Miranda* eventually; Muslims don't exactly flock to this pig-riddled planet."

"The body." Adrian rubbed his forehead.

"It's not your fault. In your line, you don't have to consider the precise disposition of corpses. I'm hoping we can sell this thing quickly, then lay low for a time and avoid any fallout from that massacre. If you like, you can return to Ottoman space with me, to Bursa where I have family, and live like the Sultan himself for a while."

"We have some time," Adrian said. "I doubt the Sheriff will think this important enough to send over the c-twenty relay." Unless Girard really was an Inquisitor, in which case the message was probably already sent and racing ahead of them at twenty times the speed of light. No need to let the Turk in on that, though.

"My thoughts exactly. Adrian?"

"What?"

"This isn't going to be a problem for you, is it? Going to Sabine?"

"No," Adrian lied. "Let's just get it done. It's about time fortune smiled on us. Especially you, covered as you are in the divine shit of God and His Prophet."

"I'll tell Nezumi to set a course out of the system." The Turk stood. "Think about staying at Bursa for a few months, Adrian. A sunny town on the coast surrounded by olive groves. If we do well in the market, you might even buy a wife."

The ship's systems hummed.

If someone saw the *Miranda* from a short astronomical distance she would appear to be one creeping speck of light among thousands. Pull back a little further and her motion relative to the stars would stop fully, and she would be lost to the eye.

Transiting a planetary system could take days or weeks depending on its size. The crew spent much of its time traveling between the habitable zone and the outer edge. On the fringe, where gravity from stars and planets weakened, c-twenty travel—travel at effectively twenty times the speed of light—could begin and end safely. Smooth, flat spacetime meant greater accuracy in reaching the programmed destination, or, as Bernt explained it once, "You won't get far riding a girl with a massive ass."

"Full stop." Nezumi announced their arrival at the initial navigation point. The multitude of status displays, gauges, and instruments cast a warm glow on the pilot's face.

Adrian watched the ritual, always fascinated by the amount of switch-turning and button-pressing required to go somewhere.

Nezumi reached up to an overhead panel, engaged the attitude-hold, and turned a switch to change its mode from STD to PRE. This told the computer to use a more precise, but more processor-intensive program for station-keeping.

"If this kit fucks up," Bernt had said of the attitude-hold system, "we could stuff ourselves up God's asshole."

It would take the computer about two minutes to fire the maneuvering thrusters in microbursts until the ship's orientation and velocity were optimum for creating the bubble.

"What's for lunch?" the pilot asked.

"Beef and spinach," Bernt said.

"Shit. Again?"

"*Ja*, I would rather eat dirt."

"There's enough filth in your mouth already," Adrian said.

Bernt's no-doubt sparkling reply was stayed by a green light that blinked on the autopilot panel, signaling that the computer believed the ship to be stable.

"Gravimeter on." Bernt engaged the delicate instrument that measured the acceleration of the ship. "All axes within margin."

The pilot keyed the intercom. "Ready for c-twenty, chief."

A few seconds passed before Mustafa found an intercom box. "Proceed."

"Wait for me!" A more excited voice broke in, followed by the echoes of running feet. Mariel loved to watch the warp bubble form around the ship.

Unlike liftoff and ascent in an atmosphere, faster than light travel was smooth. The only hint of it happening was the changed tone of the noise suffusing the ship, unless one could see outside.

"Aye, chief, waiting for the navigator." Nezumi stood by.

She ran onto the bridge and ducked under the pilot's console, slipped into a narrow crawlspace and squeezed out into the small space between the back of the instruments and the nose glazing. "Ready!"

Nezumi nodded at Bernt who opened a black and yellow-striped panel on his console and pressed the button underneath.

The background noise pitched up an octave. Starlight from thousands of pinpoints curved around the ship to form a luminous bubble.

The ALC drive, fed by exotic matter collected in the *Miranda's* fuel cells, then worked its man-made miracle. Space-time in front of the ship contracted, while that behind expanded. The front of the incandescent sphere shifted blue, and the rear half turned red. The *Miranda* squeezed out of normal space-time and effectively fell to her destination at twenty times the speed of light.

A clock next to the ALC panel began to count down. It would be 312 hours, twenty-seven minutes, and three seconds until they appeared at their destination, back in normal space-time near Saint Peter's Star and its green fourth planet, Bethany.

Nezumi keyed the intercom. "We're on our way, chief."

"Very good."

The pilot and engineer secured their stations and left for the galley and their undervalued beef and spinach lunch.

Adrian stayed behind, waiting for Mariel to crawl out from behind the instrument panel.

He watched her wriggle out, noticing that she'd done her hair up in intricate braids. Those were new.

Seeing him waiting, she plopped down in the adjacent seat, the rippling blue light from the bubble turning the flight deck into a surreal aquatic scene.

"Are you painting your lips?" he asked.

"You noticed! Do you like it?"

"I—"

"I did my hair, too, see?" She held up her braid. "I saw a woman in an old holo with hair like this. I think it makes me look older."

"It's lovely." Truly, she did clean up into an attractive young lady.

"I need to go shopping when we get to Civitate Dei. I need shoes, and a new white dress, and a new red dress, and—"

"Red? That's a little sultry, isn't it?"

"Pink, then?" She raised her eyebrows.

"That sounds nice." He gathered up his courage. This shouldn't have been so difficult to talk about. "Mariel, how long have you… been a woman?"

"Oh, four or five months now."

That coincided with the worsening of her symptoms. He should have made the connection—the intense physiological changes brought on by her maturation might easily aggravate the hidden defect.

"Adrian?" She pulled her legs up under herself and turned to face him.

"Love?"

"I found an article about fingerprints in your medical pad, and I think it's almost impossible that mine would be able to open that box."

"Maybe you're special?" Tread carefully—don't lie to her.

"Well, obviously." She kissed him on the cheek and ran off down the corridor.

Strange. She'd normally tear such a non-answer apart.

CHAPTER 07

Sabine entered the Old City as the tenth bell struck on a cloud-less morning. A southerly breeze tousled her hair and raised goose bumps on her arms. The gusts rolled in off the ocean far to the south, skimmed over a green quilt of farmland, and swept the hot summer haze from the city. In their wake, the first rapturous days of autumn.

Time to order harvest ale and cider.

The beautiful weather drew thousands to the holy city, not only to worship, but to visit among the gardens, share rumors and gossip, and plot. Sabine passed conspiracies of all sizes on her way to Saint Mary's. Tight-faced merchants scheming for coin, tittering wives weaving intricate strategies to ruin one another, common politicians. Sprinkled in, conspicuous in their desire to remain unseen, were the most dangerous: the dark loners whose ever-shifting aims could only be guessed at. The conspiracies of one.

Even now she was being shadowed—poorly—by one of them. A dusky man in a threadbare maroon coat and plaid breeches patched at the knees. She'd twice turned and twice he averted his eyes from her. If he weren't a pervert, he was someone's agent.

She ascended the steps leading to the cathedral doors, wide-open, inviting. Swiss Guards with long, burnished halberds stood at attention in front of white banners embroidered with the coat of arms of the Holy See: the keys of St. Peter, crossed, and sur-mounted by the papal tiara. All against a deep red shield.

Plaid-pants didn't follow her in.

Saint Mary's was awe-inspiring not just as the heart of Chris-tianity, but also as the former headquarters of the Earth Union's Colonial Authority. Now decorated in lacquered wood and silk, the engineering itself was the structure's most exotic aspect: stainless steel, titanium, paraluminum, and other materials that were expensive or impossible to produce now were used in ways that seemed to defy physical laws. The nave was cavernous, the shining walls angling up to the sky, to the clear pyramid at the peak, where the lion-shaped nebula of Saint Mark often shone.

Sad that God's beautiful house had become the womb of indul-gence, simony, and graft.

There were four confessionals on each side of the room, and Sabine walked to the third one on the right. It was occupied, so she sat on a nearby pew. The benches were hard and forced her back straight up.

She watched the people in the cathedral for a few minutes, until the door to her confessional opened and a man came out, looking thoroughly ashamed. She took his place, enclosing herself in the dark little space where the truth lurked.

"Bless me, Father, it has been two months since my last con-fession," she said. "I accuse myself of the following sins."

The priest on the other side of the screen coughed.

"I have smuggled goods and traded in *Machina*."

"What category?"

"Mostly *Vulgaris*. Some might have been *Suspicax*. I have also engaged in extortion for money."

"Who did you extort?" the priest asked.

"A thieving Hansa banker."

"How much did you get?"

"One hundred and twenty."

"Hmm. Perhaps it was God's will that he lost some of his ill-gotten coin, eh? For your penance—"

"Wait, Father. I have more."

"Oh? Please continue."

"Breaking and entering, assault, espionage, blackmail, conspiracy to commit kidnapping, usury—"

"Daughter?"

"Yes, Father?"

"Crime and sin aren't necessarily the same."

"Surely it's a sin to commit crime in God's name?"

"God forgives you for the sins you commit for His cause. Daughter, you dutifully bring me your list of deeds done in the Emperor's service, but this is still your true confession, and you never reveal anything personal. It makes me wonder, are you all right?"

"What do you mean?"

"Most people come here to tell me about their boring sexual peccadilloes and infidelities. This morning a woman was in tears because she was lustful and touched herself on a Sunday."

"Father, I'm not the type of woman who peccadilloes," she said in an embarrassed whisper.

"Suit yourself. For your penance, say five Our Fathers and think on the repugnance of your actions in the eyes of God."

She closed her eyes. "I am sorry for offending Thee, God, and I promise that, someday, I will sin no more. Amen."

"Amen," the priest said. "Now, I've looked into the Conti family. As you said, there's an Archbishop on Levant by that name. He's an octogenarian, and as far as I can tell, the Bishops of his Diocese run things for him. He has several children by two different women, neither of them his wife. There is an Alisa Conti, but there isn't much information on her. With the relay down, it'll be difficult to dig up more without sending someone there."

"What about Anne Kresimir?"

"Yes, lovely woman. A Missionary Sister. I walked over to the convent and had her pointed out to me."

"Anything unusual about her?"

"Not that I could tell. Is there anything particular you're thinking of?"

"Did she seem happy?"

"Actually, yes, she did. She was working in the garden and singing rather cheerfully."

"Thank you, Father."

"My pleasure as always. Long live the Emperor."

"Long live the Emperor."

Out of the confessional, out of the cathedral, and there was plaid-pants again, loitering on the steps with many others.

Enough of this.

She walked towards him, head in the sky, brushing shoulders with him as she passed.

"Oh! Pardon me, sir." She put her hand on his arm.

He hesitated before tipping his hat. "It was my fault, Madam."

Bloody Saracen.

She fluttered to the base of the steps and smiled at a Swiss Guard. "Sergeant?"

"Yes, madam?"

"That man in the maroon and plaid stole two silver quattros from the offering. He put them in his left coat pocket. I've never seen such effrontery in all my life."

The sergeant and his cohort scowled and strode up the steps. They bracketed plaid-pants and the sergeant jammed his hand in the incriminated coat pocket, withdrawing the pair of 'stolen' quattros. The guards collared the thief and dragged him off, his protests ignored.

Mary Frances took a deep breath and knocked on the door to Cardinal Duval's private suite. She fidgeted and held her eyes down, not looking at the camera mounted in the ceiling. She felt him looking at her.

"Enter." His voice was hollow and scratchy through the speaker.

She punched in her code, and the light on the keypad flashed from red to green. The paraluminum slab door retracted silently into the wall.

She passed through the lavish rooms until she stood at the threshold of his bed chamber.

"Come in my dear," Duval said without looking at her. "What brings you at this late hour?"

"Father, you've received an urgent message on the relay."

"From whom?"

"Sheriff Jollan, Saint Anthony, Gereon," she said. They used the relay cautiously, because the ancient transmitters were prone to failure and difficult for even the most experienced Hansa technicians to repair. The Holy See lost direct contact with Levant decades ago, and more recently several worlds under the rule of the Holy Roman Emperor had dropped from the relay.

The Cardinal looked up from the leather-bound Bible he was reading. He hesitated. The Bible shook slightly as he held it open.

Mary Frances stared at his hands, skin like old velum with a web of black veins just under the surface. Why so slow to respond? Unlike him. Whether happy or angry, he always spoke aggressively.

"What's happening in that cesspool?" Steadiness returned to his hands.

She activated her glass pad. The screen lit up with blocks of eight alphanumeric characters, each separated by one space.

Things changed inside her head. The jumble of confused thoughts that forever tumbled and bounced, each vying for her attention, suddenly lined up in formation like soldiers on parade.

She focused on the formula for decoding the message. Others would do this by hand, but she could decrypt the blocks almost in real-time as she read. Such a task was a blessing from God. All became silent—the countless conversations with herself, the tangential imaginings, the disjointed music.

She related the contents of the message.

At the mention of Deacon Girard's death, Duval marked his page with a purple silk ribbon and set the book aside. "Did you know Philippe Girard?" he asked.

"I met him once, father. A rather short man with garish taste in clothing. I remember that he wouldn't speak with me."

"I expect not. Girard wasn't fond of women. He took great satisfaction in the prosecution of witches, and every woman was suspect."

"No one is above suspicion."

Duval dismissed the point with a flick of his wrist. "I sent him to Gereon to procure a relic from a black-marketeer so that I might bring it under my protection."

"Under *your* protection, father? Not that of the Holy Office?"

"Some heresies are so foul that their very existence must be kept a secret from the greater Church. It is my burden to know them all."

"I would have gone to Gereon for you, father. I would have brought the relic back. I would carry your burden." Her voice quivered. Had she displeased him? How? She tried so hard to make him happy. Where did she fail?

"I know. The Lucas matter was more important, so I gave the lesser task to Girard."

The lesser task. Relief washed over her. "I might still set things right."

"Yes, you just might. Broadcast a message on the relay. Tell our men to look for this ship, the *Miranda*. Use my private code."

"I'll send the message at once, father." She turned to leave.

"Wait. Daughter, come to me," he said.

She walked to his bedside and took his outstretched hand, wrinkled and dry.

"This is very important to me, and therefore to the entire Church. Find the relic and bring it to me quietly. You will not fail."

"I will not fail."

He picked up a glass pad, and showed her a picture of a Black Box of the type in which *Machina* were sometimes found.

The picture had clearly been taken inside the Inquisition's storage vault. The box itself? No different from other's she'd seen. "What's inside?"

He ignored the question. "Note the label engraved in the top: ASCNT. You're looking for another Black Box just like this one.

It may be aboard the *Miranda*—find it and bring it directly to me. Do not toy with it, examine it, or try to open it. Say it."

"I will acquire it and bring it directly to you. I will not toy with it or examine it. I will not open it." What was wrong with him? He knew the power of her memory, that once a thing was said it was never forgotten.

"I declare the crew of the *Miranda* guilty in absentia of possessing *Machina Infernus*, but their punishment is secondary. Recover the box, then quietly remove them. Go now."

CHAPTER 08

On the first Sunday after entering the bubble, the crew gathered in the galley, temporarily transformed into a chapel by the addition of a white cloth over the table and a little bowl of consecrated oil.

Adrian stood before the congregation wearing the black robes of the Order, with the eight-pointed cross sewn to the chest in white. Mariel, along with Bernt, Lars, and the boatswain's mates sat quietly in front while Mustafa and Nezumi observed discreetly from the back.

How odd would life be if this sort of harmony were the norm? This only existed aboard *Miranda* because everyone had a job to do, and survival in the depths of space was never guaranteed. The larger the group and the more secure, the more prone to schism.

When was the last time you acted as a priest? Do you have enough faith left to do it? He looked inward and found little, but Mariel and the crew waited.

"Saint Michael the Archangel," Adrian said, "defend us in battle; be our protection against the wickedness and snares of the nonbelievers. May God rebuke them, we pray: and do thou, O Prince of the heavenly host, by the power of God, thrust into

Hell all the heathen spirits who prowl about His creation seeking the ruin of souls. Amen."

"Amen," said the solemn chorus.

Mustafa and Nezumi exchanged bemused glances.

"Today we confirm Mariel as a soldier of Christ."

She rose and stood in front of him.

She'd engineered her hair into one long, intricate braid that draped over her left shoulder. Her dress was…different. She'd taken in the waist, and she filled it out more fully than he remembered. With red lips and subtly lined eyes, she looked like a grown woman.

"What do you choose as your confirmation name?" Adrian asked.

"Sophia. After the Martyr."

The story of Saint Sophia the Martyr was morbid, but there were few happy choices among the canonized. On Earth, not long after Christ brought the New Covenant, a pious woman named Sophia had three daughters whom she named Faith, Hope, and Love. The Roman Emperor at the time, a non-believer of wicked temperament named Hadrian, was jealous of the girls' steadfast devotion to Christ. He called them before the Imperial throne to recognize his *auctoritas principis* and the supremacy of Rome's pantheon of gods. When they refused to submit, Hadrian had each girl tortured and killed, one after the other, while Sophia watched. Throughout the ordeal, the girls' faith never wavered, and their mother encouraged them to embrace their martyrdom with joy.

Adrian wetted his finger with consecrated oil and made the sign of the cross on her forehead. "Sophia, be sealed with the Gift of the Holy Spirit."

"Amen."

He raised his open hand and swung as if to hit her, but stopped short and merely touched her lightly on the cheek. The mock assault symbolized her new, adult role as a soldier of Christ.

"You're responsible for your actions, now," he said in a lower voice.

"I know. I won't disappoint you."

The assembled crew stood. Adrian looked them over. "Glory be to the Father, and to the Son, and to the Holy Spirit, as it was in the beginning, is now, and ever shall be, universe without end. Amen."

"Amen."

Tomas the young Spaniard raised his hand.

"Yes?"

The boatswain's mate stood. "Brother, Gilly and I thought it might be nice if you'd lead us in a prayer for Koray. That is, if you think it's appropriate, him being a Turk and all."

"The Muslim doesn't believe in intercession, Tomas. No amount of prayer will sway his god's judgment...but I'll try to say something decent." Most of the prayers Adrian knew by heart were rites offered before battle, to make a last general confession and set one's heart right before facing death.

Think of something. Anything.

"Mary, or Maryam," Adrian said, "is honored by Christian and Muslim alike. Let us take the opportunity, as we think of Koray, to reflect on those things we have in common, rather than those that separate us. *Ave Maria, gratia plena, Dominus tecum. Benedicta tu in mulieribus, et benedictus fructus ventris tui, Iesus. Sancta Maria, Mater Dei, ora pro nobis peccatoribus, nunc, et in hora mortis nostrae.* Amen."

"Amen," the front row repeated.

The Christians among the crew came forward to congratulate Mariel. Mustafa and Nezumi joined them after a decent interval.

"It was a wonderful ceremony," Mustafa said, "and you handled Tomas' request most deftly. But, tell me, what does it mean to be confirmed?"

Adrian looked at Mariel and nodded for her to proceed.

"It means I'm old enough to understand good and evil, and so now I can fight and shed my blood for Christ."

"I see," Mustafa said, stroking his chin. "Let's hope that won't be necessary."

"That you can doesn't mean you will," Adrian said.

"Shall we put on a little brunch?" Mustafa asked. "I think I have some sparkling wine hidden around here somewhere."

"I'm cooking," Lars said. "Steak and eggs for us. What are you having, Mustafa?"

"Just the eggs for me, I think. From a clean pan, if you please."

"Can we have a game?" Mariel asked, always excited by the prospect of some camaraderie and sport.

"Of course," Mustafa said. "What do you suggest, your ladyship?"

"Thus Sayeth Methuselah."

"I'm always handicapped in that one," Mustafa said with a grin.

Someone would say a Bible verse, and the man—or woman—next to him had to identify the speaker. If they failed, they drank.

Adrian wondered if Mariel knew what the adult crewmen drank when they failed. She only ever had tea, or watered-down ale. The game had another level.

Nezumi opened a cabinet and brought out a clear glass bottle, its cork sealed by a dip in red wax.

"Adrian, you start as usual," Mustafa said.

As Mariel always sat to his right, she was always first player. On this day, he couldn't resist the temptation to knavery, and scrounged his memory for something obscure.

"The Lord your God hath multiplied you, and, behold, ye are this day as the stars of heaven for multitude."

She thought about it, nose scrunched and lips pursed. "Thus sayeth Jesus?" she said.

"Moses, I'm afraid." He feigned commiseration.

She reached for her mug of ale.

Adrian put his hand on hers. "Not so fast, love. We've been letting you cheat."

He took the bottle of clear liquor and poured out a dram, which he pushed in front of her with his finger.

She looked at him, then to the cup, and back to him.

He nodded.

She imitated what she had seen the men do for years, tilted it back and swallowed the whole shot.

Her eyes opened wide, rings of shocked white surrounding her brown irises. She gasped and exhaled, and as she did so Adrian imagined her breathing fire like the dragons in the old stories of knights and ladies.

"Oh! Bugger me!" she shouted between coughs.

"The last words of Lot's wife, I believe," Adrian said, patting her on the back.

The crew erupted in laughter and applause, welcoming her as a full and equal member.

She pressed her fingers to her temples, and shut her eyes tight.

No. For Christ's sake, why now? This was supposed to be a happy occasion.

"I want to lie down," she said, standing up from the table. As she did, she began to sway, leaned to one side, and tipped over.

Adrian's outstretched arm caught her.

"The room's spinning," she said.

It wouldn't be long before her head began to ache, the pain ramping up quickly to a level she couldn't tolerate. At first the spells were rare, with months between them. Now she was lucky to go a fortnight without having one.

He picked her up in his arms and carried her to her room, where he pulled her shoes off and put her in bed. He turned down the lights, and lowered the thermostat before leaving to retrieve his medical kit.

When he returned, she was crying and talking to herself.

"Where are we?" she asked.

He took her hand in his. He was sure she couldn't understand him when this wave overcame her, but he answered anyway. "We're in your room, on the *Miranda*, love."

Her left hand held fast to his. Then, in a bizarre manifestation, her right hand madly tried to pry them apart.

"Crome yellow tangle" she said, a tear running down her cheek.

The delirium would last for the duration, which in the worst case had been two days.

He drew a dose of opium into a syringe, took her arm firmly, and found a vein.

Soon she was still, breathing softly, adrift somewhere the pain couldn't follow.

He sat down on the bed beside her, wiped away the remnants of her tears, and put his hand on her head.

"I'm going to fix this," he said. "Today's darkness can't survive in the white light of tomorrow."

He kissed Mariel softly on the forehead.

Two days later, a web of wires and electronic debris streamed from the relic.

"What the hell did you do to it?" Adrian demanded.

Bernt's face flushed. "You would not understand."

"Enlighten *me*, then," Mustafa said. "This is all…temporary, yes?"

"Of course," the engineer said, his voice heavy with frustration. "I bypassed the wireless charging system and connected it to the ship's auxiliary bus. No easy task, but from now on it can be powered through this." He pointed at a red cable running from the glass to an AC outlet.

"Can we access it now?" Mustafa asked.

Bernt looked at an array of graphs and numbers on his computer. "No. It's powered, but the contents remain encrypted."

"Is Mariel up and about?" Mustafa asked Adrian.

"She was gorging herself on cheese and biscuits earlier."

Mustafa went to the intercom box. "Lady Mariel to the cargo hold, if you please."

"Good idea," Adrian said. "Get a real technician on the job."

Bernt exploded in German. "*You asshole! Fuck you!*"

Adrian leaned on the workbench and laughed. His face was still red when Mariel entered the hold.

"What foolishness is this?" she asked, falling into laughter herself.

Adrian shook his head. Mariel had been in the grip of her mind's corrosion for thirty hours, only emerging early that morning. How did her spirits stay so high?

"Be a dear and activate our glass, will you?" Mustafa asked. "If it worked once, perhaps your touch will again perform a miracle."

She swiped her finger down the edge of the glass.

A message appeared on the screen. "Unauthorized use of this protected device is a violation of Earth Union law punishable by fine, imprisonment, or both. If this device has been found, please return it to your organization's information security officer. Remember: cybersecurity is a shared responsibility and we each have a role to play."

"Fuck you," Bernt muttered at the glass.

Adrian took the glass from Mariel, and scanned the content listing.

ASCNT Program Participant Field Retrofit 2820-12A.

"I think it's a medical tool," he said, hedging a bit. "The index says it's for the 'cortical reorganization of defective neural pathways of the parietal lobe presenting in participants with GENIE versions prior to fourteen point zero.'"

"What did you just say?" Mustafa asked.

"Cortical reorganization of—"

"But what was that about a genie? Version fourteen? That sounds like computer jargon."

"I don't know, Mustafa. I know that the parietal lobe is a region of the brain, but neuroscience is a dark art and everything I've read about it was censored. Whole chapters removed. That's why we're going to Sabine."

The Turk pursed his lips and scrunched his eyebrows. "What do you mean 'that's why we're going to Sabine?' We needed Sabine because of the encryption, but young Mariel has taken care of that."

Damn. "To realize the most coin we need to know exactly what the damn thing is, right?"

"Right…"

"Does anyone here know exactly what it is?"

"No," the Turk said. "No, you're right. We're going to need her expertise regardless. I'm optimistic about the value of this thing and its data, though. Anything of a medical nature is highly sought after."

"That's true," Adrian said. "So we need to make sure we understand what we have before we even think about selling it. I'm going to read through the documentation and see whether I can make sense of any of it while we're en route."

Adrian watched Nezumi and Bernt maneuver the ship into the proper reentry angle. A large LED display on the engineer's panel showed their orbital velocity: 15,000 km/h.

The main engine pods were rotated through 180-degrees, pointing the huge MOA thrusters forward.

"Retro-fire in ten," Nezumi said.

"Okay, TPS cryo green," Bernt replied.

"Hold on," Nezumi said for the benefit of the passengers. He fired the main engines. The ship immediately groaned and vibrated. Velocity decreased rapidly to 12,000 km/h.

The ship eased into the upper atmosphere and the crew were pushed down into their anti-G chairs. Only about twice standard G—not at all uncomfortable—though the chairs could carry much more weight in an emergency.

Speed bled down to 6,000 km/h while the temperature on the bottom of the hull ramped up to a warm 600 degrees K. The

Apex engineers fitted the ship with a clever system of vanes and diffusers to control the boundary layer—the two centimeters or so of air closest to the hull—so that while they flew at five times the speed of sound, the ride was near as smooth as in a vacuum.

"Altitude one-hundred. Jets on." Nezumi activated the supersonic ramjets that allowed them to maintain precise control of their reentry speed, altitude, and heading. The main engines then rotated back to a more aerodynamic position.

Bernt monitored the cryogenic Thermal Protection System. "Temp steady six-two-nine." The TPS piped cooling fluid through the inner hull, protecting the ship from extreme heat sources, including the fireball that would be experienced in an emergency reentry.

"Altitude twenty-two," Nezumi said. The ship leveled off, her speed now a mere 1,150 km/h, and the pilot pointed them towards their destination, Civitate Dei.

"Delta one five, *Miranda*." Nezumi radioed the landing field.

"*Miranda*, delta one five, copy," a static-fringed voice replied.

"Request permission to initiate final descent."

"*Miranda*, permission granted, proceed on heading one one three, landing pad six."

"Copy one one three, pad six, *Miranda* out."

They hurtled toward the landing pad. The vast plain of steel-reinforced concrete—three meters thick—covered over one hundred acres, allowing twenty or more ships of the *Miranda's* size to alight at the same time. Around the perimeter were low bunkers housing the traffic control centers for the field, and the tracking station that monitored the sensors deployed throughout the system.

Nezumi rotated the engine pods and used the thrust vectoring to bring the ship in over pad six. With his characteristic flourish, he came in fast and didn't enter a hover until the ship was only a few meters from the ground. The instant the ship's forward velocity ceased, he dropped her to the concrete where the massive, hydraulically-dampened landing struts compressed as they took up the weight.

"All hands to the galley." Mustafa's summons came over the intercom within a minute of touchdown.

Any assemblage normally took a long time to form up, the crew staggering slowly to the mess hall in various states of inebriation and undress. Today everyone was standing in the hold before Mustafa himself arrived.

"Our records are in order, yes?" Mustafa asked Adrian.

"Of course. I'll check us in at the assessor's office. When I get back, we'll go find Sabine."

"Good," the Turk said. "Lars, you'll take one of your mates and pay our fees for two days, no more, then have our water and liquid nitrogen topped up. Everyone else, stay aboard."

Mariel took Adrian's hand. "Can I come with you?"

"Is there any chance I can persuade you to stay here, without earning days of pouting and scorn?"

"I think you know the answer to that."

CHAPTER 09

The carriage swept Adrian and Mariel up and around the hill from which the Old City overlooked the New.

His black Hospitaler's uniform, with the silver Maltese cross pinned to either side of a Mandarin collar, earned them the right to ride all the way to the inner gates of the citadel.

"I like it when you wear that," she said, smoothing out a wrinkle on his tunic.

The formal attire of a knight was less than comfortable, with the tunic's high collar, the wool breeches, and the tall, stiff riding boots. That it was all black didn't help, but today a cool, late-summer breeze brought relief.

The carriage stopped, and the pair jumped out in front of the huge, arched gateway.

A detachment of Swiss Guards in colorful diamond-patterned uniforms and shining breastplates kept watch, examining each person as they entered.

Mariel dallied behind him.

"Get up here and walk beside me, on my right," he said. She deserved some time to run around, but here in the Old City their duty required a more serious demeanor.

She caught up with him and matched his stride.

"Open any doors we come to, and if anyone of common appearance comes too close to me, insert yourself between us menacingly." He looked at her. "As menacingly as you can, anyway."

"Why?" she asked.

"It started long ago with squires trying to outdo each other in displaying affection for their knights. Now it's our contribution to church theatrics."

"Don't worry, Adrian, I'll protect you from the mob."

The ceremonial and public duties of a squire rarely found their way into Mariel's tutelage. Never, actually. "Just think of Dame Rebeka and act like she would."

If ceremony were left out of her training, history was not. Rebeka, the first woman to be knighted in the Order of Saint John over two-hundred years ago, became the role model for a female warrior.

"You want me to kill the next dozen Saracens I see, rally the knights, and save the town from pillage?"

"I swear to God if you were a boy I'd knock the sass out of you with the back of my hand."

She latched onto his arm in a way that wasn't at all proper for a squire. "Then it's a good thing I'm a woman, and not a boy. Though, if you want to be more physical with me, I think I could tolerate it."

"What?" he asked with a startled twitch, but their arrival at the office of the Secretariat interrupted his already-shaken train of thought.

She ran to open the door.

They made their way past a few robed priests to an office with a brass plaque identifying the *Cursus Ecclesia*, the Church's courier service.

"Good afternoon, Brother." A pretty girl behind a wooden counter greeted him. She wore a green dress with a tan bodice and stood with her hands behind her back.

"Good afternoon," Adrian replied.

"We don't see enough Knights of Saint John on Bethany, Brother. Not nearly enough." The clerk studied him from head to toe with no pretense of discretion.

"Is there a problem?" Mariel stepped in front of him, confronting the clerk and spoiling her inspection.

A bit too aggressive. He put his hand on her shoulder. "I'm Adrian of Tarsus," he told the clerk. "Pull box six-one-six."

"Certainly Brother, box six-one-six. I'll be back shortly." She disappeared through a door behind her.

"What are you expecting?" Mariel asked.

"My stipend." As a Knight-Lieutenant he received one silver quattro per week while errant, plus an extra quarter to feed and clothe his squire.

"Maybe we could visit just one or two shops, then?"

The clerk returned with a small metal strongbox. She unlocked it and turned it to face Adrian.

There was the expected stack of promissory notes stamped and signed by the Exchequer. Not expected, though, was a letter on heavy yellow paper, folded three times and sealed with red wax. The wax bore the image of Gabriel, patron of the *Cursus*. Under the letter, a small leather-wrapped box.

"What is it?" Mariel asked, as excited by the sealed letter as Adrian was puzzled.

"I don't know."

"Who's it from?"

"I don't know." He took the promissory notes and put them in his satchel, set the smaller box on the counter, then pushed the strong box back to the clerk.

"Sign here, Brother." The girl put the log book in front of Adrian, who jotted his name.

"Open it," Mariel said.

"Why so eager for bad news?"

"It's good news. I know it."

"Nothing good ever crosses the relay." He shook his head slowly, then broke the seal and unfolded the letter.

After a moment Mariel was bouncing on her toes. "Well?"

"I don't understand it."

"Understand what?" She snatched the letter from his hand and her eyes darted back and forth down the page. "You've been promoted to Knight-Commander! Oh, that's wonderful." She jumped up and gave him a hug.

The girl behind the counter raised an eyebrow.

"No. There's something wrong. A man like me can't hold that rank."

"What do you mean, 'a man like you?'"

"Not only low-born but an orphaned bastard. They reserve higher rank for those with a pedigree as well as distinction in battle."

"You've distinguished yourself in battle. I've seen your shield."

"Have you been digging through my things?" he asked, annoyed. His armor and shield were in a trunk stowed in a dark corner of the *Miranda's* hold.

"When you told me how knights record their battle history on the insides of their shields, I pulled yours out and read it. It's long."

"It's irrelevant to this." He held up the letter.

"Well, I'll be happy for you even if you won't. My knight is a Commander."

He couldn't help notice the brightness of her smile, and for a moment he felt his own emotions thaw.

"What's in the other box?" she asked.

He pulled the top off, revealing a velvet-lined interior and two gleaming objects.

"A ring!" Mariel reached in and snatched the silver signet. It bore the Maltese Cross, carved finely into a flat, square surface. A single ruby sat at the center of the cross.

"A Commander's insignia of rank," he said.

She took up his hand and a slipped the ring onto his finger, giving it a twist to get it in position, then pulled his arm to move his hand into the light where the signet shone bright and the facets of the ruby sparkled. "Very fine. What else did they send?"

From the box he pulled a pair of glass and paraluminum tags attached to a thin necklace.

"New identification," he said before she could ask.

"We should celebrate with an ale," she said.

"Should we now, love?"

They left the Secretariat, merging with the throng of pedestrians in the street.

The Tithe Assessor's office was the same as every other, only larger, and busier. Coins chimed as they were counted and bagged. Behind the desks, the same tired, bored, and cantankerous clerks found on every other planet. They might have been clones.

Officers of the Church could go to the head of the line, and Adrian availed himself of the privilege.

A tall, thin gaunt of a merchant in a green cloak huffed as Adrian cut in front of him. The man had probably been in line for over an hour, and Adrian pretended not to notice the expression of displeasure.

Mariel did not.

"Show some respect," she said to the man. "And back up. Give the Knight-*Commander* some room."

Adrian turned and watched her stare the merchant down until he complied. Had she been alone, the scene would have been comic, but with him standing behind her the dynamic changed completely. The merchant's eyes went to the ground and he took a small, probably unconscious step back in submission.

"My apologies, Sir Knight," the man said.

"Warmly accepted, sir," Adrian replied. He'd have to speak with her about laying it on so thick, but still, she had backbone and that put her ahead of many men.

"Next!" the clerk called out.

Adrian and Mariel took their place in front of the desk.

"Declaring for the *Miranda*," Adrian said, "EC-1611."

The clerk repeated the *Miranda's* identification code under his breath as he entered it into the computer. "What are you declaring?"

"This is a provisioning stop. Nothing to declare from our previous port, St. Anthony, Gereon."

"Right. Easy one then." The clerk read his screen for a few seconds. "You're not scheduled for a customs inspection."

"Excellent." A bit of good luck.

"Oh, that's why." The clerk scrolled down the screen. "No inspection because you've been pre-authorized."

"Pre-authorized by whom?"

"H-O-I."

Bloody hell. The hair on Adrian's body stood up. *Holy Office of the Inquisition.*

"Anything else?" the clerk asked.

Half an hour later they exited their carriage at the edge of the landing field and walked to the ship.

The cargo ramp hung open, and Tomas stood nonchalant at its base smoking a pipe.

"Are we all good?" Adrian asked when they reached the ramp.

"Sure," Tomas said. "Customs is on-board, though."

"What?"

"Routine inspection. Nothing to worry about, Brother, we're clean."

"Damn it." Adrian ran up the ramp. Inside, he found a crowd.

Four men in the crimson uniform of the Customs Service milled in the hold, poking at crates and barrels. Mustafa and Nezumi stood watching them.

"Who's in charge here?" Adrian demanded.

"I am...sir." One of the men strolled over. Of middling height and olive complexion, his posture was brash. Proud.

"What's the meaning of this?"

"Customs inspection, sir. I'm Sergeant Barbieri." The Sergeant's voice was slack and he smelled of prosciutto. A close look revealed the sleeves of his tunic were too short, and his black hair a touch too long for Papal service.

Adrian's practiced eye picked up another quirk. Sergeant Barbieri was unarmed, but he stood like a man accustomed to the weight of a sword on his belt. So did the rest of the inspection team, all of them slightly out of uniform in one way or another.

Condottieri.

"I've just come from the assessor's office, and there was no inspection scheduled," Adrian said.

"There must be some mistake, sir."

"Indeed, and I fear you're making it." Adrian took a step toward the Sergeant, who backed up almost in unison. No swordsman wanted to be close-pressed, no matter how cheap.

"We're just finishing in the hold, sir. All we lack is to take a look around the engineering and crew spaces."

"Good, then. I'll escort you."

The other 'inspectors' were wandering back, forming a loose ring around Adrian and the Sergeant.

"I'm…not sure that's appropriate, sir," Barbieri said.

"Why not, Sergeant? We're on the same side."

Barbieri slapped his palm against the side of his thigh and looked around. "Very well, sir. Let's start in the crew quarters."

They found nothing there. They wouldn't. Adrian was well aware of Mustafa's two smuggling holes. One was in a large wine barrel—full of real wine—with a hidden compartment running down the center. The second was inside a broken hot-water heater in the engineering bay. Barbieri and his crew swarmed over that space next.

The poorly-disguised soldiers of fortune looked at the environmental control systems, condensers, and fresh-water tanks as if they were experts on spacecraft systems. The Sergeant wrapped his knuckles on the first, working, hot-water heater and received a dull thud. The second unit returned a hollow chime.

"That one's down," Adrian said. "Engineer says he needs a new pressure regulator."

"These old things need a lot of upkeep," Barbieri observed, moving along.

"Yes they do."

Barbieri turned back. "Let me just take a look. Due diligence, sir." Damn. "Of course."

The Sergeant opened the inspection panel and shined a light inside.

Adrian's view was blocked. His body tensed.

"Interesting," Barbieri said.

"What?"

"This tank's very clean. Doesn't look like it's been used in a long time."

"Like I said, it's been down."

"Right. Well, I think we've seen everything, sir."

Adrian led Barbieri and his men to hold, stopping them at the top of the ramp. "I need my certification."

"Yes," Barbieri said, squirming. "Sir, I've left my forms back at the office. I'll have to send a man over with it."

"Right. Be sure that you do, Sergeant."

Sabine's morning routine at the Bee's Knees included scrubbing, followed by cleaning and scouring. Though the evening staff went over the pub thoroughly when they closed the doors at midnight, there was always room for more detailing, more wood polish, and a good airing out.

She didn't serve meals until midday, but she opened the front door at eight bells so the men who worked at night could wander in, relax, and have an ale. They came in dirty and tired, smelling of burnt coal and oil, tannin, and blood. It took only a whiff to tell the blacksmiths, leather-workers, and butchers apart.

A handful sat at the bar now, jovial, talking, waiting for service.

Where was Maria? Sabine had sent the young Romany serving-girl to fetch a couple of buckets of water to scrub the floor in the entry.

"What will you gentlemen be drinking this morning?" she asked as she went behind the bar.

"Gentlemen?" one of them asked. "Oy! Miss Sabine, you know there ain't one gentleman among us."

"Not in this lot, God help us," another said. The group of men laughed heartily and slapped each other on the backs.

"Old Alfred could pass for a ponce," a younger man said, whereupon an older man, presumably Old Alfred, whacked him on the head.

"Well, Roger Murdock," Sabine said to the leader, giving the group an exaggerated wink and smile as she leaned on the bar, "you may smell of ash and tar, and you may lack the gilding of the bourgeois, but when you walk in my door you're squires and gentle men all."

"Hear, hear!" the group exclaimed. "Ale, all around!"

"Coming up," Sabine said, then left though the kitchen door.

She rounded up some mugs, put one under the tap, and grabbed the handle.

Somehow, she couldn't turn it. She stopped and leaned against the large keg. A dull ache grew in her neck, then spread through her shoulders, back and legs, until it painfully squeezed her whole body.

She rested her head on the top of the barrel.

How long had it been since Lucas' party? Days. Ten? Or more? She couldn't remember her last real sleep, but her body made it clear that rest was long overdue.

Lucas.

Alisa Conti.

The Kresimirs.

Selim Bey.

Her life was wrapped up with libertines and heathens. For what? To Hell with them all.

No…no. Don't give up.

Footsteps jarred her. The sound came from the alley door that the serving-girl left open.

"Maria—" Sabine turned.

The silhouette of a man filled the doorway.

"Bar's 'round the other side," she said, and began to draw an ale, forcing her hand to open the tap.

"I know that, Miss Adler."

The voice oozed a Turkish accent, condescending and laced with gall.

"Serhan Kaş." She set the mug down hard and walked to the center of the kitchen. She had no formal contact with the Ambassador, Selim Bey. Why was his man here?

Serhan entered and took a few steps toward her.

"What do you want? An ale? Maybe I can fry up a ham steak for you?"

Serhan's right eye twitched and narrowed. "Selim Bey bade me visit you."

The man was filthy. Not his person, which was impeccably-groomed, but his soul. A Janissary, he enforced the Ambassador's will in the Saracen district with typical cruelty. The authorities in the Holy City tended to ignore what the Muslims did to each other, as long as it didn't spill out of their boundaries. Naturally, none of them would dare complain to the constabulary.

Serhan looked at her with a heavy gaze, as if to push her down on her knees by will alone.

He wouldn't dare attack her here, would he? "What does the Ambassador want?" She held her head up. Show no fear, as when confronted by a dog.

"Selim Bey demands to know why you killed Reymont Lucas."

So, they did make her for Lucas' killer.

"Impudent. Ridiculous." Except it was plausible, depending on how much the Ambassador knew about the Grey Cloaks. "Lucas was a friend. I also bought beer and ale from him. I certainly didn't kill him." She shook her head. "This is pointless. Does Selim Bey think that I'd admit to the deed if I *did* kill him?"

"Lucas' killer has cost us a considerable sum. His Majesty the Sultan will be enraged." Serhan walked closer to her. Slow and haughty. Mocking her in her own place.

His proximity was uncomfortable. Repellant. Sabine squared her shoulders, stood her ground. "I don't know anything about the Sultan's finances. Nor do I care." Was he trying to intimidate her, or would he attack? She couldn't rule the latter out.

"You should care." His breath was warm in her face.

She glanced to her right, to a preparation table where a long carving knife lay just out of reach. Should she scream, alert the men at the bar? Could they even reach her in time?

"This attack cannot, and will not, be forgotten," he said, leaning his mouth close to her ear.

"Get out of my place."

He grinned, showing teeth stained by the hashish pipe. "Your place? The only place for you is locked in the *harem*, pregnant, or becoming pregnant." A strand of black saliva ran between is lips.

"Get out!"

There was sound at the back door.

A woman gasped.

Sabine heard a bucket hitting the floor, and the sloshing of water.

Maria.

"You get away from her! Get out of the kitchen!" the girl shouted.

"We'll meet again, after Selim Bey decides how to deal with you," Serhan whispered. He left the kitchen, pushing roughly past Maria.

"Are you all right, Miss? Who was that dirty Saracen?"

"No one, Maria. No one. Be a dear, would you, and draw up some ale for the men at the bar."

"Aye, Miss."

What the hell was the reason for that show? Sabine leaned against a table and let out an exasperated breath. They thought she killed Lucas, but they weren't sure. Selim Bey knew he had to be careful, had to be certain before he risked killing a Christian. Five thousand, though. For that, would he act on suspicion alone?

Mary Frances kneeled and picked up the mysterious paper. Slipped under her door sometime during afternoon prayer, it was coarse, folded, with no seals.

She opened it, and her mind locked onto the blocks of five characters, random on the surface but strictly ordered underneath.

Enciphered, but not using Duval's method.

Intriguing.

Soothing.

The enigma seized and held her attention.

Hand written, probably by a woman given the light, precise strokes. She held the page under her nose. The ink was dry, but its phenol odor of peated whiskey was still strong. No more than a day old.

The last line was writ plain. 'And they tarried till they were ashamed: and, behold, he opened not the doors of the parlor; therefore they took a key, and opened them: and, behold, their lord was fallen down dead on the earth.'

Old Testament. Something from the interminable dull histories of the Israelites. Why?

She sat at her small desk and opened a well-worn Bible bound in red leather. A gift from Cardinal Duval on her twelfth birthday, each beautifully illuminated page had been read, studied, sifted countless times.

Joshua, Judges, Samuel, or Kings?

Judges, she determined after some study. Book three, verse twenty-five.

The book told of Ehud ben-Gera, who murdered Eglon, King of Moab, in the name of the Lord by thrusting a dagger into the monarch's enormous gut. The wound oozed excrement from the king's bowels before his prodigious rolls of fat closed upon the blade so tightly that it could not be withdrawn. Ha!

But what was the point of this scatological tale?

Ehud tricked Eglon into sending his servants away—a king really ought to know better than that. The servants tarried—fools—until well after Ehud escaped. Finally they took a key, opened the door to the parlor, and discovered their lord dead.

A key. It could be a Vigenère cipher, mathematically quaint, but effective. If the key were JUDGES…no, it was too short. This sort of code required an alphabetic key, no numerals or other symbols, the longer the better. JUDGESTHREE?

Perhaps.

Yes.

The five-letter blocks melted like little lead ingots, her mind molding them into something golden.

KYWNS MIYVT EAYGG RVPRE PAREf orthy self thou and all thy company that are assembled unto thee and be thou a guard unto them. Thou shalt ascend and come like a storm, thou shalt be like a cloud to cover the land, thou, and all thy bands and many people with thee.

Mary Frances snorted. More obfuscation, a most delicious tease. Her hand went to her stomach, from which a warm tingle began to spread.

The message continued. 'Find ascnt, know it and know the truth, act decisively. A sword upon the liars.'

Ascnt? Ascent? An error in the encoding? No, it was the same as the relic Duval coveted. ASCNT.

Who sent this? No matter, it began a hunt, a search for something that a man sought to hide, and so *must* be dragged into the light. What was the lie, and who was the liar?

The message already memorized, she held the paper over the single candle that burned in the room, the flame consuming the witness.

She ran down the quiet hall, out into the Old City on bare feet. There was one great repository of ancient knowledge. She would dig there for this tantalizing ASCNT and its truths, and like Ehud ben-Gera, she would be God's judge of it.

CHAPTER 10

The *Miranda's* shore party approached the Bee's Knees. Far down the cobbled street, the pub's weather-worn shingle, painted with the image of a lanky-legged bumblebee, rocked in the breeze.

Adrian had left his dress uniform on the *Miranda*, and returned to his normal attire: a loose-sleeved white linen shirt worn under a tough jerkin of red-brown leather, closed up the front by four brass-buckled straps.

He felt a tug at his sleeve.

"Do you think Sabine will remember us?" Mariel asked.

"I'm sure she'll remember you. I'll wager you're the only young lady who's ever blown up a keg of ale in her tap room."

"That wasn't my fault." Her innocent smile screamed guilt.

"Say it enough and it might become true."

"It was that old dog Berry that caused it. I wonder if he's still here?"

Berry was a big black hound that hung around the Bee making as much mischief as he could. Mariel had become attached to him during their brief stay two years ago.

As they walked, Adrian could see that the men's slower pace frustrated her. She sped up, stopped to wait for them, then ran again.

"Well, go on." He feigned annoyance.

Excited, she took off ahead of the group. He watched her dart inside while he and Mustafa were still a block away.

Adrian entered the Bee's tall yellow doors with somewhat more trepidation than his young charge. The noontime crowd was in high spirits as he scanned the busy room, finding Mariel sitting at the bar but no sign of Sabine.

"Did you find her?" he asked as he walked up behind Mariel.

"No, the barmaid said she's in back. Oh—there she is!"

Sabine appeared from the kitchen.

Adrian's starved eyes fell on her. Pink blouse, honey-blonde hair pulled back, and vibrant eyes the color of bright indigo dye.

Adrenaline pumped into his veins and hit with a jolt. All his senses sharpened, his heart raced. The sensation was the same tense, jittery, but acutely lucid feeling he had every time he fought.

The interior of the pub came alive in a way few could experience. The solid thunk of mugs on wooden tables on the other side of the room became clear, the chatter of twenty men and women separated and he heard each word distinctly, the heady smell of strong ale and roasting meat touched a primal nerve.

Before single combat it was critical to read the enemy's emotional state, and though war was the last thing on his mind, his habit informed him that she was on edge.

The mug of lager she carried fell to the floor.

"Adrian," she said. In an action most observers wouldn't bother to note, her hand went to her hair, neatening it, smoothing it back over her right ear.

"Sabine." That insignificant flick spoke volumes, and his apprehension vanished.

As if summoned by the smell of beer flowing freely, Berry the black dog trotted in from the street and set to lapping up the malty beverage.

Mariel jumped from her seat down into the puddle to scratch him behind the ears, for which he thanked her with a sloppy lick to the face.

"Sabine, I have returned!" Mustafa said, stepping out from behind Adrian.

"Oh God." She rolled her eyes, then they narrowed. "Adrian, you have a hell of a nerve bringing him back in here."

"What?" His elation bled out. Had he misread her?

"Everyone's back," Mariel said. "Me, Adrian, Mustafa, Lars, Bernt, Nezumi, Gilly, and Tomas. Everyone except Koray. He died."

"What happened to him?"

"He was ki—"

"Mariel, not here," Adrian said.

Mustafa strutted to the bar. "So good to see you again, my dear." Like Adrian, he had eschewed lavish clothes and looked a bit like a Dominican friar in a dark brown hooded robe.

The silence between them became tense. Mustafa's face looked like that of a nervous magician who'd realized his audience wasn't buying it.

A flailing commotion burst from the kitchen. A plump, grey-haired woman wielding a meat cleaver rushed to Sabine and harangued her.

"What's this I hear about a Saracen threatening you this morning, Miss?" the old woman asked in a thick Irish brogue. She held the cleaver aloft.

"Ruth, put that down! It was nothing."

"The hell you say! Maria told me what happened, and—" Then Ruth saw Mustafa standing next to Adrian. Her face went beet-red. "There be one o' the Saracen bastards now."

Mustafa looked behind himself.

"Yes, you, Turkey!" Ruth shouted, waving the cleaver. "Get out! And go tell all your greasy kin to keep out o' here or I'll chop your Goddamned balls off!" She brought the cleaver down on the bar with a solid thunk, leaving it wedged in the oak.

As one, the Bee's patrons turned and looked at the Turk.

Her ultimatum delivered, Ruth held her head up and returned to the kitchen.

The crowd returned to their lunches.

Sabine's eyes hardened. "Mustafa Ali Pasha, I told you never to come back here."

"She told you never to come back?" Adrian asked Mustafa.

"She did, and I didn't. For two long years. But now we have a wonderful opportunity to share."

The charismatic overture bounced off her.

"One of your opportunities is enough for a lifetime," she said, pointing an accusatory finger at him. "I'm not interested."

"You will be, trust me. Let's go talk about it."

"Get out!"

"Sabine, please." Adrian broke in.

She said nothing, staring back at him in cold reply, head tilted to the side.

"Hear us out, will you?" Adrian asked. She had to be curious, didn't she? Her curiosity was her Achilles heel.

Mariel piped up. "Please, Sabine. We have some *Machina* on the ship we need you to look at. It's probably a big heresy."

Adrian followed two paces behind the group, frowning, frustrated by his party's inability to be discreet. Mustafa led, a large brown sack with legs. Behind the Turk walked a beautiful blonde in a grey cloak, a girl with an excess of energy bumping and jumping along beside her. Even Berry had joined the parade.

The wail of engines turning up met them as they approached the landing field. Well beyond the *Miranda*, another ship prepared to depart. Its thrusters peppered them with a fine grit blown up from the concrete.

"That's Johann Froelich in the *Cyllene* going home to Frisia," Sabine said.

They trekked across the concrete apron. When they reached the *Miranda*, Mustafa walked to her port-side rear landing strut and opened a metal box attached to it. Inside was an intercom and a twelve-key pad for lowering the ramp. He pressed the intercom button. "Bernt, lower the ramp."

Silence.

"Bernt."

Nothing.

"Where in Hell is he?" Mustafa asked. "Self-flagellating again, no doubt," he added under his breath. The Turk tapped his finger on the keypad and was rewarded with a harsh buzz. He tapped again, and received the sound of another rejection.

"What's wrong?" Adrian asked.

"Nothing. I forgot my damn code." He closed his eyes. "Let's see. Two, seven, seven, five, four." He mouthed the numbers as he entered them. Finally, he received a happy chirp and an alarm sounded as the heavy ramp began to lower.

"Bernt!" Mustafa huffed up into the cargo bay, the rest of the party in tow.

The ship felt quiet despite the rumbling air conditioning and the whirr of the electrical generators. The cargo bay lights were off, but the spotlights above the workbench projected bright cones down onto its surface.

The black case sat with its top open, empty.

"Bernt!" Mustafa said again, with no better result.

"Nezumi? Tomas?" Adrian asked.

Bugger. Thievery? The Inquisition?

Adrian went to the actuator and closed the cargo bay door, then activated the lock override. Now, no one could enter the ship without Mustafa's personal code.

"Stay here," he said to the rest. He walked through a short corridor and into the nearby crew quarters. A quick check of each cabin found no one.

He drew his dagger.

Further up the hallway, in the galley, he saw the legs sprawled on the deck.

The body was face-down. He knelt and turned it over.

Tomas.

There was no wound that Adrian could see, so he checked for a pulse.

Blood still pumped.

As he confirmed that there was still life in Tomas, he was startled by movement in the opposite corridor leading to the flight deck.

Nezumi leaned against the wall, looking bewildered and holding the back of his head with one hand. "It was Bernt," the pilot said.

"What the hell happened?" Adrian spun Nezumi around by the shoulder to inspect the back of his head. No blood, but a dark bruise was forming.

"I was sitting on the flight deck. He came up behind me, like he was going to sit down at his console. I turned back to the instrument panel and the lights went out."

"Hold your eyes open." Adrian stared at Nezumi's pupils. Normal. Evenly dilated. "You'll be fine. Tomas wasn't so lucky."

Tomas still lay on the floor. Adrian kneeled over his head as Mariel and Sabine looked on. Mustafa sat in a chair, his face in his hands.

"Get him on the table." Adrian put his arms under Tomas' shoulders and turned to Mustafa. "Now, damn it! There's no time to waste."

The words came out in a battlefield roar that reverberated throughout the ship.

Sabine jumped.

Mariel stepped closer, riveted.

Mustafa hesitated, then willed himself onto his feet and hurried to grab Tomas' legs. Together, the men lifted him onto the steel table.

A buzzer sounded.

"That'll be Lars and Gilly returning," Mustafa said. "I'll let them in." He shuffled off to the cargo hold. The lowering ramp rattled the deck plates.

"Mariel," Adrian said, his voice back under control. "Go get the medical kit, will you? Hurry now, love."

She ran off down the corridor.

Lars walked into the mess hall. "What the hell happened?" he shouted.

"I'll explain it all to you soon," Mustafa said, holding the boatswain back. "Young Tomas has taken a very bad blow to his head."

Adrian examined each of the injured man's eyes. The right side was fine, but the left was dilated. He checked the left side of the skull, and soon found the point of impact.

"I need a razor."

"You can use mine." Mustafa's quarters were closest, and he pounded off to his personal lavatory.

Adrian and Sabine stood side-by-side.

"He doesn't have much time. He'll probably die," Adrian said, clenching his fist. Tomas was just twenty.

"What's wrong with him?" she asked.

"Blood is building up between his skull and brain. You can tell by the way his eye is dilated. I'll have to trephine to relieve the pressure." Thinking about the task calmed him. He released his fist.

"You're going to drill a hole in his skull?" Sabine's eyes went wide.

"Yes, I observed a trephination once, on Acre. The knight— his name was Lawrence—lived to see another battle."

She stared at him, incredulous. "Adrian, you'll kill him. You can't just drill a hole in a head!"

"If we do nothing, he'll die on this table." Determination took hold. "We have to try to save him—inaction is immoral."

"No! I know a doctor. We can send for him—"

"Sabine." He took a deep breath. Calmed himself. "Tomas' time is measured in minutes, not hours."

Mustafa shuffled in with the straight razor and a cup of frothy cream.

Adrian shaved a patch atop the wound. He ran his fingers over it, guessing the size of the hole to be opened.

Mariel was back with his bag. He pulled out a long canvas roll and spread it open on a bench. Inside were pockets holding an array of tools. He took out a syringe with a hideous steel needle attached.

"This will keep him down." He stuck the needle into a thick, brown bottle and drew out a quantity of fluid, being careful not to pull up any air. Finding a vein, he injected the drug into Tomas' arm.

"Everyone leave, now." Adrian's voice again dipped into the tone of command.

Mustafa, Nezumi, and Gilly exited for the cargo hold.

"I want to help." Mariel spoke with the speed and high pitch of a very excited young lady.

He shoved the thought aside.

"Good," he said.

"Give me something to do, too." Sabine also lingered at his side.

"Get me some alcohol," he said, nodding at the galley cabinets.

"Is that wise?"

"To clean the instruments. Christ."

"Oh. Right. Of course," she said. "Holy water, coming up." She went to rummage through the cabinets.

Adrian selected a scalpel, locking forceps, and a trepanning tool with a conical bore. These ancient tools, made of the finest quality stainless steel, were of magnificent quality compared to the modern examples one could buy. They held an edge almost forever.

Sabine found the alcohol and Adrian wrenched the stopper out, breaking the wax seal. He washed the tools and his hands, soaked a towel and carried it back to the table, where he scrubbed Tomas' head.

Wielding the scalpel he cut a semicircular flap of skin, left to right, mopping up blood with the towel.

He focused on the work, putting out of his mind the fact that Tomas was a man he knew, a friend, even. Strangely, cutting on a man to save him brought a sense of gravity he never felt when cutting to kill.

He peeled the flap of skin down, revealing bone. To hold the skin out of the way, he ran a single long thread through it and clipped on the forceps to act as a weight.

Mariel peered in over his shoulder.

"Do you see these sutures?" he asked.

"Those wavy lines in the bone?"

"Yes. That's where the bones of his skull have fused. We mustn't drill into them."

"Why are we drilling at all?"

"A blow to the head can cause bleeding between the skull and the brain. There's only so much space inside, and the pocket of blood will press the brain, squeezing it until the man dies."

He picked up the cutting bit and attached a metal handle to it. Pressing it against the bone, he turned it. The sound was scratchy, like grit under a boot-heel, and the familiar metallic smell of blood was overwhelming.

"Will it work?" Mariel asked.

"The odds aren't in his favor."

"Why do it, then?"

"A knight must have faith that if wounded, his comrades will lay siege to Hell in his defense." When a hundred knights fought together, they each knew that a hundred shields protected them.

The Order of Saint John was founded on trust and faith, and the ideas were at the root of its reputation as an invincible force.

"He isn't a knight."

She was right, but she missed the point.

"Listen, Mariel. This is how unbreakable bonds are formed between men. Not through the coercion of guild or church, but by living and dying together as sincere individuals."

Sabine put her hand on his shoulder.

He glanced at it, and she quickly withdrew it.

The bone he was cutting into would be four to six millimeters thick, so he drilled, checked his depth, and drilled further.

The work took several minutes, but then a cracking sound announced that he was through. He pulled the drill out, and with it came a circle of bone about the diameter of his small finger, and a squirt of blood. He stuck a bowl under the opening, and caught as much as he could.

"When the bleeding stops, I'll remove as much of the congealed blood as I can before we sew him up." Adrian sat and watched the blood seep from Tomas' head. Sabine was next to him on the metal bench, close enough that their shoulders touched.

"Is he still alive?" she whispered.

"His pulse is weak, but he lives."

"I'm sorry for what I said, about you killing him. You're saving his life."

"I haven't saved it yet, though. Bernt had best pray that he pulls through."

"You're going after him, then?"

"I'll find the son of a whore—" Adrian stopped short. Running a pub, she'd surely heard everything, but there was still something crude about it. "I'll find the thieving bastard. He's made it my mission."

Sabine inched closer to him. He felt her warmth.

"How will you fix the hole?" Mariel asked.

"We don't have to. The bone will heal. Grab the needle and thread, and let's see if you can close him up." He stood and let her sit in his place.

Without further instructions, she set about stitching Tomas' head back together.

Mustafa stood in front of the workbench, tired eyes fixed on the empty Black Box. "That Hansa bastard. I'll find him and rip his German balls off. I'll feed his balls to *pigs*." The rest of the crew save for Tomas surrounded him, angry and frustrated.

"One thing at a time," Adrian said. "We have to find him, first." The thought of ripping Bernt's balls off was gratifying, but not particularly helpful.

"I'd feed his balls to a monkey," Mariel said.

"Why?" Adrian asked with an eyebrow arched.

"Adrian!" Sabine's eyes were popping with anger. "What have you knaves been teaching her?"

He grinned.

"I can read and speak Latin, sew up wounds, and best Adrian in a duel," Mariel said in her own defense.

"Not without trickery. Besides, I killed you before you showed your *botta secreta*." It wouldn't be long before her boast became the truth, though.

"Back to Bernt!" Mustafa's face was as red as his slippers.

"Bernt was a Hansa with some rank, yes?" Sabine asked.

"When I hired him, he told me he was an initiate of their ninth circle, but who knows what any of their gibberish means? Why?"

"Just curious. I'd like to have a closer look at that box, now, if you please."

Sabine didn't wait for a reply before she brushed Mustafa aside and took his place at the bench. The men stood by while she examined the box at an excruciatingly slow pace. "It's a Black Box. Extremely durable, environmentally controlled, powered by a tiny micro-fusion reactor. Worth at least a hundred in gold by itself if it isn't arsed up."

"Bernt told us as much. Can the box give us any clues about the contents?" Mustafa asked, pointing at the interior cutout.

"Maybe." She put her hands on the box and looked at Mustafa with a raised eyebrow. "Was this open when you found it?"

"No, we had to rely on young Mariel's finger for that."

"Her finger opened this biometric lock?"

"Indeed it did. Bit of luck, that."

She looked at Adrian.

He did his best to warn her off that path using only his eyes and a slight shake of the head.

"There's no accounting for luck," she said. "What was inside?"

"A glass pad," Mustafa said. "Bernt said it had an unusual compute module attached to it. Adrian thinks it's a medical device."

"I wasn't able to glean its purpose, though," Adrian said.

Sabine frowned. "I need a glass, and a coupler."

"Use the glass on the shelf, there," Mustafa said, "and as far as the coupler, ah, just look through the toolbox and find what you need. Bernt kept things well organized."

After rooting around in the steel toolbox, Sabine found the two pieces of the wireless coupler. She attached one to the security module built into the strongbox, and the other to the edge of the glass. She turned on the pad and began to tap commands into it.

Adrian watched her thin fingers at work, and noted how she stuck her tongue ever so slightly out of the right side of her mouth while she concentrated.

"Okay." She continued to type. "You can only access the security module with a coupler attached. An extra bit of hardening, but, once you're connected, the root account is vulnerable. There we are."

She read the screen quietly.

"The entry log shows the last user to open the case was Wallace, Roxanne M., just a few days ago. I suppose that's you, young lady." She looked at Mariel. "The entry prior to that is dated fourteen, four, twenty-three nineteen. That's the fourteenth of April, 2319 AD."

Mustafa let out a long whistle.

"Yes. They sealed this less than a year before the Advent." She stopped typing. The crew remained silent. "That's all there is."

"We must find Bernt and the relic," Mustafa said, smacking his fist into his palm.

"I'll go after Bernt," Adrian said, "with Lars and Gilly."

Lars nodded, but Gilly turned pale, and without saying a word ran off to his quarters. Then came the sound of the lock engaging.

The room was silent.

"Nezumi, then."

"No," Mustafa said, "you can't take our pilot."

"I'll go," Mariel said.

Interesting. There was no doubt she could out-fight Bernt, or anyone he was likely to consort with.

"Don't be silly, Mariel," Sabine said. Not exactly condescending, but the way one would talk to a girl.

"What?" Mariel stared back.

"Sabine's right," Adrian said. How could he have entertained the idea for even a second?

"But I can help!"

"You can help by not arguing."

Mariel scowled at Sabine, huffed, and left the cargo hold.

"I'll go with you," Sabine said.

"No, it's too dangerous."

She laughed. "Fine, but tell me, where are you going to begin your search?"

Damn. The city was vast.

"That's what I thought. You're in luck, though, because I know where the Hansa technophiles are hiding. Your engineer is almost certainly with them."

"Where?"

"I'll take you there, and I'll send word to one of my people to meet us."

"What are we facing, besides Bernt?"

"There are three or four of them. Engineers and technicians. No match for you and Henry."

"Which is it—three or four?"

"Four."

"You're certain?"

"Yes." She nodded, then looked at him and smiled. "Yes, this'll be perfect."

He folded his arms. She was far too eager to join the hunt, especially after the greeting she'd given them earlier.

CHAPTER 11

Adrian and Sabine crossed the city as the setting sun hovered over snaking rows of old stone and timber buildings. Cooking fires lent the air a smoky tang that was almost palpable on the tongue.

Don't experience things for the first time as a memory. Adrian pushed himself to see, hear, and feel everything that passed, from the rippling of her blouse-sleeves in the breeze to the soft little breath she took each time she began to speak.

"Where did you find this relic?" she asked.

"In Saint Anthony of all places."

"Easley?" She turned and met his eyes.

"You know him?"

A few errant strands of her blonde hair meandered on the breeze. Occasionally the sunlight hit one just so, and it flared golden.

"I've heard his name, that's all. He's a minor player in the trade."

She was smooth, but a deflection was a deflection. Was it a criminal's natural caution, or something else?

"Was a minor player."

Her cinnamon perfume was in the air, its spice vying with the smoke.

"Dead?"

"Sadly." He could see the grisly severed head, with its cloudy eyes looking up at him.

"Who killed him?" she asked.

"Someone calling himself Girard." He smiled to himself. A few easy words back and forth and she'd already extracted half the story. How would she react if he told her Girard might have been an Inquisitor?

"I don't recognize the name. Not among the collectors and brokers I know, anyway. Adrian?"

"Yes?"

"You know more about this relic than you're telling me. It was in a Black Box, and your Hansa engineer was willing to hurt men he'd known for years to get it. Not to mention your daughter was able to open it."

Her sharpness was almost as arousing as her shape.

"As I said before, I think it's a medical device." Don't give her any more. Not yet.

"Hmm. I do love a mystery."

"I know. That's why I'm here."

The conversation ebbed and flowed as they walked. She told him of antics that had occurred at the Bee's Knees, and he recounted the adventures the crew of the *Miranda* had seen, with only a little embellishment. Sooner than he would have liked, they drew near the limestone blocks framing the stairwell leading down into the reservoir.

For decades after the Advent, the colony's old but efficient water reclamation system kept massive storage tanks filled with clean water. Eventually, the needs of thousands and soon tens of thousands of residents forced an expansion of infrastructure and the Church began construction of a vast underground cistern.

The grey-cloaked figure of a man stood just inside a stone portal. Tucked between a disused granary and a tired warehouse, the stairs were out of sight and largely forgot by the residents. The smell drifting up was slightly stagnant, like a still pond at the height of summer, the entire surface covered by duckweed.

"There's Henry," Sabine said.

"Everyone except Sabine calls me Harry." The man was tall and bony, with fair skin and short-cropped reddish hair. Hanging from his belt, a long blade similar to Adrian's. His eyes were wary, always moving, and he carried his body with trained poise.

Sabine hadn't lied, this man was more than an amateur swordsman. Adrian offered a hand, which Henry shook with a firm grip.

"So good to meet Sabine's Hospitaler," Henry said. "You look quite the model of a soldier of Christ."

"Don't start trouble, Henry," she said.

"I wouldn't think of it." He raised his hands in mock surrender.

"Good, then let's get these bastards."

Adrian raised an eyebrow. Get the bastards, not the relic.

"My man watching the place saw a stocky fellow go in. New to us," Henry said. "Average height, shaved head, very nondescript, really."

"That could be Bernt," Adrian said. "He's very nondescript until he opens his mouth."

Pale limestone blocks framed the steep, narrow stairwell. It became dark, and Adrian stopped to give his eyes time to adjust. The hard steps under their feet disappeared into a still pool. A hint of light snuck into the yawning cavern from above and reflected off a glass-smooth sheet of water fanning out ahead. Two flat-bottomed boats floated at the base of the steps, tied to iron rings set in the walls. More rings hung empty.

He grabbed a rope covered in slick scum, pulled one of the old boats up onto the limestone, and stepped in.

He put his arm out for Sabine. She hesitated, and he was sure that she would brush it out of the way. Then, to his surprise, she took it and allowed him to help her step down into the boat.

Henry climbed in behind her.

Adrian picked up an oar and pushed the dubious craft off the stones and out into the underground lake. "How far does it go?"

"Half a kilometer or so, cut into the limestone under Cemetery Hill."

"A lump of limestone sounds like a difficult place to bury people."

"Oh," Henry said, smiling, "there's no cemetery. Someone thought the rocks scattered over the hill looked like grave stones."

The trio floated out into the cistern, Adrian at the oars and Sabine in the bow, leaning forward, straining to see what awaited them in the darkness. Adrian put his back into it and propelled them forward. The cavern amplified each wet slap of the oars. If there were anyone concerned enough to listen, their approach would be no secret.

Minutes passed, and his shoulders began to burn from the rowing.

Little grates placed at odd intervals high overhead let some light in, and with his eyes now well adjusted he could see the old arched columns, supporting the ceiling above, glide by to the left and right. To pass the time and distract himself from the complaints of his shoulders, he counted them. One after another the thick pilings drifted by.

"Slow down, we're at the end," Sabine whispered.

He had just counted the thirty-first row of columns.

The boat drifted close to a slab wall, and Adrian used an oar to hold them off. Save for some tool-marks, the wall was smooth with no cracks or flaws, and there was no sign of the Hansa having passed.

Sweating, Adrian could sense a waft of air as it cooled his neck. "Feel that?"

"Yes," Sabine replied.

The air should have been still in the crypt-like chamber, but it moved, a light breeze created by a draft. There was an opening somewhere.

"Seems to be moving that way, to the right," Adrian said.

They didn't drift far before they found the source, a rough hole chipped out of the stone wall, large enough for a man to crawl through. Two more boats were tethered under the portal. Adrian guided them to the opening, where Henry reached out and tied the boat to a ring. Before either of the men could offer help, Sabine pulled herself up and through the hole and disappeared into the blackness beyond.

"Sabine, wait," Adrian said in an angry whisper. Damn it.

"Damn it," Henry said. "It's always like this."

"Stop dawdling and climb up," she replied.

Henry went next, then Adrian pulled himself up, crawled through several feet of rough tunnel, and rolled out to find that he was lying on cold, flat stone. No light penetrated, and it was impossible to see.

There was a click and a red beam illuminated the wall of a stone tunnel. Adrian watched Henry fiddle with the torch, widening the beam as much as he could.

They stood in a large hall, about ten meters wide. Looking left and right, Adrian couldn't see the ends of it before the walls faded out of the radius of Henry's light. He put his hand on the stone. Cold, and very smooth, no sign of having been worked by hand.

Henry pointed the light up. The ceiling was ten meters above, as flat as the walls and floors. Running along the center, a metal tube snaked between unlit diode fixtures at five meter intervals.

"Pre-Advent, for certain," Henry said. "But what for?"

"Shine the light down, Henry," Sabine said.

He dutifully pointed the light at the ground, revealing footprints in a light powder of dust.

"They go that way, which I think…" She produced a copper bit, knelt down, and rolled it across the tunnel. It veered off in the direction of the footprints and accelerated into the darkness. "Yes, there's a little slope. I wonder how they cut this passage so smoothly? They must have used a machine, this is too precise to have been done by hand."

"Let's go." Adrian took up position beside Sabine, and they descended, close behind Henry and the red light.

The unreal, absolutely square tunnel rolled downward, meter after empty meter. An odor of rain infused the humid air. Smaller tunnels, also square in profile, left the main shaft at odd intervals, but the footprints in the dust never departed from the central path. Henry illuminated each branch they passed, but, seeing no interesting features, the trio continued straight on.

After a steep stretch downward, Henry again lit up an offshoot tunnel, glanced down it, then passed it by.

"Stop," Adrian said. "Put the light back there."

"Did you see something?" Sabine asked, a little nervousness creeping into her voice.

"I'm not sure."

Henry turned the light back down the shaft.

"There. What's that?" Adrian pointed down the hall.

On the ceiling, just where the cone of their red light yielded to the darkness, a pinpoint of contrast.

A fuzzy carpet of undisturbed dust had settled in the corridor. There were no footprints leading that way.

Adrian walked toward the anomaly. Something was reflecting the light from the torch, and as he came closer, he noticed another shimmering reflection from the floor directly underneath. As he approached, he could see a pool of liquid, or metal? Illuminated in red, it looked like a puddle of bloody quicksilver.

"Any idea what it is?" Adrian asked.

"Almost like mercury," she said. "Liquid at room temp—"

A drop of the stuff fell from the ceiling and landed at their feet. There was a blink of phosphorescent light as it struck.

Then darkness. And silence. Not only a lack of sight and sound, but a null idling in his head.

Adrian's awareness returned, fuzzy, and his skin tingled. He saw a dot of white light in the center of the black nothing that surrounded him. The light expanded, all the time coherent thought hung just out of his mind's reach.

The disc of light continued to grow, turned a pleasant shade of yellow, and he felt cognizance returning. First came a rush of jumbled sights and sounds, strobes and roars, then other sensations. The smell of a fire burning dominated all, followed by pain. Scorching pain from all senses.

Soon he could see again. The shadowy tunnel, a man on his left and a woman on his right. Other sights superimposed themselves on the tunnel. Things he knew. His vile mother, men who had tormented him. Then, flames and a smoking pyre. A series of images flashed in rapid succession, from the monastery on Valetta, to the Ottoman War, and the *Miranda*.

The ghostly images faded and the tunnel came into sharp focus. He couldn't move, only stare straight ahead. In his peripheral vision, Sabine and Henry stood motionless.

Someone approached from the left. A new red light advanced towards them, and soon three shadowy figures moved in the corner of his eye, which still stared forward, unblinking. The unknown people followed in their footsteps. Precisely.

The first figure came into view.

It was Henry.

The duplicate walked up to the pool of liquid metal and stepped directly into the space the frozen Henry occupied. The two figures overlapped with one another.

Then the moving figure of Sabine walked past and merged with the frozen Sabine, and finally he felt as much as saw himself step into himself.

Then, the drip and the flash again. The three moving figures jumped back from the pool, out of the frozen bodies. There was a commotion, and finally all three figures walked off to the right, into the unexplored darkness.

Sound returned. Adrian heard his heavy breathing. His muscles contracted, pushing him away from the bizarre puddle. Sabine and Henry following suit, a bit slower.

He looked right, then left. Sabine and Henry both had shock and confusion on their faces, leaving no doubt they had experienced something, too.

"Are you two all right?" he finally asked.

"I think so," Sabine said, voice shaking.

Henry nodded.

They stood for a time.

"I saw my home," Sabine finally said, "when I was young. And then…other things."

"So did I," Adrian said. "I mean I saw the place I lived. I also saw the three of us come and go."

"Yes. We came from down there, and walked off that way." Sabine pointed to the right.

Henry shined the light on the puddle. "It must have hallucinogenic properties, but how could we all see the same thing?"

Sabine stared into it. "It wasn't like any drug I've experienced. I wonder if this is Flux?"

"What's Flux?" Adrian and Henry asked in unison.

"A heresy." She eyed Adrian. "The spacetime-unstable element that makes c-twenty speeds possible. Before its discovery, c-one was the universal speed limit."

"Valuable, then?" Henry asked.

"At the Apex, yes. Now, unless someone starts building new FTL drive cores, it's useless."

"I wonder where we went? The other group of us." Adrian said. The sense of curiosity was overwhelming, as if his mind—and something else, something outside him—was forcing him in that direction. "Let's have a look."

They pressed on, pushed and pulled by the invisible current, through the precise geometry of the tunnel until they reached its end.

After what seemed like a kilometer or more of walking they stopped, and Henry put the torch out. A light was on up ahead. The tunnel opened into a larger room, and they crept toward it.

Electric lamps suspended from the ceiling bathed the center of the room in a wide circle of blue-white light. Adrian couldn't see the far side. The walls were not only hidden in darkness, but blocked by rows of shelves and electronic equipment that hummed, blinked, and squealed in a dead language.

No sign of Bernt, nor anyone else, but as he stood at the threshold, a sense of cold familiarity struck him. The setting was eerily similar to a bunker in New Golan that he and his fellow knights had invaded a decade ago.

It was in the depths of that bunker he had found Mariel.

Silence descended on Persis Abbey at dusk, words forbidden until the next day's light hit the prismatic stained-glass windows of the east wall.

The Daughters of Our Lady of Sorrows made their home here, inside the Old City. Built post-Advent, the Abbey was of sturdy stone and timber construction rather than steel. Two stories tall with an open inner courtyard and cloister, the only outward facing windows were stained or heavily frosted, leaving the inner workings of the convent a mystery to all save those enclosed.

Sponsored by Cardinal Duval, other members of the Holy See tended to view the secretive nuns with suspicion and jealousy, but fear of the Grand Inquisitor got the better of anyone who might ask questions or think to cross their threshold uninvited.

Mary Frances was rightly proud of her role in maintaining that fear, though she didn't receive the credit she deserved from the Holy Office of the Inquisition. Not nearly, and Duval was the most miserly of the lot. Had he ever even hunted sinners? Had he left the confines of his dungeon to root out the non-conformists where they lived? No.

She lay on her bed, hands gliding over her body.

A single candle lit her cell, fighting and failing to overcome the thick darkness.

The quietest tapping at the door aroused her. She slid out of bed and pulled the heavy portal open by its iron ring.

A nun in a pure white habit stood on the other side. It was Anne Kresimir, a sleek, catty little thing. The candles in the hallway flickered, giving her dress a golden glow.

Mary Frances tilted her head, raised her sinuous arms, and placed one hand on either door jamb, displaying herself. Her thin dressing gown was nearly transparent in the soft light, and she watched Anne's brown eyes as they landed on her nipples, then fell to the dark triangle below. She let Anne stare, then tiptoed back into her murky cell.

Anne followed and closed the door behind. "Sister," she said in a whisper.

"Silence." Mary Frances looked into Anne's eyes. She slowly gathered up the long skirt of Anne's habit until she could place her hand on the novice's warmth. She ran her fingers through the silken hair she found there.

Anne swallowed a moan, but remained quiet.

Mary Frances put her hand lightly around Anne's neck. She felt the novice's pulse quicken. The cosseting of her svelte fingertips urged Anne on until she quivered and gasped.

Mary Frances brought her moist, ambrosial fingers up to Anne's mouth, where they were licked and kissed. "Now, what news have you?"

"The *Condottiere* found nothing on the *Miranda*, Sister, but they followed the ship's Hansa engineer when he left."

"Fine." Mary Frances slipped back into her bed.

Anne removed her veil and pulled her habit over her head, dropping it on the floor. She lay down and pressed herself against Mary Frances. "Their *Militium Publicanus*, this Adrian of Tarsus, is a strapping knight, Sister. I can only imagine the murder and rapine he's perpetrated among the heathens."

"Indeed?"

"I envy the Saracen women he's surely forced." Her voice was wistful. "He went with the fat Turk and another of the crew to a pub called the Bee's Knees."

Mary Frances laughed.

"I know, it's a funny name." Anne giggled.

"Yes, but funnier than that, Lady Conti knows the owner. Sabine Adler. She's a tech broker and supplied *Machina* to that old goat Reymont Lucas. How convenient."

"Will Lady Conti approach her?" Anne asked.

"She will. If their plan is to broker the relic through Sabine Adler this will become a trivial thing, but maybe we'll find some sport with your knight, eh?"

Anne shivered. "Oh, that would be wonderful." She pulled Mary Frances' gown up, and slid herself down to the foot of the bed.

CHAPTER 12

Adrian's sword cleared its scabbard with a metallic rasp.

There was no sign of Bernt or his Hansa consorts.

Looking over his shoulder at Henry, Adrian pointed to the right.

The other man nodded.

A large workbench sat directly under an intense light that beamed down in a sharp-edged cone. Electronic equipment was piled haphazardly on the bench. Outside the cone, the room was impenetrably dark.

Adrian hugged the left wall, lightly dragging his fingertips along it to stay in contact. His sword-arm extended out into the room, waiting for a flicker of shadow to give away the enemy.

Glancing back, his eyes fell on Sabine.

She stood with a blued-steel dagger in her hand. The opposing polarities of beautiful flesh and deadly steel sent a charge through him.

He put the voltaic image away, something to consider later.

She followed him into the room, three steps behind. Did that mean something, tagging behind him instead of her henchman?

Piles of junk—wires, green circuit boards, and old display panels—lay scattered about, but everything looked like a piece of something else. There was no sign of their own stolen relic.

Sabine pulled through the bits and pieces.

"Junk, junk, junk…oh!" Her face lit up.

"What?" Adrian asked.

"I think it's a neural interface, in good condition. No blood on it." She picked up the little object and stuck it in her pocket.

"Happy Christmas, then. What about our relic?"

"No, I don't see any pads here," she said, rummaging through the stuff.

Somewhere above them, a speaker burst to life with a piercing squeal, causing the muscles in Adrian's neck to stiffen.

"Hello, Fraulein Adler." The voice was a man's. High-pitched, almost tittering, not laughing but undeniably amused. "I always hoped we'd meet again. I see you've brought your grey-cloaked comrade Henry Monday with you, but who is your new friend? He doesn't look like your average Imperial busybody. He looks dangerous."

Adrian watched and listened, alert for any sign of life at the periphery of the light.

Sabine clenched her fist, but didn't respond.

"Speak up now, girl, don't be rude," the voice demanded.

"Bastard," she said under her breath.

"I'm Adrian of Tarsus, and I can speak for myself."

"Tarsus?" the voice asked. "Not Imperial. Barely under Papal control, at that. Are you a Reformist, like Fraulein Adler and Herr Monday, then?"

"Reformist?" Adrian shook his head, looking at Sabine.

"It appears not. Very interesting," the voice said. A click from the speaker ended the conversation as suddenly as it had begun.

"Reformists?" Adrian asked Sabine. "Who in Hell was that?"

"Syndic Martin Dietrich," she said, her jaw tight with anger.

"What does a Hansa Syndic have to do with you?" Syndic was the highest known rank within the League, reserved for the most brilliant engineers and the most devious traders. No one knew how many of them hid at the top of the League's gilded pyramid, but they commanded fanatical loyalty from their underlings.

The sound of feet moving in the darkness put him back on guard before she could answer.

Men appeared on two sides.

Four entered through the same tunnel Adrian and his companions had used, and four more stepped from the shadows on the opposite side of the room.

Damn. Both exits blocked.

"Eight? You said there were four." Adrian looked over his shoulder at Sabine.

"I wasn't expecting so many." Dagger at the ready, she backed towards him until they touched.

The Hansa were short, thick men with leathery faces and shaved heads. They wore the plainest dark breeches, bleached white shirts, and bulky leather boots. They advanced with smallswords.

The name was a misnomer—the blades were eighty centimeters long.

Bad position.

Shit odds.

Dire.

The rapier already in his right hand, he drew the dagger strapped to his left thigh. A final confession might be in order.

"Sabine?" he asked.

"Yes?" Her shoulders pushed against his back.

"I think about you all the time. I still love you."

"Now? You consider right now the perfect time to tell me?"

"It might be my last chance. Get under the workbench!"

For once she didn't argue, and ducked under the bench. Thank God.

Adrian seized the only advantage he had—there were so many Hansa they couldn't all attack at once. Two stepped forward as he heard the chime of sword on sword behind him. Henry would have to hold his own, for now.

A pair of thrusts came at him in unison. The attacks were so well-synchronized that he swept both weapons aside with the same parry. In the same motion, he brought the dagger around in a left hook and stabbed it into the forearm of the closest Hansa.

The wounded man let go of his sword. Adrian skewered him through the chest, and, using the implanted rapier as a lever, turned the Hansa's back to his partner and pushed, pinning the second man against the workbench.

The pinned man screamed.

Adrian looked down and saw Sabine's arm thrust out from under the bench, her dagger sunk into the man's ankle. Adapting to her helpful hand, he put all his strength behind the rapier to push it through the first Hansa's body and into the second. He slid the blade back out, and the bodies fell to the ground one after the other.

Another pair of Hansa came at him.

Adrian set his feet to receive the charge. The pile of bodies on the floor to his left forced one of his attackers to halt short while the other came on running.

After a single sharp exchange the Hansa was on the floor, bleeding from the chest.

The next one came more cautiously, in a practiced stance with sword on guard.

Adrian unleashed a rapid series of attacks and ripostes that the Hansa skillfully parried.

Not bad. Classically trained, but a weakness in many old styles was a reliance on timing and pace.

Adrian renewed the assault with the same rhythm as before, and quickly established a pattern of parries and ripostes with his opponent. Then he stole a beat, and what was a fight in 4/4 time switched to 3/4. Unable to cope with the change in signature, the Hansa's defense collapsed within two bars. A blade through the heart ended his performance.

Move!

Sensing someone behind, Adrian jumped to the side just in time to avoid gleaming metal crashing down at him. He turned and saw a bullish man with small eyes staring back at him. Dietrich?

The new opponent held a long metal staff with a forked head.

Adrian experienced the strange circumstance of having to tilt his head up to look the man in the eyes—he was well over two meters tall.

For such a hulking man he was fast, and he jammed the blunt end of his staff at Adrian's chest.

Adrian moved to parry, but was too slow by a half-tick and took the hammering impact in his sternum. He staggered back and fell.

His skull hit the steel planking and pools of light rippled in his eyes. Through the colored swirl, he felt as much as saw the Syndic looming over him. He lay prone, but his sword was still in his hand. His nerves fired to roll away.

The Syndic slammed the end of the staff down on Adrian's blade, pinning it to the floor.

There was an audible click before terminals on the end of the staff burst into a ball of blue electricity that rode up the rapier's blade and pulled Adrian down into darkness.

Adrian awoke on the ground with his right arm and shoulder numb, and a searing pain in the center of his chest.

Damn. Tied. Wrists and ankles bound tightly with rope.

He rolled and pushed himself up against a wall, hands behind his back, and looked around. The room, save for rows of metal shelves piled with bits and pieces of old technology, was empty.

The last time Adrian had been tied up and thrown in a closet was twenty-five years ago at the monastery on Valetta. Back then it had all been in fun, the squires playing knights-versus-heathens on Sunday afternoons.

His sword and dagger were gone.

The lock on the door clicked, and the Syndic entered, Bernt skulking behind him like a mischievous gnome.

"You are Adrian of Tarsus, of the Knights Hospitaler?" the Syndic asked. The man smelled like pickled garlic. He stood puffed up, chest forward, chin high. Arrogant bastard.

Dietrich leaned closer. "I asked you a question."

"I am. What does it matter to you?"

"Nothing, professionally. Personally I'm extremely curious to know how a Hospitaler came to be mixed up with a pair like Mustafa Ali and Sabine Adler. The Pope's most elite henchmen don't usually mix well with Turks and Imperials."

"Surely our Judas here has told you the story." Adrian nodded at Bernt.

"The story of a botched deal at St. Anthony?" He arched an eyebrow. "And the theft of *Machina Infernus*, all of which belong to the Holy See?"

"Which means you've now stolen it from the Holy See."

"We can't very well let it be locked up in some vault and never used, now can we? I've not seen a piece quite like this one, though. Bernt insists you're too stupid to know anything about it, but I wonder. Do you have any knowledge you might like to trade for your life?"

Adrian sat up straight and pursed his lips, making a show of considering the offer. "Well...this relic, you see..."

"Yes?"

"Its *old*. Very old." Adrian nodded.

Dietrich propped his chin up on his thumb and regarded Adrian. "No, I doubt you can tell me anything I don't already know. The secrets of this relic will be mine soon enough, and I must go finish with Fraulein Adler."

"If you—"

"Let me guess. If I harm her, you'll kill me in some extremely gruesome way." He laughed, and held his hand up to his mouth to stifle it. "If it helps at all, my plans for her are longer term than my plans for you."

What the hell was he waiting for, then?

Dietrich stood and turned. "Good bye, Adrian of Tarsus." He closed the door behind, leaving Adrian with Bernt.

Several quiet seconds passed.

"Are you waiting for me to say something?" Adrian asked.

"I'll entertain your pleas for mercy."

"What barb has lodged itself in your arse?"

Bernt stood over him. Arms folded, chin high, a look of smug satisfaction on his face. "I've wanted to kill you every day for four fucking years. Ever since you came on board with your idiotic fairy tales and pathetic devotion to a corrupt morality."

Adrian laughed.

"What's so fucking funny?" Bernt asked.

"I hope you see the irony in wanting to murder me for devotion to morality."

"Papist shit! You couldn't have an intelligent thought if I gave you one." Bernt's face flashed through several shades of red. "You and your bastard cronies want to keep us in this dark age of filth and stupidity forever, but we will *not* let you."

"Bastard cronies?" Adrian laughed. Bernt's profane characterizations made it impossible to take him seriously, even now.

"Shut up! We're going to wipe all of you fucking Papists out." Bernt swept the air with his arm. "All Papists, all Muslims, all Jews, all purged from the universe."

"Who? You and these Sodomites?" Adrian nodded at the door. "Good luck."

"Laugh now, but we know the truth of things."

"What truth is that?" Bernt seemed to want to tell him something, perhaps something the traitor thought would shatter him before he died. Good. The longer he talked, the longer Adrian had to find a way out of this.

"The Advent is a lie. Earth still exists." Bernt shook his fist at Adrian with every word.

"You know that Earth was destr—"

"No! It's still there! You keep it hidden, but the Earth and all the knowledge of mankind are still there."

Completely insane. Keep him talking, though. "Ships were sent after contact with Earth was lost. None returned."

"You have no proof of that. It's a damned lie created by Papists that's been propagated for centuries."

"Is this Earth-cult why you Hansa are so secretive about your circles of initiation?"

"Earth is the sole reason for the circles. You have no idea what the truth is." Bernt pointed his finger at his chest. "But I know."

"Tell me the truth then. The Advent is a lie. What else?" Could such a foul little turd actually know something? Doubtful—why would his overlords tell him anything? Still…

Bernt went to one of the shelves and picked up a circuit board. "This is the secret. The Earth is a shining world of pure technology, and in the *Machina* we find enlightenment."

"What kind of enlightenment?"

"A state of being in which every component has a function, and carries out that function with absolute precision until it fails. When it does, it is replaced and the system continues to run, unchanging."

"When you say 'component,' you mean person, don't you?"

"Look around. No one knows what they're supposed to be doing, what their purpose is. Mankind lurches from one war to another because the system has been corrupted, by Papists and charlatans who profit from the chaos. We must create a sustainable system, one with an inviolate hierarchy in which all components serve the whole and no component is irreplaceable."

"You want to live like *Machina*, then?"

Bernt began to speak, then stopped and started again as his tongue tripped. Finally he found words to spit out. "No more talk. I won't give you the honor of dying with an enlightened mind."

"You don't know a damned thing," Adrian said. "Your masters are no different from anyone else's. They string you along, dropping little crumbs of fiction for you to chase after, and all the while you think you're on a quest for enlightenment. Christ. You're going to be disappointed with what you find at the end. Everyone is."

Bernt drew his sword. He pressed the tip of the blade against Adrian's neck.

Adrian felt the cold steel on his throat. This would be a pathetic way to die. He pulled his legs back and prepared to thrust them at Bernt's knee. If he could break it, he might buy himself a few seconds...

"Assassin!" The cry came from the adjacent room, the word cut off with a liquid sputter. Two dull thumps followed.

Adrian looked to Bernt. "Sounds like trouble. You'd better check it out."

Bernt cursed. He turned and started towards the door, stopping short when it opened and a dark figure met him toe-to-toe. A stiletto dripping with blood left no doubt as to the aim of the new arrival. Covered in black, head wrapped with a *cheich*—a desert turban that also veiled the face—the killer left only her eyes visible. They were definitely the eyes of a woman.

"Who are you?" Bernt demanded.

The killer didn't answer, but mockingly twirled the stiletto in her fingers.

Christ. Not a woman. Mariel.

"I'll find out when I have your head!" He screamed as he swung the sword.

She easily ducked, and taunted him again with her blade.

"Stop showing off. Kill him!" Adrian said in the hard voice he used during practice.

She thrust her blade with fantastic speed. Bernt was ready. He brought the sword around, now aimed at the back of her skull. Somehow she foresaw it and ducked while slicing at his stomach. She missed by a hair, and as she recovered her guard,

Bernt swept at her legs, forcing her to jump. Her feet had barely touched the ground when he kicked her in her chest, sending her to the floor, flat on her back.

No! Move, any direction, stay in motion!

Mariel rolled, and the sword blade crashed into the floor. She jumped up, planted her feet, and attacked with a ferocious lunge to his left side, blade aimed under the rib cage.

Bernt was quick enough to avoid a mortal wound, but not to escape her sting completely. The tip of the blade penetrated his side, and as he twisted away it opened a long trench. Maybe because of the blood lubricating the stiletto's grip, she lost hold and the weapon spun to the ground.

Don't give up, you're smarter and faster.

"Now, little whore," he said, gloating, "I'll shove this up your c—"

Never linger over a kill.

She dove for the ground, recovered the dagger, and rolled onto her back.

Despite his wound Bernt remained quick, and he turned as she flashed by. As she rolled he raised his sword into the air. "Die!" He screamed in a falsetto voice.

Now, Mariel!

Before Bernt's sword moved, she crunched her abdomen and sat up, jamming the stiletto into his groin. It easily penetrated his breeches and genitals, piercing his bladder, the needle tip not halting until the twenty-centimeter blade was thrust up through the colon to slice open arteries and veins massed near the spinal cord. The wound spit blood and urine, and he collapsed on top of her, his legs twitching pathetically.

Adrian watched her crawl out from under Bernt and look around the room. Not seeing any threats, she snatched the dagger out and quickly cut his throat. The little courtesy was good form on the battlefield. Well done.

She walked up to him, bloody weapon in hand. "Are you okay?"

"Of course I am. Are you?"

She shook her head as she cut his bonds. "You underestimate me even after I rescue you from these fools."

"No, I just have a care for your safety."

"Maybe you should have a care for your own." Her voice carried an edge. "Adrian…"

"Love?"

She stepped close, and looked up into his eyes. "If you died I couldn't live. You mustn't get yourself killed. If not for you, then for me."

Adrian found his weapons on a table outside the room. "Did you see Sabine, or Henry?"

"Who's Henry?" Mariel asked

"He works for Sabine. Thin, red-haired fellow?"

She shrugged.

"Stop."

"What?"

"Let me see that arm." Her sleeve was sliced open, and he saw blood on the skin underneath.

"I don't know when that happened. I didn't feel anything."

"That's normal with a little scrape like this." The wound wasn't too deep, but it would probably leave a scar. He found himself smiling. It must have been the pride parents felt when their child showed talent as an artist, or musician. There was no time to enjoy the moment, though. "Are there any more Hansa?"

"None behind us, but the tunnels go further."

Knight and squire ran down the tunnel, checking each door in turn.

Adrian stopped at the third.

"What is it?" Mariel asked.

The room reeked with the smell of blood and other human efflux.

"Sergeant Barbieri, and his *Condottiere*," Adrian said.

"Who?" She looked around him, into the room.

"*Condottiere*. From one of the Italian charter mercenary companies. Remember the lot that came aboard the *Miranda* earlier?"

"The customs men?"

"They weren't with customs, they were hired. Looks as though we aren't the only ones who followed Bernt into this hornet's nest."

Four bodies lay on stainless steel tables, showing a range of fatal injuries. Adrian checked each, finding the remains cold and the blood still in all but the last. Barbieri himself lived, though it wasn't a blessing. The man's intestines hung from a gaping wound, spilling out onto the table beside him.

Adrian grunted and drew his dagger. "He's had it."

Barbieri's eyes flashed open, looking up at Adrian.

"Those Hansa did you in, I'm afraid," Adrian said. "I'll end it for you."

"Wait," Barbieri sputtered. "You're the one from that ship… the *Miranda*."

"That's right."

"We aren't…we weren't with customs."

"I figured that out while you were still on board. Who sent you, and why?"

Barbieri coughed up a spurt of blood. "Strange…a big hurry… she brought the uniforms and insisted we go right away."

"She?"

"Bitch who's hired us before…calls herself Anne…don't know her real name…that's it…that's all…do it now."

Adrian nodded. He slipped the dagger between ribs, into Barbieri's heart. Shortly after, the *Condottiere* died.

Mariel stared at him.

He couldn't tell whether she were shocked or engrossed. "Are you all right?"

"Why did he tell you that?"

"Who can say? Maybe it was a last gesture of camaraderie between warriors. Come on, squire, let's find Sabine."

They ran down the tunnel, stopping at a set of double doors with a faded message painted above them in blocky letters: MINING OPERATIONS. Side-by-side, they pushed through.

Into a large room with many powered-down computer consoles. There was a steel table in the center and around it were the skeletons of several chairs, the upholstery having rotted away long ago. On the far side, a vast sheet of acrylic glass formed the entire wall. He was taken aback by what he saw on the other side.

The floor fell straight down at least ten meters and fanned out into a huge rectangular bay. Parked in the bay were four enormous metal machines mounted on tracked carriages. They were square in profile, and looked as though they would just fit through the fastidiously carved tunnels in the mine. They were numbered D9-1 through D9-4, and a thin layer of white dust covered them. The room was equipped with an overhead crane, workbenches, and stands with even more high-tech equipment. Hoses and wires snaked around the floor under and among the vehicles.

A flash of blue light caught his eye. Down below in the far corner, four men hovered over two bodies strapped to metal tables. Sabine lay dead still. Henry was on the receiving end of the Syndic's electric staff.

The heavy glass blocked all sound, but Adrian could tell from the way Henry's body convulsed that he was in agony from the repeated application of electric shocks. Sabine was motionless, body limp, head turned to one side.

Do something.

Adrian scanned the operations room, looking for a way to reach them. He ran to a door with a large yellow arrow on it, pointing down. Mariel was at his heels. Inside was a vertical shaft cut from the stone, with metal stairs and controls for a powered lift mounted on the wall. Electric shit. He studied the lift controls briefly—the things were always damnably slow—then ran down the pierced steel steps.

The stairs reversed six times on the way down, and when he reached the bottom, his heart was pounding. He pushed the door open, and immediately the sounds of crackling electricity and screams reached him.

Machines blocked his view of the far side of the room. He slipped out, glancing back to ensure Mariel was still in tow.

Drawing his sword with his right hand and the long dagger with his left, he advanced down the side of one of the huge vehicles.

Henry's screaming stopped and Adrian could overhear bits of questions.

"Liar!" the Syndic shouted, then the prickly sound of electricity filled the air again and bright light strobed.

Adrian stepped around the front of the vehicle, the noise and light covering his movement. The Syndic stood a meter back from Henry, pressing the sparking end of his staff into the man's side just over the kidney. A little smoke rose as the flesh under the arc burned. The other three men looked on.

Even the odds. With a powerful overhand motion, he hurled the dagger, striking one of the Hansa dead in the back, the blade digging between the man's shoulders and dropping him to the floor with a cry and a potato-sack thud.

The Syndic and his remaining men turned.

"Kill them!" Dietrich shouted, eyes wide, fanatical, as he pulled the staff back from Henry's side, pointing at the intruders.

The two Hansa underlings drew swords and charged, one to Mariel and one to Adrian. He watched Mariel come to guard, but his own attacker forced him to turn his attention.

The Hansa attacked fast and hard.

Crisp, fast, Italian school. Adrian parried and counter-attacked, looking for the crack in the Hansa's defense. He could hear Mariel's fight to his left. He tuned it out—he felt nothing but confidence in her ability.

Focus.

Now!

The Hansa's peripheral vision seemed to be poor. Adrian forced an awkward parry, then exploited it for the kill, chopping into the man's neck from a high-outside position.

The Syndic's smug grin faded as first one, then the other of his men went down.

"Stay back," Adrian said to Mariel as she returned to guard after dispatching the henchman.

In his rage, Dietrich jammed the end of the staff into Henry's neck, at the base of his skull, and fired the arc. Henry's body convulsed, every muscle in his body tightening simultaneously and he screamed until his lungs were empty. The Syndic pulled the staff back, and Henry went limp.

"Son of a bitch!" Adrian shouted.

"That's nothing compared to what I'll do to her." He pointed the tip of his staff at Sabine.

The men faced each other—Adrian's rapier in a low guard, Dietrich's staff held at an angle, gripped with both hands like a quarterstaff. The tip of the staff crackled.

Adrian attacked. Dietrich defended aggressively, parrying and counter-attacking with much greater speed than most men could manage with a staff.

Mind the sparking bit. Adrian countered the Syndic's thrusts deftly. The staff had no guard, and he attempted to run his blade down the length and into Dietrich's hand. He nearly succeeded, but the Hansa pulled his right hand from the middle of the shaft at the last second.

The move put Adrian's weight forward and in the fraction of a second it took him to recover, Dietrich rammed the staff into his shoulder. Protected by leather, he nonetheless felt the burning surge of power and jumped back. Pain shot down his arm followed by numbness, and he gingerly maintained a tenuous grip on the rapier's hilt.

Dietrich saw the opportunity and lunged.

Adrian parried, his blade met the staff with a spark.

The Syndic stopped in the middle of his stroke, his eyes went wide.

Mariel plunged her dagger into his biceps, drawing a scream as he let go and the staff flew from his hands.

Dietrich's final mistake was to ignore the woman in the room.

Adrian ducked the flying pole and brought his left hand up to the rapier hilt to steady his hold. He lunged and thrust, putting his blade into Dietrich's stomach. Twist. Pull up. He tore open a trench several centimeters long. Blood and fluids surged out.

He stepped back and looked around, confirming that the room was empty, then let go of his sword and gripped his right arm tightly. As the numbness receded, he felt a hundred needles piercing him from the tips of his fingers to the top of his shoulder.

"Are you all right?" Mariel asked.

"Fine." He flexed his arm, watched her retrieve her stiletto and check to ensure the Syndic was dead. "Mariel, after all these years you've finally proven yourself useful."

"Ass."

Sabine lay still on the table. There was color in her skin, and she breathed, but her eyes were closed.

"Bine, can you hear me?" Adrian asked.

No reply.

He looked around, taking in the scene. Medical instruments. An articulated arm with a bright light attached. On a shelf set against the wall, a syringe and several glass bottles. She was bound to the edges of the table with leather straps. What had the sons of bitches been planning?

"I'll get Sabine. Check on Henry."

Mariel ran to the man's side and put her hand on his neck. "He isn't breathing. There's no pulse."

"Look for the relic," Adrian said as he checked Sabine, looking her over for injuries.

"There!" Mariel said. On a stainless-steel workbench sat the glass with its odd attachment.

"Take it." He unbuckled the straps holding Sabine down and pulled her to him, preparing to pick her up.

"Unhand me, knave." She squirmed. Her speech was slow and groggy.

"Come on, let's try to sit up." He took her firmly by the shoulders and eased her up, smiling wide as he realized she was unharmed.

"Fiend! I'm not…" Her words trailed off, and she yawned. "I'm not your wench to manhandle." When he had her sitting up straight, legs dangling over the side of the table, he took her by the chin and turned her face towards him.

"Sabine." He stood in front of her, close, and could see that it took some effort for her to open her eyes.

"Oh, Adrian. What news?"

"How do you feel?"

"Fine, fine." She leaned forward and slowly tipped over, her face planting in the middle of his chest. Leaning against him, she began to snore.

He hoisted her onto his shoulder. "Let's get out of here."

CHAPTER 13

Adrian inspected Mariel's wound and grinned. "Now who looks like Geoffrey?"

"It hurts more than I thought it would." She sat on the counter-top in the pale green shower frowning at the gash on her arm; the pink skin lay open and caked with congealed blood.

"When you play with swords you get cut. What matters is how you take it, and you've done well."

"When did you first get cut?"

"There were eight squires my age at the monastery." He opened the sewing kit and set out the quist butter, needle, and thread. "One morning we mustered for practice and found our wooden swords replaced with steel. The Knight-Lieutenant walked up to each of us in turn and cut us on the forearm with a dagger. 'Now you've been cut,' he said, 'so you don't have to worry about it any longer.'"

"That was cruel."

"Was it? I've not worried about it since." He opened the familiar bottle of clear liquor and handed it to her. "Drink."

She raised it to her lips. Her nose twitched when it picked up the shocking vapor, but she took a long swallow, then coughed violently.

He watched her fight to keep the strong spirit down. He was so proud of her.

She took a second, more cautious drought.

"You'll need three stitches, I think. My record is safe."

"What's your record?" she asked.

"Fifteen. This is going to hurt." He took a clean cloth, soaked it with alcohol and cleaned her cut of dried blood. He felt her muscles tighten against the pain. "Good. I'll numb it now."

He opened the jar of butter and pulled out a glop of the rank stuff. The numbing effect would set in quickly, but he started by putting a little on the surface of her cut to make it more tolerable when he pressed more into it.

"Why didn't you cut me when we started practicing?"

"That would have been cruel."

"Why is it cruel for me, but not for you?" she asked, indignant, as if he'd withheld something valuable.

"Because you're not going to let men cut you at their whim. Understand?"

She didn't respond, and he took the opportunity to finish buttering up the cut, then started putting in the stitches, one by one, with great care. The burning tingle in his right arm didn't make the job any easier.

She began to sway a little bit—the alcohol was strong—and he put a hand on her shoulder to steady her.

"Not much longer," he said. "Mariel?"

"Yes?"

"There's something I need to tell you."

"You never tell me you have something to tell me. It must be bad."

Damn. "I suppose it depends on how you look at it. If I asked you who you are, what would you say?"

"Mariel. Mariel of Tarsus. I'm *me*."

She wasn't from Tarsus. This was the first time she'd ever assumed his own borrowed surname.

"Though…"

"Go on," he said.

"I wonder who this Roxanne Wallace is, or was, and why that computer thinks I'm her."

"It doesn't matter. Few things are permanent, but you are and always will be Mariel of Tarsus."

"You can't ask me such a bizarre question and not tell me why, Adrian."

"I know why you're having the headaches, the dizziness, the cloudy vision. All of it."

She turned to face him. "Why?"

"You have a genetic problem affecting your brain. It's going to get worse if we don't fix it, but the relic we picked up on Gereon is part of the cure. We're close now. Once Sabine tells me how it works, I'll fix you up."

"Fixed? Just like that?" She waved her hand.

"If I'm right, yes. The shadow banished by the white light of tomorrow."

She smiled. "When will we know?"

"Soon, I hope."

"Adrian?"

"Love?"

"If that's what you had to say, why did you ask me who I am?"

Why indeed, if he weren't going to tell her the whole truth? "I wanted to know how you see yourself. Whether your sense of self comes from within or without."

He tied off the last stitch and wrapped a cloth bandage around her arm. "There, good as new."

She slipped off the counter, her knees buckled a little, and she wobbled.

He took her arm. "Steady on. A little of that liquor goes a long way."

With his hand gently on her elbow, it took only a few steps to guide her down the hall to her door, which he opened as she leaned against the bulkhead.

"Would you like me to sit with you for a while?" he asked.

She reached out and touched his arm as lightly as a lost feather landing on the forest floor.

He stopped short.

Standing on the tips of her toes, she pressed her young body into his chest and put her lips to his.

Frozen, he must have looked like an old statue from antiquity in the middle of some deep thought, but he stood there, scrambled, feeling vaguely stupid.

"I love you," she whispered. She then disengaged, and slipped into her room, sliding the door closed behind.

Hell.

Adrian slid open the door to his cabin and found Sabine sitting on Mariel's old bed.

He wanted to sleep, but knew he'd only lie awake trying to make sense of Mariel's inscrutable behavior. Sabine's insomnia might be a blessing.

He closed the door and set his leather satchel, containing the ASCNT pad, on the little shelf molded into the bulkhead near the door.

"I thought you were going to rest in Koray's room," he said.

"I can't."

He pushed aside the silk curtain separating the bunks and fell onto his. The bruise over his sternum ached, and his right arm still tingled. He flexed his hand.

"Does it hurt?" she asked.

"I'll survive. Look, Sabine, about your man Henry."

"He's dead, isn't he?"

"Yes, he is. He was still alive when I found you, but I was too late to save him."

She stared at her feet for several seconds. "Dietrich?"

He nodded.

"Henry was lots of things but he wasn't naive. He knew the risks and accepted them, just as we all do. It wasn't your fault."

"You're damned right. At least, it shouldn't be my fault, but thanks to you it is."

"I—"

"You should have told me everything." He raised his voice. "Did you think I wouldn't go if I knew you had an agenda?"

"I don't know."

"We'd have gone down there prepared for a Syndic and his followers. Henry might still be alive. Damn it, Sabine, what was this all about?"

"That's none of your business."

"Fine. I haven't lost anything today. I'd hate to see you get burned, though." Any good Catholic publican would have an image of Saint Martin over her bar. Sabine did not. And when he carried her out of the mine he noticed the cross around her neck was plain, not a crucifix. By themselves those things meant nothing, but, combined with Dietrich's talk of reformists, they became dangerous.

"What do you mean?" She narrowed her eyes.

He never thought about loyalty—his was instinctive. To Mariel, then to the Order, to Christendom, and to God. Strange, but disloyalty to dogma didn't offend him. "Nothing. You've nothing to fear from me, whatever it is you're hiding."

She brightened. "Dietrich was an evil man. I don't want to think about the people he killed at Merse, on Frisia."

Adrian put Sabine's motives out of his mind. After the fact, they didn't really matter. Maybe she could shed some light on something else. "Bernt said some things before he died. Things about Earth."

"Let me guess. He said that Earth wasn't destroyed in the Advent, and that the Church conspires to hide the fact."

"How do you know that?"

"The Hanseatic League hides behind the truth. They cultivate an image as a ruthless mercantile guild—and they are—but behind the facade is a sect whose devotion to technology takes on religious significance. Not all of them, mind you, but the higher up you go, the more indoctrinated they become."

He grunted. "I don't play at politics. Religious or secular."

"Too bad, because you're neck deep in it."

"You'll have to explain that."

"Mustafa Ali Pasha," she said with a wry smile.

"That's not much of an explanation."

"Tell me, how much has Mustafa netted while you've been on board the *Miranda*?"

"In gold?" It took a moment to think through four years of receipts, her close proximity making it all the harder to focus. "Seven hundred, maybe a little more. A fine profit, now that I think about it."

"Do you know where his money goes?"

"No, but I do know you told him you never wanted to do business with him again. Why are you so interested in his accounts?"

"It's easier to watch a person who thinks you're disinterested."

"You're watching him?" He looked into her eyes, penetrating their cool blue. It occurred to him how deep they were.

"He has an aunt named Ferah." She continued.

"I know. Koray was her son. What of it?"

"Her full name is *Ferah Hatun bint Abdulaziz*."

"Lady Ferah, daughter of Abdulaziz?" He leaned back on the bulkhead as he translated the title.

"The daughter of *Sultan* Abdulaziz. Fahish Ferah to others: Ferah the Bitch. She leads the Corsairs."

Adrian knew the Corsairs well. The band of criminals, escaped slaves, and rejects from the Janissaries caused lots of damage raiding Christian settlements on border planets during the last war. Now, they were a thorn in the side of the new Sultan.

"We were on-world when Abdulaziz died." He put the pieces together. "If Mustafa is related to the old Sultan, even distantly, he might be a target for the usurpers. That explains why we left in such a hurry."

"They told everyone the old Sultan died peacefully, but it isn't true. He was murdered, and the Grand Vizier, Osman, seized the throne. Nasty business. They found Abdulaziz with his bollocks shoved down his throat."

"That's why I don't play at politics."

Without warning she stood, straightened her blouse and crossed the room in two steps. Her wine-colored skirt stretched tightly over her artfully curved bottom as she sat down next to him.

"The Corsairs are in open revolt against Osman and Mustafa sends a lot of gold back to planets they control. We're certain he's backing Ferah's insurgency."

"Who is 'we'? The sodding Publican's Guild?"

"We are the loyal subjects of the Holy Roman Emperor." She took a deep breath, and with a flick of her hips slid over next to him, bringing their thighs and shoulders into contact. "Listen. The Khanate presses Osman on one side, the Corsairs on the other. So long as they're bleeding each other, they can't turn their eyes back to Christendom."

"Tell me about these loyal Imperial subjects."

"That's a discussion for another time."

Against his better judgment, he felt aroused at a deeper level than ever before. Was it the combination of beauty and zeal? "You're trying to tell me that if Mustafa profits from the sale of this relic, it could tip the balance between the Sultan and the Corsairs?"

"We need to know more, that's one of my jobs. The Sultan is desperate for hard currency and a major deal fell through recently, so, if the Corsairs get their hands on enough, it could break the stalemate."

Their voices were conspiratorially low. "Relics. Religion. Hansa. Corsairs. Why are you really sitting here?"

"In the mine, you said you still love me, but…"

"It's true." Still true, despite what she'd done. Was real love so invulnerable?

"Sometimes I wish I could live these past few years over," she said.

He felt her lean against him and relax.

She spoke so softly. "This fighting will never end. I feel as if I've traded happiness for a bit part in an overlong folly. A few days ago I had a man beaten nearly to death for a worthless scrap of information. And now...now I've killed Henry."

The parts of his leg and shoulder that pressed against hers burned like flesh on a coal stove. His eyes were grappled and pulled down to the cleft of her breasts, pressed wonderfully up and tightly together by her corset. She was as beautiful as that summer after-noon when Mustafa and he had walked into the Bee for the first time.

Adrian found himself holding the woman he loved, sitting in his bed with his arm around her, alone. Her head rested on his shoulder.

He was too tired to move.

He closed his eyes and enjoyed the warmth of her body next to his. She twitched a little, and he heard the sound of quiet crying. He looked down at her, but he couldn't see her face. She clutched at his shirt and the sobbing started in earnest.

Hell. Do something.

"Bine?"

She continued to cry, chest heaving, and she balled her little hand into a fist and beat feebly on his breast.

He winced as she pounded the bruise left by Dietrich's staff.

"Bine, what is it?" Was this some sort of strategy?

After a time, she sniffed and spoke. "I'm okay, Adrian, I just need to get this out."

"All right then."

She patted has chest and after a few minutes it passed.

"If I can do anything…" he began.

"No, no dear. Sometimes a woman just needs to cry, like men need to pound their fists on the wall or roar at passersby. I'll pull myself together."

"Just sit here with me," he said.

Soon after, he was asleep.

"Lars!" Mustafa roared at the top of his lungs.

The howl reverberated throughout the ship.

Adrian woke up with Sabine beside him, a slender arm draped across his chest. He started to wriggle out of the bed, carefully, trying not to wake her.

She stopped him with her hand. "Let them handle it."

"Sure as I do, they'll catch the ship on fire." He opened the door and stuck his head out into the hall. To his left, he could see Mustafa fuming in the galley.

From the cargo bay, Lars ran towards the sound of the alarm. He sprinted through the crew quarters, past Adrian. He entered the mess at full tilt, and met Mustafa who was standing with his hands on his hips, a pile of black fur at his feet.

"What's the matter?" Lars asked.

"Why is this animal on my ship?"

Berry lifted his head up and growled at the Turk.

"He must have come in with you earlier."

"Get it out. Immediately."

Berry stood up and trotted out of the mess hall to the crew quarters.

"Go after it." Mustafa harried Lars as they followed behind.

The dog stopped at Mariel's door and pawed at it, scratching it with his nails. The door slid open and he walked inside, then turned around, stuck his head out, and snorted at Mustafa. The door slid closed.

"That animal rebuked me!"

"Smartly," Lars said.

"On board my own ship!"

"Indeed."

Mustafa made a move to open the door but Lars blocked him.

"You can't just go barging into her ladyship's room."

"Oh…yes, of course." He thrust a righteous finger into the air. "This is far from over. You will apprehend and expel that creature at the first opportunity."

"Aye, at the first opportunity."

Adrian shook his head as he closed the door, and returned to Sabine's side. "Mariel's made friends with your dog. Mustafa is furiously flummoxed. Possibly even flummoxed furiously."

"That's cute, Mariel and Berry. He's not my dog but he loiters around the Bee constantly. It's strange that he came all the way out here." She took his hand in hers. "Your daughter is lovely, by the way."

The subject was destined to come up eventually, but what to say? Sabine's help was crucial, and, as had been proven earlier, no partnership could stand on a foundation of mistrust. He'd make the gesture—see how far the truth would get him. "Mariel isn't my daughter."

"What?" She looked up.

"She's an orphan, like me. I treat her like my daughter, but she knows she isn't."

"I had no idea. The way she looks at you—I'd never have suspected."

He nodded. "The sick irony is that, if I had followed my orders, she'd be dead."

"Your orders?"

"This was ten years ago, give or take. The war was still on. We'd retaken Acre and fought off the Turks at Levant. We were spread thin—not just the Order but the regular army, too. I remember being surprised when they took ten of us from the garrison and put us under Knight-Commander Lazcaris."

"Is he related to Grand Master Lazcaris?" she asked.

"He is Grand Master Lazcaris."

"You have friends in high places."

"I have superiors in high places. I didn't dwell on it then, but they gave us equipment that didn't have the cross sewn on, or anything else that would connect us with the Order."

"I'd have been suspicious."

"Because you're good at politics. We rode to New Golan—this was before they found gold in the mountains. It was a wretched little town."

"Now it's a wretched big town."

"All we knew was that we were looking for a group of Hansa that had splintered off from the Syndicate. We spread some coin around and found a talkative whore. She pointed one out, and we followed him back to their hole. An old bunker. Pre-Advent."

"Then what?"

"None of them survived. Excepting Mariel, though she wasn't one of *them*."

"You were supposed to kill her?" She leaned forward.

"No one said to kill all the little girls we found—our orders were more general."

Sabine nodded.

"The fighting was all but over. We were searching room-to-room for stragglers, and I walked into a control center. The air was frigid, and it was dark. She was sitting there on the floor, naked, in the middle of a labyrinth of computers flashing blue light on us. I raised my sword, but I couldn't follow through. She was about four years old."

There was no need to tell her about the other children he found there. The ones in formaldehyde tanks.

"How did you get her out of there? And why didn't you tell me this before?" she asked.

"It wasn't hard. The border planets are full of orphans and street children, and I was able to get her entered on the Order's rolls as a squire. The bribe was pathetically small. The scribe probably thought I wanted her for…well, to Hell with him, anyway. My next assignment was to the garrison at ash-Sham, the Jasmine City, and then I talked my way aboard the *Miranda*."

"It's an amazing story, Adrian. You saved her from who knows what? Bloody Hansa can't be trusted for a moment."

"Bine. Here's the important part." He looked her in the eyes. "Mariel is sick, and that relic holds the cure. Mustafa doesn't know. He thinks we're going to sell it, but I—Mariel and I—need your help to figure out how it works."

"You aren't going to sell it, and Mustafa doesn't know that yet?" she asked.

"Just so."

"Of course I'm going to help. We'll bring it to the Bee where my tools are. I'll examine it there, but, Adrian?"

"Yes?"

"There's something I need in return."

"Tell me."

"There's a Saracen who wants to kill me, and I need you to talk him out of it."

CHAPTER 14

Adrian entered the *Mimar Hamam*, the largest of the steam baths in the Ottoman enclave.

Just off the dusty main street and hidden behind a bakery, there was no sign to identify the bath, only a highly polished maple door with old brass fixtures. Secluded and protected by an aura of taboo among Christians, the *hamam* served as the court of the Sultan's Ambassador, Selim Bey.

Behind the door, a room covered in ornate, blue and white Seljuk tiles with intricate patterns in relief. A sleepy old attendant sitting on a stool opened one eye, closed it, then stood up, startled, it seemed, by the sight of the Crusader cross on Adrian's dark uniform.

Adrian spoke Turkish. "Tell Selim Bey that Adrian of Tarsus, Knight of Saint John, would speak with him."

Without a word, the old man ran through a silk curtain into the depths of the *hamam*.

Ottoman men and women all used the local baths, but the *Mimar Hamam* served male customers only, according to Sabine.

The bathing custom was a part of Ottoman culture Adrian respected. Cleanliness was not only aesthetic, it was critical to maintaining the effectiveness of an army in the field.

The Order of Saint John adopted baths at its outposts, pleasantly opening them to both brothers and sisters. Such an arrangement would be scandalous on Bethany or any other core Christian world, but members of the Order didn't fraternize with each other sexually, obviating the need for segregation. The family was stronger together.

The attendant returned. "His Majesty's Ambassador Selim Bey bids you welcome, and invites you to join him in the *hararat*."

Adrian walked through the curtain into a dressing room. The ritual involved warm, hot, and cool rooms. The *hararat*, or hot room, would traditionally be dry, with a temperature of ninety degrees centigrade. Even in the dressing room he could smell the pine pitch burned twice a day to enhance the contemplative mood.

He undressed and handed his clothes and possessions to the attendant. There was no chance of anything going missing—punishment for thievery was severe. He quickly wrapped a towel around his waist. It was gauche to display one's genitals at a reputable *hamam*, and, despite the popular notions of amorous *tellak* boys and sodomy, liaisons arranged in the heat of the steam rooms were consummated elsewhere.

The temperature jumped as he walked down a short corridor to the warm room.

Inside, two men sat on a wooden bench with a marble chess board between them. They glanced up, faces briefly puzzled before the curiosity melted away and they returned to the game. Others ignored him completely, engaged in an intensely quiet conversation.

The *hararat* was the next room. The dry heat was a rare pleasure, the one memory of his home at Tarsus he could think of fondly.

"Adrian of Tarsus, Knight of Saint John, I presume?" The man lay face-down on the hot-stone, a massive block of marble polished to a high gloss in the center of the room.

"I am. And you are Selim Bey, Ambassador of the Ottoman Sultan?"

The man rolled over on his back. "Indeed. You are the first Christian ever to call on me here. To what do I owe the unexpected pleasure?"

The title *Bey* was an honorific, like Mustafa's dubious title *Pasha*. The word originally meant chieftain, and was roughly equivalent in prestige to a Christian baron.

"May I first ask if you are Selim Üzümcü, General of *Sipahis* at the White Desert?"

"I am. Were you at the battle, knight?"

"I was. I remember you gave safe passage to the civilians of Qari to evacuate to Tayyshan before you laid siege. It was an honorable gesture—my brothers and I didn't know your name at the time, but we spoke highly of you."

Selim Bey sat up. "My officers and I marveled at your order's unbreakable defense."

Adrian sat on a bench and leaned against the wood-paneled wall. The heat was sublime. "I'm here on behalf of Sabine Adler."

Selim Bey laughed, hearty, from the bottom of his chest. "That woman never ceases to surprise. Now she commands the loyalty of the Knights Hospitaler?"

Before the mention of Sabine's name, the Ambassador was loose, relaxed. After, his muscles tensed. Interesting.

"She has my loyalty. I'm not here on behalf of the Order."

"That is good to know. What, then, can I do for you, Adrian of Tarsus?"

"She's afraid you want to kill her, and asked me to persuade you not to."

"Ah. I should not be surprised. I suspect that Miss Adler murdered Reymont Lucas as a…shall we call it a political expediency? That said, I've given no orders to harm her."

"I'm to assure you that she did not kill Lucas, and that she's working to track down the culprit. She knows that Lucas was poisoned, and that the poison was delivered via the wine he bought for the party."

"That's interesting, but I must ask, why is she so certain I'm going to kill her?" The Ambassador raised an eyebrow.

"You sent a man to threaten her. This Serhan Kaş."

"I did no such thing. Why would I threaten someone I intend to kill anyway? It would serve no purpose but to alert them."

"Your man went to the Bee and tried to intimidate her into confessing."

"I gave no orders for that. I will see what Serhan has to say about it. In the meantime, I give you my word that Miss Adler will not be harmed. By me or my men, anyway. I cannot speak for other enemies she may have." He grinned.

"Your word is all I need, Ambassador." Adrian stood and offered his hand, which Selim Bey took in a firm grip.

There was one thing that didn't make sense.

"Ambassador, why would you call Lucas' death a political expediency?"

"Sabine Adler is a Grey Cloak." He shrugged.

Of course. Sabine spoke of herself as a loyal subject. Who were more loyal to the Holy Roman Emperor than his spies and anti-Papal and agitators?

Who are you?

Mary Frances lay on the edge of her bed, glass pad in hand, staring at a still image of the puzzling young woman from the *Miranda*. She ran the image through filters, trying to sharpen it, but to little effect—she'd have to get a look at her in person.

Surely it was someone she knew? The girl's pixelated face had tickled the back of her mind since she first saw her in the field surveillance video she'd sent Anne out to the customs office to acquire.

Her austere, whitewashed room in the abbey was dark and cool, but she lay naked on top of the blanket.

"Aren't you cold?" Anne asked. She stuck her arm out from under the covers, putting her hand on Mary Frances' firm stomach.

"No. God's love warms me."

Anne rolled onto her side, tracing a delicate circle around Mary Frances' navel. "Sister, aren't you afraid God will be angry with us. For this?"

"Those rules are for followers, not leaders."

"You're a leader, but I'm not." Anne gently cupped Mary Frances breast, kissed the nipple, and feigned to suckle.

Mary Frances lay the glass down. "I want you to give up on the fool Missionary Sisters, and join me here."

"One must be sponsored by Cardinal Duval, or another of the Inquisitors, to join the Daughters of Our Lady of Sorrows."

"You'll have no trouble finding a sponsor. I'll see to that."

"Then it's a done thing." Anne smiled. "You're frustrated, Mary, I can tell. Is it because of the mystery letter?"

"Yes. I found information about the ASCNT Program. Sure it's a grand heresy but I fail to see the relevance of an initiative dead for over a thousand years and the lost technology behind it."

"Relevance to what, my love?"

"To me. Someone felt that I, specifically, should know of this."

Anne picked up the pad. "Hmm. What are you working on here?" She held the sheet of glass out at arm's length, looking at the unknown woman. "Admiring yourself?"

"What?"

"How old were you when this picture was taken?" Anne asked. The question was a bit of fleshy bait, and her tongue a barbed hook.

The cool air of the room turned frigid. Mary Frances sat up and tore the pad from Anne's grip.

The hair? She had never worn hers that way. The clothes? Never owned them. But the face—yes, Anne was right. It *was* her face, some years younger, but so, so alike.

When Mary Frances was with Anne, the clamor in her head retreated. Now it returned screaming, deafening her. Despite the noise, she did the math.

ASCNT.

The hair on her body stood up, and her skin frosted.

"Get out."

"Sister?"

"I love you, Anne, but if you don't leave this room at once, it's certain I'll harm you."

"I'll take that risk, my love." Anne put her arm around Mary Frances, gently. "To help you."

"You help me? With what?"

"Mmm. You've been lied to about who you are. Used by someone you trusted so much."

Duval.

He sent an inferior agent to Gereon. He forbade her even to touch the relic he tasked her with retrieving. And then, this… this *false thing* appears on the *Miranda*, the very ship carrying it.

"A sword upon the liars," Anne said.

Bile frothed in Mary Frances' stomach. She wanted to vomit, leaned over the side of the bed, but the purge didn't come. Blood rushed to her head, and with it rage. She slipped a flat dagger from under the down-stuffed mattress.

"Liars." She rolled on top of Anne and pressed the blade to her throat. "Of whom you are one!"

Anne frowned, more a pout than a show of fear or displeasure. "Oh, Mary, I've not lied to you. I love you. So too does your Holy Father who sent me to you."

"Why?"

"To help you free yourself from the grip of a false prophet. We want you to be free to find yourself. To find the power they've denied you."

Mary Frances felt Anne's hands on her back, stroking her. She kept the razor steel against Anne's throat. "What power?"

"Put the knife down, my love, please?"

Mary Frances' body pressed down on Anne's, heat and sweat building between them. Her breasts swayed, nipples brushing lightly over Anne's bare chest, tickling and teasing them erect.

"You slipped the letter under my door. You've known about this all along."

"I had to let you discover the truth yourself, lest you reject it out of virtuous loyalty. Now, together, we can deliver justice to the deceiver," Anne said, "and then the Holy Father will send you on a pilgrimage—it will be miraculous."

Mary Frances dropped the knife on the floor. "A pilgrimage?"

"A hunt for the huntress." Anne spread her legs, letting Mary Frances' body nestle between her thighs.

"Anne, tell me what to think." She rested her head on Anne's chest.

"Don't think." Anne ran her fingers gently through Mary Frances' hair. "Trust in your captain, your leader, the Holy Father."

"Don't think." The bedlam in her head spun down.

"That's it. I'll tell you everything you need to know. About ASCNT, about yourself, and about this Adrian of Tarsus."

CHAPTER 15

The young barmaids at the Bee's Knees ferried mugs of frothy-headed ale, occasionally disappearing into the kitchen to emerge seconds later hefting large pewter plates laden with piles of roast beef and potatoes.

Adrian watched Sabine walk to the public bar, admiring the velvety sway of her hips. She returned with a mug in each hand.

"Red ale," she said, holding one of the pewter mugs up.

"You remembered." The ale was cool and wonderfully strong with hops.

"You like red ale, undercooked steak and overcooked potatoes. You also have a fondness for bread pudding."

"Don't forget my fondness for saucy blonde publicans."

She eased up to him. Close. Took a slow drink of ale and licked her lips. "Follow me."

Trailing her up the sturdy oaken steps was quite rewarding in his view. They ascended several flights, to the third floor of the old building, where she unlocked her door with a brass key. Before she entered, she ran her finger down the side of the jamb, causing a soft tone to sound somewhere inside.

He followed her in, across a polished wood floor inlaid with an intricate cross-hatch. The apartment was small but lush, with walls painted a warm off-white and dressed with creamy silk woven in a delicate floral pattern.

She struck a match and lit candles, making the silk seem to glow. "No electrics?" he asked.

She pursed her lips and blew out the long match. "Candle light is so much more pleasant. I'll be back in a moment."

He dropped into a large, high-backed chair with an ornately carved frame. It felt like a throne, and it occurred to him that this was the first time he'd ever been inside the walls of her castle. Two years ago he'd tried to be gentleman, respecting the rules of courtship he'd read in an old book. The approach proved foolish— they hadn't trained him to be a gentleman and he should never have tried to act like one. It'd probably made her feel foolish, too.

That was then.

Something in the room smelled good. Pure, cool, and sugared. So unlike the city outside. He couldn't put his eyes on the source, but, if pale blue had a smell, that would be it.

She returned with a little wooden box, heavily varnished with a small metal clasp. On the sofa, she opened it and removed a small aluminum device that looked like a DNA drive, but onto which were grafted additional electronics.

He took the ASCNT pad out of his satchel and handed it to her. The strange accessory clicked onto its bottom and she ran her finger down the right side of the screen to activate it. Normally, a glass would recognize its owner's finger-swipe and come to life, as when Mariel unlocked this one on the ship.

"This," she said as she pointed to the attached device, "will give us root access to the glass after a moment."

Just as she promised, the screen lit up. Amber-colored text on a black background.

"Now I can add our fingerprints to the security module."

"Mustafa was right when he said you're no mere publican."

"Thank you." She smiled. "Come over here and put your finger on this."

He raised an eyebrow, then walked over and sat down beside her. "Where?"

She held the glass in front of him and pointed to a circle in the center of the screen. "Right there. That's the spot…good."

With his fingerprint captured she restarted the pad.

"I looked through this on the ship," Adrian said, "but it's as if someone took an Apex computer manual and a treatise on neurology and mixed the pages up. It's practically unreadable."

"I won't be able to help with the medical side, but I know someone who can. Right now, let's try to figure out what this extra compute module is for."

Adrian watched Sabine work. He'd lived the last ten years with the knowledge that he'd lose Mariel. He never gave up hope, but as time crept by he felt the probability of his succeeding shrink ever smaller, until recently it seemed as if he were carrying on with the quest so that, when she was gone, he could assure himself he'd done everything humanly possible. Now, for the first time, he felt reality shift and that bit of hope he had clung to began to grow.

"This is interesting," she said.

"What?"

"This thing is an ultra-high bandwidth near-field comm module."

"Right." He nodded. "What's that?"

"Rare. Very rare." She continued to browse through the pad's menus.

He waited. Her sweet scent was an infernal distraction and he found his attention torn between the data pad and the complex curves of her ear.

"Here's something," she said, sitting upright.

"What is it?"

"A status screen listing neural interfaces paired with the comm module. Adrian, do you know what this is?"

"I was hoping you—"

Before he could finish, she jumped up and ran to the other room, returning with a small metal disc only a few millimeters in diameter.

"Remember this?" she asked. "The Christmas gift I found in the mine?" She placed it next to the glass and pressed a button on the screen labeled 'pair.'

A new serial number appeared on the list of neural interfaces.

"This is *Infernus*, Adrian, chrome-plated *Infernus*. Oh, yes." She put her hand on his arm and squeezed. "This glass communicates with brain implants."

"Truly?" He hooked his arm around her so he could lean closer and look at the screen. "What does it—how does it?" He stumbled over the question. "How will it help Mariel?"

"I don't know. No one's had an implant for centuries, so I can't say what functions it performs. I want my cousin Enn to look at it."

Exciting. Frustrating. Arousing. He couldn't be near her any longer without talking about it.

He took the glass from her hand and tossed it onto a chair. "Sabine, about the last time I was here—"

"Oh for the love of God, Adrian," she said, exasperated. "Can't you just put your hands on me?"

Yes?

He reached out and pulled her close, pressing his lips to hers.

She draped her hand on his shoulder and kissed him, her tongue lightly playing around the circle of his lips. "Finally," she whispered.

His arms closed around her, encompassing her narrow shoulders, his hands coming to rest on the soft curves of her back. He returned her kiss, his tongue gently penetrating her mouth. Their lips lingered until they parted for air, then he scooped her weightless body up into his arms.

"Through there." She pointed.

She nipped at his neck and ears on the way.

Her light touch was intense, charging him and standing the hair of his body on end. He laid her head on the pillow, never taking his eyes from hers, transfixed by the azure diamonds. Soon his weight was gently shifted onto her. He played his lips on hers as he slipped a hand between their bodies to hold her breast.

Her corset foiled the attempt.

He pushed back, unbuttoned his tunic and threw it to the floor.

Her velvet armor was held closed by busks, little steel strips with tiny loops on one side and posts on the other. They were a knave's box to undo, and he fumbled with them.

"Watch," she took his hands and moved them to her hips. Then, her slim, elegant fingers slipped each pin from its restraining loop, one by one. As each came undone, the corset opened slightly, reveling her vulnerable belly. It popped apart as the last captive pin slipped from its loop with an audible ping, and her perfect round breasts offered themselves to him.

The only barrier between her chest and his hands was a wisp of a fine chemise, and he could see a dark spot atop each breast with a brave, hard nipple standing on each summit, aching under the silk. He bent down to kiss her again, nudging his left thigh into the warm vale at the junction of her legs.

She fluttered under his touch. "Why couldn't you have—"

A furious knocking on the apartment's door startled Adrian upright. What the hell?

Sabine sat up beside him.

"Adrian?" Came the call from the stairwell outside.

Mariel. What's happened now?

"Adrian?" she called again.

"One damn minute!" He rolled off the bed and set about tucking his shirt in.

Sabine picked up her clothes and scurried to get into them.

He left the bedroom stumbling over the rug and opened the door.

"Adrian—" Mariel began, then stopped and studied him up and down.

Looking down at himself, he found that he wasn't at all together. "What is it?"

Her face flushed, and he saw a flash of anger.

"What are you doing?" she asked.

"Let her in, dear," Sabine said from behind him.

He looked back. Somehow she had gotten herself together much more completely than he, looking almost unmolested. He stood back, and Mariel entered, giving them both a close inspection.

"Are you—" Mariel's expression wobbled between outrage and pain as she looked at them both. "With *her*?"

Sabine turned to Adrian and waited for him to respond.

"Never mind us. Why are you here?" he asked with an edge on his voice.

Mariel hesitated for a moment, her eyes narrow and her hands trembling ever so slightly. "Mustafa went mad and left the ship."

"What?"

"Mus—"

"Why?"

"I don't—"

"Where did he go?"

Mariel bit her lip. She looked at Adrian, the strange anguish in her eyes putting him at a loss for words.

"Please, Mariel," Sabine said, voice calm. "Sit down and tell us what happened."

Adrian watched Mariel's eyelids quiver as she walked to the sofa. Something was terribly wrong, and while he knew she'd do her duty, sit, and tell the story, he wouldn't hold her captive in such discomfiture.

"No," he said. "Go back to the ship. I'll be there as soon as I can."

"Oh God, Adrian. How could you?" Mariel asked, before breaking into tears. She ran out, brushing past a barmaid who had just reached the door.

Christ. He listened to the sound of her footsteps fade down the stairs.

"Message for you, Miss," the barmaid said. She handed a piece of paper to Sabine.

She read it, and quietly looked at the ceiling, waving the piece of paper like a fan.

"Bine?" Adrian asked.

"There's a messenger downstairs. She wants to arrange a meeting between us, and Lady Alisa Conti."

CHAPTER 16

In the shadow of *Miranda's* hull, the familiar flashing lights and alarms sounded and the powerful hydraulic struts lowered the ramp to the ground.

To Adrian's surprise, Tomas awaited them at the top.

"How are you feeling, old man?" Adrian asked.

"Back of my head is throbbing. Must have drunk too much of Mustafa's cheap wine last night. Lars says you saved my life. Thank you."

"No need for that. You should lie down, though. Stay off your feet for a few days." Adrian walked to the control box and raised the ramp. "No swabbing of the deck."

"Aye," Lars agreed, entering the hold. "I was just trying to convince him of that." The boatswain turned to Tomas. "Now do what your doctor says—take your medicine and lie down."

Tomas trundled off to his quarters.

"Is Mariel here?" Adrian asked Lars.

"She was. Ran in, left this for you." The older man pulled a folded letter out of his pocket and handed it to Adrian. "I haven't seen her since."

Adrian unfolded the paper and read it. Anger and confusion swirled together. Why was this happening? He stood and stared at the note before folding it back up and putting it in his satchel.

"What is it?" Sabine asked.

"Mariel. What time is it?"

"Just after six local," Lars answered.

Adrian turned and walked to the mess hall without speaking. He pulled a bottle of wine from the cooler, uncorked it and filled three cups to the top.

Sabine and Lars caught up.

"What about Mariel?" Sabine asked.

"Nothing. I'll deal with it, Bine. Lars, what the hell is this about Mustafa leaving?" He took a deep drink.

"I've been sacked, I couldn't care less," the boatswain said, taking a swallow.

"Sacked? What are you talking about?" Adrian asked.

"I told him he was being stupid and he sacked me." Lars shrugged.

"Back up and start from the beginning. You know he wouldn't do that unless…well, I can't imagine him ever doing it."

"Right, Brother." Lars put his cup down. "I heard the ramp lower and went to check on it. Mustafa had let some Saracen boy into the ship and was talking to him in their language. It sounded heated but you never can tell with them."

"And?"

"The whole thing stank, so I stopped him and asked what he was doing. He wouldn't say—told me it was none of my damn business. I told him not to be stupid—not to run off by himself— and he fired me."

"Is the ramp camera working?" Adrian asked.

"It should be." The Boatswain walked to a console, folded down the keyboard and began to navigate the ship's status screens. He opened the security menu and selected the camera labeled RAMP1. The *Miranda* was originally equipped with many cameras to monitor activity inside and out, but only of few of them were operational. This camera sat above the control box on the landing strut, and its wide field of view encompassed the loading ramp and the area at its base. A digital image appeared on the screen showing the empty concrete slab the ship currently rested on.

"Roll it back," Adrian said.

Lars scanned back through the recording. High-speed images showed the movements of the crew in reverse for the past several hours until finally they came to the scene of a lithe Turkish boy walking up to the control box.

Lars pressed a button and normal speed playback began. There was no sound with the video, so they watched in silence.

The boy put his face fully in-frame. He was young, no more than thirteen. Words were exchanged with someone over the intercom.

Lights began to flash and the cargo ramp lowered into view. The boy ran up into the ship.

"I met them in the hold about here," Lars said after skipping forward a few minutes.

There was movement on the screen again. Mustafa walked down the ramp, the boy beside him. Before they walked out of view, Mustafa stopped and turned back to the ship. He pointed at someone, or something, and spoke, then made an exaggerated shooing motion with his arm.

Adrian looked at Lars for an explanation.

"I don't know, Brother. By this time, I'd been told to be off the ship first thing in the morning."

Then the object of Mustafa's apparent ire came into view. Berry walked down onto the concrete, pink tongue hanging from the right side of his mouth, and confronted the pair. Mustafa kicked at the dog with his pudgy leg. Berry easily avoided the attack, and eventually the frustrated Turk and the boy left. Berry stood for a few seconds, then trotted off after them.

"Roll that back a bit, Lars," Adrian said.

The boatswain scanned back a few seconds.

"Stop," Adrian said. He pointed at the screen. "Look at the boy."

The unknown boy was about one and a half meters tall, with light brown skin and dark hair. He was thin, but not frail, and wore a simple robe with tan and brown stripes.

"Look at his feet," Adrian said.

"Clogs. With wooden soles," Sabine said. "He's a *tellak.*"

The young bath house attendants spent hours a day in the steam rooms, and protected their feet from the hot stone and tile with wooden-soled slippers.

"Find the bath house with the boys, and we'll likely find Mustafa," Adrian said.

"There are two others besides the *Mimar Hamam,*" Sabine offered. "One is for women."

"I'll find him." Adrian said. "But first, I've got to take care of another problem. I'll be back soon."

"I'll go with you," Sabine said.

"No. Don't worry, I won't be far away." He looked up at the ceiling.

Adrian pulled himself up and through the *Miranda's* top hatch. The early evening air was crisp, and the wind rippled across the wide, clear landing field.

He clambered onto the ship's back intent on scolding Mariel for disloyalty. For abandoning her post, neglect of duty, and insubordination. For retreating.

The thoughts vanished when he walked up behind her.

She sat on the alloy plating, dangling her feet over the side of the ship.

Despite being a squire duly entered into the Order's rolls, she wasn't a soldier and she would never be one.

He wouldn't allow it.

It wasn't the right thing for her—she was capable of more. The standards the Order held him to were well and good for a warrior, but far too low for her.

"Mariel?" He reached down and offered his hand.

"Adrian, you came." She wiped her eye, then took his hand and stood up, close to him. She wrapped her arms around him and rested her head on his chest.

Was this clinginess part of becoming a woman? "Of course I did. You knew I wouldn't let you leave my side. You realize, though, that to properly run away you have to actually run, to somewhere away?"

"I know. But don't you realize that I'd never run from you?" She broke down, her face buried in his chest.

He did know it, making this all the more surreal. He put his hand gently on the back of her head, resolved to soak up her tears until she had gotten them all out.

"I suppose we need to talk about this," he said.

She nodded.

"I just assumed that because you never had a mother you wouldn't be upset if I tried to make a relationship with someone. No one's being displaced, or left behind."

"Oh, Adrian. This isn't about mothers and fathers, it's about you and me. Why won't you love *me*?" she asked, a desperate shout buried in her quiet voice.

Where in Hell was this coming from? "I do love you. For the last ten years I've shown you all the love I could. As if you were my own child I've loved you."

"That's what's wrong." She took his hand. "I never was your child."

Understanding hit him harder than any blade or arrow could. That was the dark heart of it.

"You know exactly how to be a man, Adrian. You're the man a woman dreams about."

This went far deeper than he'd realized.

"You've never known me as anything but a grown man, but I've seen you as a little girl. Taken care of you. It shapes my feelings for you. Elevates them above all that."

She shut her eyes, and he watched her fighting away tears. He fought the same battle, much further from the surface.

"Won't you kiss me, just one time, as you would a woman?" she asked.

No. At what point does one stop indulging ones daughter? Surely this was it, but his heart was irretrievably dedicated to her happiness. At the expense of his own conscience, though?

At any expense.

"Will that truly make you happy?"

"I don't know. I only know that I desperately want you to."

Could anything he did possibly make it more painful? This must be the bottom.

She looked up at his face in anticipation.

He put his arm around her, hand on her back between her shoulders and drew her close.

Her heart beat fast.

A hand went to her hip, and he leaned down.

She stood on the tips of her toes.

Their lips met.

He held her tight, and kissed her as he would a woman.

CHAPTER 17

"What do you mean, 'erratic?'" Adrian asked, waiting next to Sabine in front of a battered old door in perhaps the filthiest, most dilapidated neighborhood in the city.

"You never know what you'll find in here." Sabine shrugged and knocked on the door a second time.

A metallic click signaled the unbolting of the lock, followed by the scraping of wood as a bar raised. The door opened, revealing Enndolynn in the blue and gold, nearly transparent silk garb of a *harem* girl. She wore a little embroidered vest that barely covered her breasts, shining gold wrist and arm bands, and *zills*—finger cymbals.

A pale Christian woman dancing in the Oryantal style?

She waved them into the house, where the exotic sound of an Ottoman quartet oozed from a hidden speaker, and the air smelled of incense.

Adrian looked at Sabine, who rolled her eyes.

"Welcome cousin," Enn said, affecting a heavy Turkish accent. "Who is this rock-hard yeoman? A new slave-concubine? Perhaps you've brought him to share with me?" She danced close to Adrian, her hips gyrating with the music.

"No on all counts," Sabine said in her most serious voice. "Except the hardness."

Enn laughed out loud and shut the door, dropping the wooden bar back into position. She turned to Adrian. "That's the first lewd thing she's ever said."

"That's not what I meant," Sabine said, blushing.

"May I know the name of the man who's stoked Sabine Isolde Adler's passion?" Enn asked, putting her hand on Adrian's chest.

"Adrian of Tarsus," he answered.

"Knight of the Order of Saint John," Sabine said, her voice full of satisfaction.

"Oh my, a Crusader." Enn gave Sabine a curious eye as she continued to dance around Adrian, chattering away with the finger-cymbals. "Tell me. What do you do with the poor little Saracen girls you capture?"

Enn wasn't only erratic, she was also more than a little annoying.

He drew the dagger strapped to his thigh. "Sometimes the throat." He ran his finger above the edge of the blade, then touched the point. "Sometimes the heart."

Enn stepped back, giving up her accent in the process. "Truly?"

Adrian gave her a noncommittal shrug. He sheathed the blade.

"We have work for you, Enn," Sabine said, holding up the ASCNT pad.

She frowned and let out a frustrated huff. "Just when this was getting interesting. What do you need?" She took the glass.

"This is an admin tool for neural implants. We need to know how it works, and what it does." Sabine unlocked the device.

Enn snatched the glass and tapped the screen several times. She started reading, scrolling through the pages while an awkward amount of time passed.

With no warning she turned and walked to the back of the house and went up the stairs.

Adrian looked at Sabine. "If that's erratic, I'd hate to see mad."

"Sometimes she's normal. Sort of. Adrian?"

"Bine?"

"Those Saracen girls. You didn't really…" She drew her finger across her throat.

He put a finger to his lips. "We 'Crusaders' have a reputation to maintain."

They climbed the creaking stairs to the attic laboratory and found Enn sitting at her desk with a pad in each hand, apparently reading from both simultaneously.

"Where did you say you got this?" Enn asked as they walked in.

"We didn't," Adrian said.

Enn continued to read.

Adrian took a place on the old, threadbare settee and held his hand out for Sabine. She joined him, leaning against him with her legs pulled up beside her.

The bells of the cathedral rang, eight deep knells.

"We've a meeting at midnight," Sabine said.

If Enn heard, she didn't acknowledge it.

After an uncertain amount of time—it felt like an hour or more, but nine bells had not yet rung—Enn turned in her chair.

"Congratulations, you've found it," she said.

"Found what?" Adrian asked.

"The original sin."

Adrian leaned forward. "This isn't a joke. Men are dead because of this."

"I wasn't making a joke."

"Tell us what you've found, cousin," Sabine said, her soft manner cooling the warmer tempers.

Adrian sat back.

"I thought this ASCNT Program sounded familiar, so I searched through the G-fragment." She turned to Sabine. "The Library fragment you gave me after that Yirmi business a few years back."

"I remember," Sabine said.

"It's just a footnote, and the link is dead, but look here." Enn handed the glass to Sabine, and pointed to a specific line.

"'See ASCNT Program charter document.' Okay. Enn, this footnote is in an article dealing with 'genetic conservation.' What does that mean?"

"I don't know, but the study of genetics is what the Ecumenical Council was referring to when they spoke of *Machina Infernus* 'defacing the human soul.' Hence, your original sin." Enn shook her head and frowned. "We need a more complete version of the library."

Both women looked at Adrian.

"C-NOC," Enn said.

"Sea knock?" Adrian asked.

"The Colonial Network Operations Center. The hub of the ancient computer network, and the resting place of the most complete copy of the World Library in existence. Or so they say—I wouldn't presume to know anything about it." She looked at Adrian askance.

"It's no secret that it exists," Sabine said, "at least not to those of us interested in such things. But only ranking clerics are allowed to use it."

"I know about the library." Adrian said. "The thinking is that only those who are sure in their faith can risk exposure to the heresies it contains."

Enn laughed and glanced at Sabine, who also smiled.

"You find it amusing?" Adrian asked, staring at Enn. "Hidden somewhere in that library is the recipe for destroying civilization. Again."

"Then why are you so eager to sift through it?"

"I'm only interested in this." He stabbed at the glass with his finger.

"Right, children." Sabine broke in. "Let's focus on that." She gave Enn a prickly eye.

"Fine." Enn clenched her jaw. She seemed like the sort of person who adopted any position that would spark a volatile argument, regardless whether she subscribed to it or not.

"How do we get into this damned C-NOC?" Adrian asked.

"First," Enn said, "you won't get through the door unless you're a diocesan Bishop or better."

"Adrian is a Knight-Lieutenant," Sabine said to Enn, then turned to Adrian. "Where does that put you?"

Adrian hesitated, thinking back to his visit to the *Cursus Ecclesia*.

"What is it?" Enn asked, leaning forward.

"A Knight-Lieutenant in the Order has the same precedence as a pastor, or a parish priest."

"You don't have enough muscle," Enn said, shaking her head.

"But I'm not a Lieutenant. Not anymore."

"What do you mean?" Sabine asked.

"I received word of my promotion to Knight-Commander when I arrived here." He held up his hand, displaying the signet.

"Adrian, that's wonderful," Sabine said with no small amount of satisfaction. In fact, she sounded proud of him.

"That's impossible," Enn said. "You're no Lord. Not even a Baronet. Not even a banneret, for that matter. You're nobody."

Sabine scowled at Enn. "Cousin—"

"Even so," Adrian said, "the order came from Valetta, with all the proper seals and accouterments."

Enn ran her hands through her hair, then scratched her head. "It can't be a coincidence. You show up needing high-level access, and a promotion is waiting for you?"

The whole thing was perplexing, sure, but the connection she made didn't work. "We only found the relic about two weeks before we arrived here. Even if someone learned of it, and learned of us, the timing doesn't work."

"Don't let Enn pull you in with her paranoia, Commander. I'm happy for you and I'm sure the promotion is a reward for, what is it, thirty years of service to the Order?"

"About thirty, yes." Thirty years. It didn't seem like it.

"You don't look that old," Enn said. "I would have put you at thirty-five."

"That's about right. I came to the Order at a young age. Four, five. I don't know exactly."

"Oh? You've not known anything else, have you?"

"No."

"Once we're inside—" Sabine began.

"We?" Adrian asked.

"I'm going with you, Commander. Once we're inside, we'll have our work cut out for us. We'll have to query out the information on ASCNT, but it's probably in the government secure annex."

"Tough to crack," Enn said.

"What's the secure annex?" Adrian asked.

"The World Library contained more or less everything that mankind knew," Enn explained, "but just like now, the best stuff was secret. The annex was the high-security sub-cloud used by the Earth Union government. We find fragments of it occasionally, but decryption is tricky."

"Why?"

"Math," Enn said. "I can't say how long it will take to crack."

Adrian leaned back. "That won't work. Being in there for too long is sure to draw attention."

"No doubt they've turned off the near-field wireless, too," Sabine said, "or we could copy off what we need and crunch it at our leisure."

"What if we could reconnect it to the network?" Adrian asked.

"It wouldn't do us any good." Enn shook her head. "We'd still need a second terminal, somewhere else on the network to hack in from."

"What kind of terminal?"

There was silence as the ladies considered the question. Sabine finally answered. "A glass pad won't do. We'll need a workstation, and it'll need to be on the colonial backbone. If there are any firewalls between, the time it would take to break through would put us back at square one."

CHAPTER 18

Mary Frances flicked her hand in the field of blue light projected by the holographic keyboard, setting in motion a series of timed events in the Holy See's security system.

Minutes later, she stood in front of a little-used door on the side of the Palace of the Holy Office hidden by a trellis and curtain of white roses.

She noted the red light on the security camera.

At the appointed moment, the door lock clicked and she pressed the lever with her gloved hand.

Up the back stairs to the third floor. All the cameras showed red.

There was no attendant outside Duval's office at this hour and she entered, activating the hidden latch in the bookcase and sliding it aside. The stairwell light was already on. She pulled the bookcase back into position, then dropped a wooden bar into place to prevent it opening from the outside. She descended the steps.

In the steel dungeon below, a Swiss Guard in full regalia stood watch by the only other exit. His eyes stared straight ahead, boring into the opposite wall.

"The Cardinal is here?" she asked.

"Yes, Sister. Cell four."

"Anyone else?"

"No, Sister."

"Leave us."

The guard snapped to full attention, clicked his heels sharply, and turned to leave the room.

She reached around, and with a quick, precise swipe of her blade opened his throat.

Mary Frances entered a code into the door control panel, locking it and overriding the external keypad.

She walked toward the fourth cell, from which she could hear the Cardinal's soft, fatherly voice educating a prisoner.

She stopped in front of the black oven used to heat the tools of persuasion needed to prod the wayward back to the light. Its electric heating elements were cold now, but with the flip of a switch, they would rise to twelve hundred degrees in a matter of seconds. On racks next to the oven hung the special instruments, many different types, each suitable to punish a specific offense.

Iron rods and brands in many hooked and barbed configurations. The Heretic's Fork. A Spanish spider with razor-sharp claws to shred the breasts of witches. And, Mary Frances' favorite, the wicked and versatile Pear of Anguish. Fitting punishment for those who spoke heresy, but also sodomites and whores.

She picked up one of the brass fruit. In its closed position, it fit comfortably in her palm. Turning a small key at its base drove a screw that made the innocuous orb slowly blossom, four petals inexorably spreading.

She closed the Pear and picked up the Dragon's Tongs. A pair of vicious pliers, the ends shaped like the head of a mythical beast, its mouth full of spikes and blades.

She hid both tools under her cloak.

The door of the fourth cell was open; Cardinal Duval sat on a stool, deep in prayer in front of a woman's body still embraced by the iron band of the Scavenger's Daughter. Wrapping around her back and shins, it compressed the victim into a little ball. When cinched down tightly, breathing became impossible.

"Father," she said.

Duval jumped, startled. "Mary Frances, I didn't hear you."

"What happened here?"

"We lost another soul. She refused to confess. Refused to repent." There was sadness in his voice, but not in his eyes.

"Souls are the reason I'm here."

"Indeed?"

"How many souls are there, father?" She stood over him, looking at the dead heretic.

"I suppose there are as many souls as there are people, no more, no less."

"Each one unique?"

"Yes, each is a unique creation of God." He stood. "What brings on these questions?"

"What if a person isn't a creation of God, but of man? Would that person have a soul? Would she be unique?"

His face darkened. His eyes seemed to sink into his skull, and he took on a wrinkled apparition of age she had never seen before. "Man cannot create man," he said with an edge on his tongue.

"You lie!"

"Lie? How can I lie to you? I've taught you everything you know about the truth. I define the truth for you!" By the end, he was at full, enraged, roar.

She gripped the iron handles of the tongs tightly under her cloak. An image of him chained to the wall flashed in her mind.

"Well?" the Cardinal demanded.

She snapped out of her fantasy.

"Answer me! How can a man who creates truth *ever* be a liar?" His hand reached out and grasped her by the jaw, squeezing her mouth, and shaking her head.

There was strength in him, despite his age. She had all but forgot his methods of discipline. She thought he had changed, become kinder, but no. It was she who had changed, her will broken and tamed. The violence had only ended because she submitted to him.

"You told me I was special," she cried.

He let go of her, pulled back and hit her mightily with his open hand.

"Ignorant bitch," he said under his breath. "I've told you over and over how special you are. I've made everything you've ever done a success whether it was or wasn't." Again he slapped her, harder, the sound ringing off the cell walls. "For this, I am a liar?"

Tears streamed down her face. "I'm not special. I'm one of many. Who knows how many there are just like me?"

He struck at her, back and forth across her face. Her head rocked violently from side to side with each blow. The pain had never bothered her, but the disapproval, the blame, and the disgrace of failure, these slashed at her mind.

But, if she were a creation of man, and had no soul, then was there nothing to save, no reason to submit?

Duval's open palm, red from the assault, smashed her again.

She shoved him away with one strong arm, sending him backpedaling until he tripped over his long Cardinal's robe and fell onto his back.

"I'll have you flayed," he shouted. "Guard!"

She sprang on him, slamming his head into the steel floor. "No guards can hear you." She pinned him to the floor, hand on his throat. "Now confess, liar."

He struggled, but her young muscles, lovingly engineered for strength and agility millennia ago, kept him down.

"Confess!"

"Never. My conscience is clear."

From her robe she produced the Dragons Tongs, holding them above his face. "You'll confess. Everyone does."

"No—"

She jammed the hideous tongs into his mouth, grabbing hold of his tongue in the beast's serrated, razor-sharp teeth.

He screamed and fought to push her off, but she only squeezed down tighter on the handle.

He clawed at her face, shook his head like a dog. His struggle only made the dragon's teeth rip deeper into his tongue.

Blood flowed from the punctured organ down into Duval's throat, where his breathing caused it to sputter and spray from his mouth.

"Confess your sins against God…and me." Still crushing down with the tongs, she again demanded contrition.

He continued to scream, unintelligibly with the sharp tool in his mouth, and fought against her.

"No? Allow me to persuade you." She pulled back slowly on the tongs. At first, his tongue was drawn out, but soon it was fully stretched and the dragon's teeth cut it to bloody ribbons as she pulled the instrument straight out.

He writhed and screamed under her, blood spattering her face, the remnants of his shredded tongue hanging from his mouth, twitching pathetically.

"I...lied." Sputtering and crying, he confessed.

She tossed the tongs aside and pulled the pear from under her cloak. She jammed the orb into his mouth, breaking teeth, and turned the key, slowly.

Lying helpless on his back, the tool pried his mouth open. Lips and cheeks stretched, until finally she had forced his jaw as far open as it could naturally go.

Muscles tore and bone snapped.

He gurgled, tried to breathe and fought to swallow the blood filling up his throat. A violent ejection of breath sent a red spatter into her face, then, his body convulsed as pooling blood washed back into his lungs, drowning him.

CHAPTER 19

"How does this thing work?" Adrian asked. The odd little lump of flesh-colored plastic lay in his palm.

"Put it in your ear, like this." Sabine helped him place the device. "Now you can hear the rest of the team. It's an open mic, so everything you say will be broadcast."

"Adrian." Lars' voice came over the earpiece. "Miss Enndolynn and I are in the control center now. We're working on getting the computer online."

"Any trouble getting down there?"

"No...no, just a lot of corpses. I, uh...I saw Bernt."

"Good, let us know when you're ready."

The sun was setting and the air turning chilly as they made their way through the gates of the Old City. Adrian's new signet put them through the guard post with hardly a glance, and they made their way through the thinning crowd to St. Mary's.

Purple and orange twilight reflected off the tall structure, fading as Adrian led Sabine across the courtyard to a smaller building just south of the cathedral. The Papal Archives. Formerly, the Colonial Network Operations Center.

Through the entire walk, Adrian listened to a stream of low chatter in his ear as Enn and Lars worked on the computer deep below in the mine. Finally, he heard the words they were waiting for.

"That's it," Lars said. "We're online."

"And our IPv9 address confirms we're on the backbone," Enn said a few seconds later.

The computer in the mining operations center proved to be on a trusted network segment. Behind the firewalls, it was a forgotten gateway to the Church's network.

"Fine work," Sabine whispered. "We're going inside."

The Swiss Guard at the Archive door looked at them with more skepticism than his compatriots at the gate, but, once again, they passed inspection.

"So far so good," Sabine said.

"The real test comes next," Adrian said.

The temperature rose inside, the air processed by a central conditioning system. Past the small entry chamber, whitewashed and brightly lit by diodes, a monk with a shaved head and brown robes sat behind a stainless steel counter. There was one door leading deeper inside, closed and watched over by another Swiss Guard.

"May I help you, sir?" the monk asked.

"I'm Knight-Commander Adrian of Tarsus. This is Sister Prudence. We're here from Valetta to use the library."

"Very good, sir. May I see your identification?"

Adrian pulled his ID tags from under his shirt and removed their chain from his neck. He waved one of the aluminum and glass tags over a sensor on the counter.

"Thank you, Commander," the monk said. "Sister, please present your identification."

Adrian measured his breathing. Sabine wore the habit of a Raphaelite Sister, an order dedicated to healing and allied with the Knights Hospitaler. Perhaps it was a little loose, but coifed and veiled the disguise didn't look entirely contrived. It was just that she made far too beautiful a nun.

Sabine held up her rosary, to which was attached another ID tag. She waved it above the sensor.

The tag was one from Adrian's old set. Sabine and Enn insisted that they had reprogrammed it and that it would correctly identify Sister Prudence Weiss.

Nothing happened.

The monk watched the blank screen. "Try again, Sister, sometimes it doesn't read."

Still nothing.

The monk reached over the counter, took the tag, and held it right down on the reader, moving it back and forth. "There we are."

Adrian's body unwound.

"Oh, Sister, is this your first visit to the Holy City?"

"Uhm…yes…why do you ask, Brother?"

"Your identification is good, but we have no record of you in the local security database."

"Oh?" Sabine's voice trembled ever so slightly.

"Don't worry, Sister, it happens when a person takes their vows on another planet. The system will fill in the blanks the next time we run an administrative batch over the relay. For now, as long as the Knight-Commander is willing to vouch for you…"

"Of course," Adrian said.

"Thank you, Commander. Head down to sub-level four. Brother George is on duty in the Library. He'll help you with your query." He pressed a button hidden under the counter, and the door unlocked with a click.

"Thank you, Brother," Adrian said.

"Yes, thank you so much, Brother." Sabine smiled.

They were in, the door closed and locked behind them.

"We're inside," Sabine whispered.

The building had five sub-levels. They took a set of winding stairs down to a door with a large '4' painted in red and stepped out into the Library's antechamber. Another Swiss Guard stood at rest beside the door.

The lower level was noticeably colder than above, with lower lighting and an omnipresent, pitched drone in the background that Adrian recognized as the sound of a large computer system.

Across the room, behind a small desk, sat a large monk with a bushy beard and close-cropped hair. He picked at the remains of a chicken breast on a pewter plate and stared at a computer screen set up with a chess game.

The monk moved his bishop. "Take that, wench," he said with a laugh.

The computer immediately countered, and a flat, vaguely female electronic voice announced the result. "Knight takes bishop. Checkmate."

"Damn and blast!" The monk slammed his fist on the desk, just as he noticed Adrian and Sabine approaching.

"Brother George?" Adrian asked.

"Oh, pardon me Sir Knight, and Sister." He nodded to Sabine and quickly reached to turn the game off. "Yes, I'm Brother George, how may I help you?"

"We need to research a medical problem in the Library," Adrian said.

"Well, you've come to the right place, then." George giggled. "In fact, it's the only place."

"Yes," Adrian said slowly, nodding. "That's why we came all the way from Valetta."

"Ah, yes, just a little library humor you know." George looked at the floor.

"No harm in that, Brother." Sabine smiled warmly at George, then turned to Adrian and glared. "God hates an old sourpuss."

George's face turned up. "That's exactly how I interpret the scripture, Sister. In Lamentations, for example—"

"Brother George." Adrian interrupted. "Let's discuss Lamentations after we conclude our research."

"Of course, of course. My apologies."

"We certainly will discuss it." Sabine leaned close to George and spoke in a faux whisper, all the while looking at Adrian. "Whether Knight-Commander Grumpy wants to or not."

Damn it.

"Well then, do you have a writ?" George asked.

What the hell was a writ? "No."

"No problem, no problem. We can query *ad hoc*, as they say. What annex will you need?"

Adrian looked to Sabine.

"The government secure annex, Brother, specifically the Universal Health Organization databases, but we'll probably need to join other tables as well."

She handled that rather expertly.

"Very good. You've worked with the Library before, then?" George asked.

"Oh…no, no I haven't. The Mother Superior gave me those instructions."

"I see. Well since you're new to the system, I'll need to review the access rules with you." George took a leather-bound book from the desk and opened it to the first page. The contents were hand written, and intricately illuminated. The book was two centimeters thick.

Perfect. Adrian pulled a pair of chairs up to the desk, waited for Sabine to sit, then dropped himself onto a hard wooden seat as George began to pontificate.

"One: You shall use the information in this Library solely to advance the goals and interests of the Holy Church. Two: You recognize that the Library contains incorrect information with no basis in theological fact. Three: Exposure to such information is at your own peril. Four: Dissemination of heresy is a crime punishable by death. Five: If you believe you have disseminated heresy in error, please contact the Holy Office of the Inquisition. Six..."

Who would turn himself over to the Inquisition? Why yes, I did preach heresy, but it was only a little one, on accident I swear. Probably the same people who self-flagellate. They get bored of it and decide to move up to autoerotic immolation.

"Fourteen. No food or drink is allowed inside the Library..."

Adrian glanced at Sabine, who was giving her full attention to the liturgy of rules. He could smell her. Cinnamon. That damn perfume again. Funny that no amount of heat, cold, exhaustion, or pain had ever distracted him from his work, but the faint smell from this particular woman's body stirred his mind like a spoon in pudding.

Sabine glanced at him, smiled.

Hell. Caught ogling Sister Prudence.

"Any questions?" George asked.

"What?" The end of the Brother's speech extinguished Adrian's carnal thoughts.

"Do you have any questions about the rules, Commander?"

"No, we don't," Sabine said. "They're perfectly clear and reasonable."

"Good then. Follow me into the Library and I'll assist you with your query." George stood.

"That's probably not a good idea, Brother," Adrian said. He pointed to the remains of George's chicken. "We'll have to look at some images of a nasty flesh-eating disease. Might not sit well with you after dinner."

"Well." George hesitated. "I suppose I had best be strong. I am supposed to attend all visitors." He waved his arm at a steel door painted a deep crimson with the coat of arms of the Holy See overlaid in gold.

"Of course, you have to do your duty," Adrian said.

George opened the door for them. "Uhm, Commander?"

"Yes?"

"What exactly does a flesh-eating disease look like?"

"Imagine a nice turkey leg that you've eaten the greasy skin off and chewed away most of the soft meat, then imagine it putrefied, black, with copious pus oozing—"

"I see."

"—sometimes maggots—"

"I see, well, I think I'll just watch you on the security camera. If you need anything, just wave."

The interior of the Library was stark. A white room, with row after row of black cabinets. Lights on the cabinets flashed randomly, flickering off the glass wall that separated the storage cloud from the terminal room. Underneath it all, a cold chill and the continuous whirr of cooling fans.

"This is it," Sabine said, staring at the rows of high-capacity DNA storage systems. Her sensual, fully adult face took on the aspect of a child anticipating the opening of a mysterious present.

"I've never understood how so much of this stuff continues to run, after all this time," Adrian said.

"It's a mystery. On the one hand, it was extremely well-made in the late colonial period, when planned obsolescence was out of fashion. On the other, everything fails eventually. I suspect that the Hansa are more than just paranoid repair-men. They may have developed some capacity to create new parts."

"Create new? That would run afoul of the maintenance-only doctrine. Does the Church know?"

"Wouldn't they have to?"

He shook his head. "Let's finish. This has been far too easy—something's bound to go wrong."

"It only seems easy because our plan is a good one."

"Tell him, cousin," Enn said over the radio. Her voice crackling as the signal passed through meters of rock and metal. "I'm in their surveillance system. Let me know when you're ready."

Sabine sat at the terminal, in a thickly padded leather chair. Adrian took up a position behind the chair, standing over her.

"Record us now," Sabine said. She waited a moment, then began to type using the virtual keypad, a wide box of blue laser-light floating under the terminal that registered the delicate movements of her fingers and hands in three-dimensional space.

"Look up necrotizing fasciitis," Adrian said.

She strung together a query and entered it.

The Library returned a long article and a selection of photographs.

"Oh, that's disgusting," she said, looking at a man's necrotized leg, dark red with irregular chunks eaten away.

"Avoid working in fields fertilized with human filth, if you can."

"Fine, that's good," Enn said. "I'm looping this video…now. Get to work."

"Right," Sabine answered. From a little pouch hidden under her habit, she produced two paraluminum tubes, about five centimeters long and one in diameter. They folded open lengthwise, revealing complex circuitry on the inside.

She got down on her knees, opened an access panel beneath the terminal, and poked her head inside. "This terminal is hardwired to the Library for security. We have to bridge the signal to the network that the rest of the complex uses. Look around; find a data port."

"I thought most everything was wireless before the Advent."

"Yes, but for high-security applications they used wires. Just think, all those centuries ago, universal-government apostates and radical individualists were trying to do just what we're doing now."

"Things never really change." He looked around the room, and found an unused port on the wall. "Here."

Sabine popped back out of the terminal cabinet. "The first collar is attached." She scurried to the port Adrian found, plugged in a cable, then clamped the second collar around it. Within a second, a blue light illuminated on the collar. "Yes! Enn, we're online here, can you see the bridge on your side?"

The blue light on the collar began to flash irregularly.

"Got it," Enn replied. "And I can see the Library terminal."

"We'll start our cover queries, let me know when you're done," Sabine said. She sat back down at the terminal, and began sending new queries related to necrotizing fasciitis.

Adrian rattled off additional medical terms to search for, and soon they built a convincing search string narrowing down a rare fungal infection with symptoms similar to a flesh-eating bacteria. All of this would be logged by the system in case anyone chose to follow-up. Enn's surreptitious activity, on the other hand, would be far more difficult to detect. At least according to Enn and Sabine.

"Some of this is unbelievable," Enn said.

"Focus on what we came for," Adrian said, irritated.

"Focus, Enn," Sabine said, just as the door popped open and Brother George stuck his head in.

"What's that?" George asked.

"Focus…*in* on the problem, Knight-Commander," Sabine said.

Adrian moved to block George's view. The coupler under the terminal was out of sight, but the other one…

"How goes your search?" George asked.

"Fine," Adrian said. "Just fine. We've just learned about a specific type of maggot that can be used to eat away the desiccated flesh of—"

"Excellent! Let me know if I can be of assistance." He pulled out quickly and closed the door.

"How long have we been in here?" Adrian asked Sabine.

She checked the clock on the terminal. "Half an hour."

"Surely she's got it by now?"

"I had the ASCNT data ten minutes ago," Enn said over the radio. "I'm downloading other things now."

"Damn it, cousin! We're done here," Sabine said with a balled fist. She got back on the floor and began to undo the bridge collar inside the terminal.

Adrian watched her arse wiggle under the black habit as she worked.

There was a knock on the door. "Is it safe to come in? No maggots on the screen?" George asked.

Hell. "One moment," Adrian said, loud enough to be heard through the door.

Sabine continued to fiddle with the collar.

Another knock on the door, this time sharp and impatient.

Sabine slid out and jumped back into the chair. "Okay."

Adrian opened the door a few centimeters. Brother George stood on the other side.

"Pardon me, Commander, but I need to know if you're almost done. A representative from the Holy Office of the Inquisition is waiting to use the system." George nodded his head towards a nun standing in the antechamber with her back to the men.

"Yes, of course," Adrian said. "Sister Prudence, finish up and meet me outside, will you?"

"Yes, Commander."

Adrian stepped out of the terminal room and closed the door behind.

The nun turned to face him.

They looked at each other for a moment.

Adrian found himself lost in the shape of her face, the angle of her nose, and the set of her lips. Familiar. Her habit framed her face in an odd way, but—her eyes! They were frosty and cold but the same shade of honey brown as Mariel's. God, she was one of them.

"Knight-Commander." She enunciated the words slowly, with slick precision. "I wasn't expecting to find a warrior here."

"The Order dabbles in medicine, as well, Sister..."

"Mary Frances." She curtseyed. Perhaps a little exaggerated, perhaps not, then slid up and stood very close.

Brother George slipped hurriedly out of range.

Mary Frances' close proximity repelled Adrian as if they were opposite poles of a magnet. He stood firm, even leaned forward a bit in defiance, and locked his eyes to hers. The difference in size between them was such that she could have hidden in his shadow.

The door to the terminal room opened, and Adrian heard Sabine walk out. She passed by quickly, head down, and made for the stairs. The entire time, Mary Frances and he remained locked in a bizarre contest of scrutiny.

Adrian finally broke it off. "It seems we're finished, Sister."

"Tell me, Commander, what's your name?"

"Adrian."

"Knight-Commander Adrian. Well, I want you to listen to me very carefully. I know who you are, and what you have. Oh yes, and I know of your young lady aboard the *Miranda*, too. We'll meet again very soon, and when we do it will be to your great advantage, and that of Miss Adler and the girl, to support my proposal. Ignore this advice, and you'll all roast before dawn— you last."

Enn's attic window was open, and Adrian sat on the sill watching the people on the street below and musing on the opium-perfumed breeze.

Funny how knowing a thing and comprehending a thing were two separate experiences.

He watched Sabine remove the nun's veil and shake out her blonde hair. She wriggled out of the rest of the habit, revealing a much more attractive evening dress underneath.

"Copies?" he asked.

"Genetic copies," Enn replied, "but not quite identical. You have to understand that their developmental paths begin to diverge the moment the eggs are fertilized. It's the same with twins—they develop independently even in the same womb."

Neither Adrian nor Sabine spoke.

He'd known since that day in the bunker at New Golan that Mariel was the product of experimentation with unearthed Apex technology. He knew that her strange illness was down to an engineer's mistake made over a thousand years ago—or maybe it was deliberate, just to see what would happen. Regardless, seeing it documented so objectively, from the passionless conception to the loveless birth, made it all the sadder.

"With that said," Enn continued, "the artificial wombs used in the program would likely make gestation more consistent."

"Why would anyone want to do that?" Sabine finally asked. "Weren't there billions of people on Earth before the Advent? Why make more?"

"According to the information we pulled, the purpose wasn't so much to create people, but to create better people."

Adrian shook his head. "How could they imagine that such an endeavor wouldn't break the covenant?"

Sabine leaned on his shoulder. "I don't think they saw themselves as being party to any covenant, dear. At the Apex, this was all they had left to put their faith in."

"Even the name of their program—ASCNT—sounds like a challenge," Enn said. "I suppose they thought they were being clever. It means Advanced Somatic Cell Nuclear Transfer, which was the technique they used to create the clones."

"How does it work?" Adrian asked. "I know enough about biology to believe they could make a flesh and blood body, but how did they create souls for these people?"

"I'm afraid that knowledge may be lost to us, if it ever existed," Enn said. "Or maybe we don't really understand the nature of souls."

"Yes," he said, "I'm beginning to think that a lot of our understanding is flawed."

"Heresy, Knight-Commander."

Adrian bristled, then relaxed. She was right, in both her expressed and implied points.

Sabine leaned over and whispered in his ear. "You're starting to see the world like a reformist."

It was both fascinating and repulsive, but there was a practical point to their obtaining the knowledge.

"How do I use that to put Mariel right?" He pointed at the retrofit pad.

"Now that gets interesting," Enn said. "The glass pairs with neural implants, and apparently—because I have no idea how this is possible—blocks some defective nerve pathways and stimulates the growth of new, healthy cells."

"Hell, if they can create a body and put a soul in it, why shouldn't they be able to do that too? Tell me about these implants. How do I get one for Mariel?"

"The question is, how do you successfully put it in? You're going to need an Apex medical facility for that."

"Christ," he said, rubbing his head.

"Don't despair, Commander," Enn said with a smile. "I think there's one left."

"What? Where?"

"I'm working on that. There's more data to decrypt—we've only scratched the surface—but based on what I've read so far, there was a base for the cloning program. I just can't seem to find the details."

CHAPTER 20

Adrian flagged down a carriage and held the door open for Sabine. He rapped his knuckles on the roof and called out their destination, South Gate, to the driver. With a lurch they began to move, accompanied by the clopping of hooves on cobblestone. Scenes from the New City flashed by in the windows. Throngs of men and women walked the streets, going home, or to a pub, or somewhere less reputable.

"Bine, there's another problem."

"Of course there is, Commander." She smiled.

"What?"

"When you finally run out of problems, you'll be dead." She laughed. "What's happened now?"

Sabine was giddy. She must have truly thrived on these intrigues.

"That nun from the Library? She's onto us."

"She told you that?"

"She did."

"But she didn't arrest us. That means she's scheming at something."

"She also said we'd see her again soon, and that I'm to back her proposal—whatever that is—under threat of execution. All our executions."

"Well then. What's your plan, Commander?"

"Confound the enemy with my complete lack of a plan?"

"Roll the dice, eh? I love that you can tolerate both the regimented and the random." She took his arm and snuggled up next to him.

South Gate was two places. In the first, the name referred to one of four huge portals through the stone and earthwork walls surrounding the Old City. More generally, it was the district surrounding the southern gate. Blue and cold on the Old side of the wall, it was red and passionate on the New side, packed with Inns, pubs, and theaters. Then, tucked behind, physically as well as in men's minds, the brothels, gambling halls, and dens. What elevated South Gate above the City's other pockets of sin were the clientele. Young, arrogant, born to the families of Cardinals and Barons, inheritors of wealth and power.

Neither Adrian nor Sabine belonged there.

The carriage stopped and deposited them on a busy street corner. As soon as Adrian had helped Sabine down, he was jostled by a pair of teetering revelers who forced their way into the carriage demanding the driver deliver them to 'papa.' Unable to extract clearer directions, the driver took off slowly, no doubt content to earn a few extra silver for nothing more than circling the block until his passengers sobered.

Sabine straightened herself, hooked her left arm through his right, and set off.

"I believe you're enjoying this, m'lady."

"Truly. I'll be the only woman here tonight on the arm of a Knight of Saint John. I might as well enjoy it."

He relaxed and allowed her to guide him along the way.

The Murky Affair was true to its name. Folded behind three other buildings, they reached it via a moonlit alley, along the way passing a few loitering figures whose activities were shrouded from view by deep shadows. Adrian couldn't escape the feeling that someone was watching them, but in the fog of the night it was impossible to know.

The alley wove around between the buildings making it difficult to tell which were which. Sabine took them directly to the unmarked entrance from which roared the throbbing, boiling din of an ebullient crowd.

The interior was just as dark and confounding, maybe more so. Adrian couldn't tell the purpose of the establishment. There was no bar that he could see, no tables. Men and women walked in and out of the yellow lamplight, some with drinks or food in their hands. All were besotted to one degree or another. The rumble of a hundred whispered, secret conversations seemed to make the room vibrate, and occasionally a sharp burst of laughter or loud exclamation exploded above the murmuring. Draped over it all, the sweaty, musky smell of people.

The crowd pushed in on him, smothering him. Adrian had been lost in masses of men before, but in battle it was the commander's duty to see the legions and make sense of it. The commander creates order from chaos. The soldier simply picks one man out of the thousands, turns his whole being to killing that man, then moves on to the next, then again, and again.

He slowed. Hemmed in by standing bodies, their faces flashing in and out of light. Sibilant whispering burned in his ears. His left hand began to fall downward of its own will. Its fingers opened, and the tip of his index finger touched the sharp point of the conical skull-crusher on his dagger's grip.

Pick one. Kill him. Then another.

He felt a light hand on his elbow. Suddenly, the crowd seemed to fall back, though they didn't move at all. The noise dropped to a tolerable level, and he breathed easily.

"Adrian, come on, this way." Sabine led him to a staircase to the side of the room that was guarded by a pair of large men.

"Miss Adler," one of the men announced.

"Back again," she replied, handing him a silver quattro. "This one is with me." She pointed to Adrian with her eyes.

The two men stood aside, and Adrian followed her up the stairs.

"You're a regular?" he asked.

"There's business here from time to time."

They walked up two flights of stairs, leaving the addling din of the crowd. The upper floor was smaller, far less crowded, filled with smoke. Diodes provided a low light, but never shone on the tables, where patrons disappeared into the shadows. Occasionally someone would take a draw from a cigar, and the bright red ember at its tip would strobe like a lighthouse's beacon, warning the traveler to steer wide.

Sabine led him to an empty table where he sat at her right hand.

"How do you find anyone in here?" he asked.

"We don't. The person who arranged the meeting will find us."

A barmaid came and held up two fingers. Sabine nodded, and the girl left without saying a word.

"This place is a sort of *terra nullius* inside the City," Sabine said.

"Who keeps the peace?"

"The Church, the League. Other powerful interests. They all use it, and anyone who creates a disturbance comes to regret it."

The barmaid returned and set two pewter mugs in front of them. Adrian took a whiff of the dark liquid inside.

He felt Sabine's hand on his arm.

"I think they've found us," she said.

Two cloaked figures floated to the table. Through the shadow and smoke Adrian strained to pick out details. It wasn't until the figures' hands came into clear view that he knew they were women.

They sat, turned their shaded faces from Sabine to Adrian, then pulled the hoods back.

Mary Frances and another woman, Anne, the messenger she'd sent to the Bee's Knees to arrange the meeting.

"Lady Conti." Sabine said. "And Anne, was it?"

"Indeed," the lady said, giving Adrian a warning glance. "I'm pleased you accepted my invitation, Miss Adler. And please, call me Mary Frances, Lady Conti is just a friend."

"What do you want?" Sabine asked.

"I originally thought you would broker the Commander's relic, but the situation has changed." Mary Frances looked at Anne. "Now, I need partners."

"Partners for what?"

"The expedition to Anance, of course."

Adrian flinched as something touched the inside of his left thigh. A little foot? It felt around and began to trace a path inward. His eyes flashed away from Mary Frances and found Anne staring back at him.

She licked her lips as her foot rubbed him.

"I think you've made a mistake, Mary Frances. I don't know of any Anance," Sabine said.

"That's because I erased everything about it from the Library before you broke in, including the last known coordinates and velocity vectors of its star."

Anne's bare foot slowly stroked him. He reached down and took it gently in his hand, massaging her sole with his thumb.

She grinned and pursed her lips.

"I'm afraid I still don't follow you," Sabine said.

"Let me lay it out, then." Mary Frances paused and looked deliberately at both Sabine and Adrian. "You have a relic of the ASCNT Program. To put it to use, you need the medical facilities at the ASCNT base on Anance. Only I can provide you its location. Simple enough, yes?"

Adrian crushed down on Anne's foot, squeezing it without mercy. She bolted upright.

With a flick of his thumb, he pushed her little toe back over itself, as far as he could without snapping it off.

Anne gasped, stifled a yelp, and wrenched her foot from his grasp. To his surprise, she looked up at him with the glow of a woman who had just reached a climax.

"Why do you want to go there?" Adrian asked Mary Frances.

"Apex technology. And…your relic may be of use to me as well."

"You have the same headaches, vertigo, and dementia that Mariel does?"

"Not exactly, my mind is…but the specifics don't matter."

Adrian nodded. Her very existence was a heresy. She couldn't be acting for the Church, much less the Inquisition. "Another passenger makes no difference to me, but if you have the coordinates why do you need us?"

"Convenience, anonymity, and you, Commander," Anne said.

"Why me?"

Anne smiled back at him.

Sabine gave the nun a thoughtful look. "Is your name Anne Kresimir?"

"That's right."

"But, your father, he thinks—"

"Yes, my dear old father. You and your hooligans smashed the shit out of the old bastard. Good on you."

Sabine stared at her, blank-faced.

"You haven't answered my question," Adrian said to Anne. "Why me?"

Anne shook her head and smiled as if the answer were obvious. "You're the model of a soldier of Christ, Adrian. You come from nothing, the Church is your everything. The Holy Father trusts men like you."

The Holy Father?

The great bell-tower at the City center struck the first of fourteen deep knells to mark the turning of the planetary day. Adrian and Sabine rode in a carriage, returning to Enn's apartment.

Sabine's giddy excitement was gone. She stared quietly out the window.

"What's wrong, Bine?" He reached out and took her hand.

"I love the excitement, Adrian. The thrill of a midnight rendezvous in a dark alley. The game of following, being followed, and shaking them off. The danger is like the drugs Enn cooks up in her lab. These people, though, are beyond evil. They aren't on any Crusade—they aren't fighting for anything. They're just sadists. That's all."

"I know. I see it more and more."

"I think I'm finished with it."

"Maybe it's time to settle down?"

"Is that an offer?"

The sound of an arrow hitting a man was a solid noise, palpable, felt as much as heard by those nearby. Their driver screamed.

Move!

Adrian grabbed Sabine and crashed through the coach's little wooden door. He landed with her on his chest and flipped to cover her from the storm of arrows that splintered the carriage. The missiles punched through its thin wooden frame and shattered on the cobblestones around them. Splinters and bits of fabric from the upholstery peppered them before the horse bolted and charged off, dragging the perforated carriage on its side.

A dozen arrows, rapid fire, high angle.

The rooftops.

How many archers?

A skilled bowman could fire once every four seconds.

He yanked Sabine onto her feet and thrust her into the closest doorway, kicking the door in just as another wave of arrows began to strike around them. His arms wrapped around her, he shielded her with his back and pushed her inside.

The thunk of arrows smashing into the door frame reverberated down the corridor, dark streaks rushed by, one passing close enough to draw blood from his neck before striking the floor and chattering into the darkness.

A long hallway. An apartment block.

"Are you hit?" he asked her.

"No, no I'm all right."

"Come on." He prodded her down the hallway, glancing behind, expecting the ambushers to appear at the door any second.

None did.

They reached the end and another door. Arrows that had slid up the hall now lay snapped and split at its base. He pressed her firmly against the wall, then, using the heavy door for cover he pulled it slightly open and peered out.

Two arrows splintered the wood only centimeters from his face, and he flung it closed again.

Damn it! Flanked.

"Up," he shouted as he took her by the hand and ran for a set of rickety stairs.

Four flights to the top floor.

He spotted a window at the end of the hallway and heard the clatter of four, maybe five pairs of boots down below, converging at the landing.

He desperately wanted to stop and have it out with the attackers, to run them through with steel and watch the life drain out of them, but his need to protect her overrode all other thoughts.

In that instant he realized just how much he truly loved her. Enough to show an enemy his back.

They ran to the window, opened the latch, and shoved. The outside was caked with paint, sealing it shut. He put his boot to it and it burst open, sending bits of broken glass flying onto the clay roof tiles one level below.

Their assailants were near the top of the stairs now. He jumped and landed on the slick terra-cotta tiles, crushing several. He held his arms up and motioned for her to jump.

He caught her easily, but the angle and slipperiness of the tiles undermined him. He lost his footing just as she fell into his arms. He landed on his back with Sabine on top, and they slid down the roof just as a fresh salvo of arrows rained on the window.

The pursuers arrived to meet the projectiles. The leader took two shafts in the chest and staggered out, rolling down the roof behind Adrian and Sabine.

With nothing to grab, Adrian went over the edge and landed on his back three meters below, on the ground floor roof. The impact of his head on the tile knocked him senseless and Sabine, light as she was, took the wind out him when his chest broke her fall. Sharp tile fragments pelted them, and finally the body of the dead man rolled over the edge and struck both of them.

The mayhem was too much for the roof, which gave way and dropped all three bodies in a cloud of dust and debris onto the floor of the apartment below.

He was dazed—maybe unconscious—for a moment.

"Adrian!" Sabine shook him by the shoulders, unwittingly bashing his head against the floor even more.

"Bine. Bine. Stop." He struggled to breathe. His chest and abdomen throbbed.

"You're alive!"

"Yes. Just...stop trying to revive me." He forced himself up. A body lay near his feet, and there was someone else...on the left! His hand went for the dagger at his hip, but Sabine stopped him in mid-draw.

"No, no, dear, it's just the man who lives here. It's all right." She held his arm tight. "It's all right."

The old man backed into the corner with a half-frightened half-outraged look on his face.

They'd fallen on the poor fellow's table, crushing it along with his dinner and several bottles of liquor. Cheap liquor with a noxious, nose-burning reek.

Adrian concentrated on his own body, moving his legs and arms, checking his shoulders and back. Miraculously, nothing was broken.

He turned to the body that had fallen on top of them. At first glance, the man looked like a mercenary. Maybe even a Landser, but something wasn't right. The skin—dark.

Adrian slid over to the body and, using his dagger, slit the left shirt sleeve open from wrist to elbow. He pulled it apart and revealed a tattoo—a crescent rising over a pair of crossed scimitars. The mark of the Janissaries.

"What the hell?" he said aloud.

"Shit, he's a Saracen," Sabine said as she looked over his shoulder.

Footsteps echoed outside and shadows flitted across the apartment's lone window. Soon a fist was beating on the door.

"Come out! We know you are inside!" The voice was high-pitched, heavily accented, a Turk.

Selim Bey had lied to him. Son of a Goddamned whore.

The man outside pounded his fist again.

"Okay damn you! We break it down!"

"Persistent little bastards, aren't they?" Sabine asked.

"Get the hell out before they smash my door!" the old man screamed from the corner.

There was a loud bang as something, or someone, crashed into the door. It was sturdy oak, but the frame cracked slightly with the impact.

Another, heavier crash followed. The Turks must have decided to double-team it. The door frame gave some more, long cracks forming.

"How many are there?" Sabine asked.

"At least four followed us up the stairs. Then there are the archers." Adrian moved over and stood in front of the door, about four paces back from it. He drew his dagger and gripped it blade-down.

"What are you doing?" she asked.

The Turks again slammed themselves into the door. This time the frame buckled and split. The door was barely hanging on. They would break through on the next effort.

"Now you die!" came a scream from outside.

Adrian pushed off with his right leg. He took three powerful steps toward the door, roaring.

The door frame burst and he pushed the heavy plank forward a meter before colliding with the oncoming Turks.

He drove them back and pushed the whole pile over. The door—bits of the splintered frame still attached—fell back on the stunned Turks.

There were two other men in the hall.

One on each side.

Surprised.

Adrian grabbed the first one by the collar. He pulled the man in close and drove the point of his dagger down into the junction of his neck and shoulder. The twenty centimeters of keen, tapered steel punctured the muscles of the neck and sunk deep, into the Turk's heart.

Dead.

A short-blade has no defensive value. The only tactic to employ with it is unrestrained assault.

The next Turk thrust his sword at Adrian's chest.

Parry.

Charge!

Adrian was inside the man's reach. He drove him to the ground, raised the dagger and jammed it down into the Turk's eye, penetrating the thin skull behind, carving and stirring up the soft brain inside.

Dead.

Don't linger. Adrian expected the two men under the door to be up and ready to fight, but when he jumped to his feet he found the hall empty, the broken door lying flat on the floor.

He looked left and right.

Sabine, blonde hair tousled, stuck her head out of the apartment doorway. "I believe they found Christ and fled."

"It's never too late. Are you okay?"

"Yes. I turned my ankle in the fall, I think."

"Let me see."

She pulled her dress up for him to look. No bruising or swelling. A sprain.

"How's the old man?" He nodded towards the apartment.

She stuck her head back into the room for a second, then replied, "looting the body."

"Right. Let's get out through the back, there must be more of them."

She winced when she tried to walk, so he pulled her arm around his shoulder and eased the weight off her hurt side, but the difference in height between them made it comical.

He picked her up in his arms and walked to the back door, looking out into the dark of a narrow street.

CHAPTER 21

"I'm coming with you, Adrian," Sabine said.

"No."

"I am."

"Like hell. You shouldn't be here at all." Adrian stood in front of a bakery in the Ottoman district, the smell of *simits* in the oven tickling his nose. Just up the way was the door to the *Mimar Hamam*.

Sabine leaned half-out of the carriage, her sun-lit blonde hair a beacon for every assassin in the quarter. Mariel was inside pouting over being made to come along, but she was the only person he could rely on to look after the other stubborn woman.

Family life.

"Stay in the damned carriage. And you, Mariel, you're a grown woman and I expect you to act like it."

Both women looked back at him as if he'd just said the stupidest thing since Jephthah's vow.

"Fine. You're a squire in the Order of Saint John and I expect you to act like *that*." The upside was that he could vent his anger on Selim Bey before he killed the bastard.

"What are you going to do in there?" Sabine asked. "Kill them all?"

"I'm going to defend you aggressively. If they all happen to die…" But before he could set off for the *hamam* he saw something entirely unexpected.

Berry the dog trotted up the street, straight to the carriage, wagging his tail and holding a fez in his mouth. He ran up to Adrian, sat on the cobblestones, and dropped the fez at the knight's feet.

Adrian picked up the unique hat—bright red velvet, gold tassel, and a large size to accommodate Mustafa's thick skull.

"Berry!" Mariel jumped from the carriage and rubbed the dog's head. "You found Mustafa!"

Berry barked happily.

"He found his hat, anyway," Adrian said. "Hopefully there's a lot more of him nearby." He looked at the dog, incredulous. "You know, the Saracens think that black dogs are possessed by demons."

Berry growled.

"I didn't say it was my opinion."

Mariel took the fez from Adrian's hand. She kneeled down and held it in front of Berry's nose. "Can you find Mustafa?" she asked.

The dog stood and sniffed around.

"That's not going to—"

Berry seemed to catch a scent, and started off down the street, nose to the ground.

"Work," Adrian said. He turned to Sabine, who also watched Berry.

"Damn it." He and Sabine set out after Mariel and the dog.

Berry crossed over two streets and trotted north. As they walked, the streets became busier, and the smell of spices and incense grew stronger.

"We're headed for the Carshi Bazaar," Sabine said. "It'll be crowded."

They walked faster, not letting Mariel and the dog stray more than a few meters in front of them.

The bazaar spread over ten blocks, two streets wide, like a plush Oryantal throw-rug. Tiny compared to the sprawling covered markets in Ottoman cities, it was nonetheless impressive for its colorful awnings, exotic aromas, and the wandering herd of foreigners who flowed in and out of the shops and stalls.

They passed racks full of gold bracelets and chains, rows of fanciful shoes, and piles of ornate rugs and carpets. Bolts of silk were stacked six-high, and everywhere there were baubles and trinkets of brass, silver, and leather.

Berry snaked his way around and through people's legs, with Mariel close behind. They came to an intersection, and the dog stopped and put his nose in the air, trying to find the scent.

"There's no way he can follow one scent in the midst of this," Adrian said to Sabine. Besides the smells of spice, incense, and freshly tanned leather, there was the warm odor of baking bread and roasting chicken. It was an assault on the nose, and Adrian felt his own sense of smell waning.

As soon as he said it, though, the dog was back on the trail, crossing over to the next street.

"Don't underestimate old Berry's nose," Sabine said, laughing, as they pushed their way through the crowd.

Adrian looked back and realized he was holding her hand, having taken it unconsciously sometime after they entered the busy market.

Berry led them over to the next street, then north again before he slowed to a walk, tongue hanging from his mouth, panting.

"Where is he, Berry?" Mariel asked. She scratched him behind the ear. "Where is that fat little Mustafa?"

The dog grumbled and whined, then walked over to a carpet-merchant's stall, sat down, and barked.

An old man sat in a wooden chair tipped back on two legs, his feet up on a stack of rugs. At the sound of the dog barking, he startled, let out a cry, and fell over backwards. Then came a stream of fairly serious Turkish curses and oaths.

The man stood up and dusted himself, then looked around for his fez. He found the well-worn cap, brushed it off on his shirt sleeve and returned it to his head. He studied Adrian and his companions for a moment, then smiled broadly.

"What a lovely Christian family," he said, clasping his hands. "A beautiful day to buy a rug, my lord. I see you have brought your lovely wife and daughter, and your no-doubt faithful and friendly hound."

Berry growled.

"I am Farhat, and I would be pleased to sell you one of the finest rugs in the City of God." He waved his hand at his wares.

"Yes, perhaps we'll have a look," Adrian said. Still holding Sabine's hand, they strolled to Farhat's stall. "Does anything catch your eye, love?"

"Oh indeed, my lord," Sabine said with facetious emphasis on the title. "There are so many fancy patterns and wonderful colors. We simply must have one for the salon."

The rugs were stacked outdoors and covered by an orange canvas awning. The shade hung from poles attached to the side of a building whose ground floor walls were made of a light-colored stone.

Sabine and Farhat began to pull through the stacks.

"Mariel, be a dear and help your mother pick out a rug," Adrian said.

Mariel glanced from Sabine to Adrian, eyes narrowed. She huffed, pointed a finger at him, and mouthed what he thought was "bastard" before positioning herself on the other side of Farhat where she and Sabine could play tennis with his attention.

A large red and gold carpet hung from an iron bar mounted on the side of the building. Adrian meandered over to it and peeked behind. An open doorway led inside. He looked back at the women and Farhat, then slipped behind the rug and into the dark.

More rugs were stacked inside, and the whole dim room smelled like a wet sheep.

He crossed the wooden floor and entered a doorway into a short hall. At one end, an empty kitchen with a pink clay oven sitting cold. At the other, steep and narrow stairs leading both up and down. The floor creaked as he approached the stairs. He stopped and listened at the landing. From below, a voice. A woman, speaking Turkish with the speed and ferocity of a dervish. He couldn't quite make out the words.

Adrian descended the stairs as softly as he could, placing his feet carefully to avoid giving himself away by a creak.

The woman's voice grew louder. Animated. Angry. He tried to translate her words, but she spoke so quickly he couldn't keep up. Then, she stopped. There were a few seconds of silence before she continued.

"Mustafa Ali, you are a rat!" she said, with heavy emphasis on the rat.

Adrian's feet touched down on the stone floor of the basement. He crept forward, hugging the rough wooden wall, until he was standing outside the room the voices came from.

"Rat is so harsh," Mustafa said. "Could we agree that I'm more of a...mouse?"

"Dog!" The crisp sound of a face being slapped echoed down hall. "When were you planning to tell Ferah Hatun of this calamity?"

"I was hoping you might do that," Mustafa said, voice low.

"What?" the woman asked. "Do you know what she'll do to the bearer of this news?"

"Well, yes, actually. That's why I want someone else to deliver it."

"You'll make a fine eunuch, Mustafa Ali."

"See!" Mustafa said. "That's exactly why you should tell her for me—you don't have any balls to lose."

Adrian slipped the dagger out of its sheath.

He peeked around the door frame, and saw Mustafa standing with a cup in his hand. In front of the Turk was a woman with long black hair, and well-tanned arms sticking out of the sleeves of a blue silk dress. Her back was to the door.

Fatal mistake.

He raised the dagger to the level of the woman's neck, and moved in on her.

Mustafa's eyes bulged and nearly popped out of his skull at the sight of Adrian filling the doorway. He waved his hands furiously, dropping his wine-filled cup, and stammered, "No, no, no!"

Adrian stopped short behind the woman, blade in the air.

She turned, saw him poised over her, and shrieked as she ran to hide behind Mustafa.

Not a terrible plan, as he offered ample cover.

"Mustafa Ali! Do your duty as a man and protect me from this assassin!" She stuck her arm out around his belly and pointed at Adrian. When Mustafa didn't move she felt around for the curved *jambiya* on his waist, drew it, and held it up for him to take.

There was a moment of silence.

She jabbed the dagger up in the air in front of Mustafa again. When he refused to take it, she shot up behind him and put it to his throat.

"Wha—" Mustafa started.

"Take another step and Mustafa dies!" she shouted.

Adrian looked at her face, serious, then to Mustafa, quivering, before bursting into laughter.

"Ayla, please put the knife down," Mustafa said.

"What makes you think I care enough about him to stop you?" Adrian asked, still laughing, as he sheathed his blade.

"You are useless even as a hostage," the woman said to Mustafa. She dropped the dagger to the floor.

"Ayla, come out from behind me and let me introduce you to Adrian of Tarsus, Knight of Saint John and my ship's *Militium Publicanus.*"

She complied, and Adrian saw her clearly for the first time. Her face was a thin oval, smooth and bronzed. Her eyes were big and brown, like almonds, and her lips full and red. An exotic beauty, hot and volatile—a leopardess—she sized him up from under kinked eyebrows.

"Adrian, this is my cousin Ayla."

"A pleasure, Miss," Adrian said.

"What are you doing here?" she asked.

"I was going to look for Mustafa in the *hamam*, but his trail led here."

She frowned and thought about it. "Why are you after Mustafa Ali?"

Adrian glared at Mustafa. "To prevent him from doing something stupid."

"Ha!" Ayla threw her hands in the air. "You are too late for that by far."

"What's he done?"

"Mustafa, tell this man of your incompetence." She waved a finger at Adrian.

Mustafa took a deep breath. "My dear, I haven't been honest with you."

"That's hardly a surprise."

"No. Yes. It's true that I don't practice strict honesty with anyone, but there's something specific I've lied to you about, and I want to tell you now because it might get us killed." All the normal cheer and frivolity were gone from the Turk's face.

"You'd best tell me, then."

"Koray wasn't my cousin."

"I don't want to know what you two did behind closed doors." Adrian held up a hand to stop the Turk.

"No. God no. He wasn't even close to my type. No, Koray was the cousin of the Sultan. The real Sultan. Abdulaziz."

Adrian didn't play at politics and the importance of the revelation crept up on him slowly. "Koray would have been in the line of succession, albeit pretty damn far down the line."

"There were others in direct line, but you can imagine their fates once Osman gained the support of the Janissaries and House Guard." Mustafa shook his head.

"You're saying that Koray was the rightful Sultan?"

"It's complicated, but he could have made a claim in the absence of a more direct successor. At the very least, he could have been someone for those fighting Osman to rally around."

"I don't know what to think." He looked at Ayla and back to Mustafa. "Why does that endanger us? Surely we're safer with him gone?"

"Koray wasn't my cousin, but Ferah the Bitch is most definitely my aunt. She entrusted Koray to me for his safety."

"I see. Vengeful, is she?"

"You have no idea."

"She has a right to be vengeful, and a duty." Ayla said to Mustafa. "You were to see to his safety. No assassin could reach him inside a spacecraft, lost in the void."

Adrian looked away from them. Time to come clean. "Koray's death is my fault."

"Your fault?" Mustafa and Ayla asked simultaneously.

"I talked you into going to Gereon because I'd heard a rumor about the relic when we were at Acre. When we arrived, I tipped Easley to the fact you were there with gold to spend."

"Why didn't you just tell me?" Mustafa asked, his voice revealing an unexpected dejection. "You've never been shy about working off-the-books."

"This is different. Mariel..."

"Oh," Mustafa said, understanding coming to him. "This has to do with her problems, doesn't it? Some sort of Apex treatment? Damn it, Adrian, you should have told me. She's practically my niece."

"I had my reasons, but...I'm sorry. I'll explain, but not here. Not now."

"This does not absolve you, Mustafa Ali," Ayla said. "Koray was your responsibility. I would not want to be in your shoes when you deliver the news to Ferah Hatun."

"One thing at a time," Adrian said. "We need Mustafa back on the ship."

"No one's stopping him from leaving."

Adrian rubbed his temples. "Let's go, then."

Ayla drew a startled breath and stepped back from the men.

Farhat, the rug dealer, braced himself in the door frame. The old man breathed heavy and clutched at his side with a bloody hand, with the end of a black crossbow bolt sticking out through his fingers.

"Janissaries," he said, struggling against the pain, before he fell to the floor.

CHAPTER 22

A dead Saracen lay crumpled on the ground among the rugs, a dagger's handle protruding from his chest. Adrian kneeled and drew the steel out, releasing a final spurt of blood from the wound. He studied the weapon; one he'd seen before.

"Mariel got this one," he said to no one in particular. Ayla and Mustafa stood behind him.

He squeezed the handle of the dagger with his fist. Hate he hadn't felt for years suddenly choked him.

"What lunacy is this?" Ayla asked. She pulled a crossbow bolt out of a stack of rugs and held it up. "Janissaries kidnapping Christians on the streets of their holy city? Selim Bey will provoke a Crusade right here, and for what?"

"He must've taken them to the *hamam*." Adrian set off in the direction of the bath.

"Wait," Ayla said. "He would not have taken captives there. It's too public."

Adrian turned to face her, pointing the dagger at her. "Where, then?"

"My men are everywhere; this will have been observed. Come inside." She ducked back through the hanging carpet.

Adrian continued toward the bath house.

Mustafa ran after him, chugging until he could throw himself in front of Adrian and hold up his hands. "Stop, stop. If Ayla says they aren't at the *hamam*, they aren't at the *hamam*."

Adrian stopped. "Who the hell is she, anyway?"

"My cousin…" the Turk hesitated. "And an agent of my aunt, Ferah Hatun."

"A Corsair? Do you think she can find them?"

"I'm certain of it, my dear, come along." Mustafa urged Adrian back to the curtain.

They descended into the basement, where Farhat was lying on the floor, breathing heavily. A pair of younger women and a boy kneeled beside him.

"Ismail," Ayla said to the boy, "fetch a doctor at once."

"No," Adrian ordered. "I'll take care of him. You focus on finding Mariel and Sabine." His tone left her no room for argument, a fact she noted with a flick of her eyebrow and a curious smile.

"Mustafa?" he asked.

"Yes?"

"I'm going to need my trunk. Not the one in my cabin, the old one in the cargo hold. Quickly."

"I'll take some boys and retrieve it," the Turk said.

"Quickly," Adrian said as Mustafa trotted out.

Adrian crouched on one knee beside Farhat and inspected the wooden shaft sticking out of his side. The bolt-head had pulled the material of the old man's silk shirt into the wound.

"You're lucky, old man," Adrian said, "this'll come out easy." He turned to Ayla. "I'll need something clean to dress this with."

When she left the room, Adrian drew the dagger on his thigh and held it in front of Farhat. "Like I said, it'll come out easy, but it's still going to hurt like hell." He shoved the leather-wrapped handle of the blade into the man's mouth, then grabbed the bolt firmly and looked Farhat in the eyes.

Farhat nodded and closed his eyes tightly.

A violent jerk and the blood-slicked projectile was out. The old man's body convulsed. He screamed as he bit down on the leather. He breathed hard and fast, and Adrian pinned him to the ground while holding pressure on the wound. When Ayla returned with the bandages, he wrapped them tight while Farhat cursed.

Mariel and Sabine in the hands of heathens.

Torture, rape, slavery, and death were the only outcomes.

Were the Muslims more brutal than Christians? Not on the surface. Indeed, they gave the impression of being more practical about it all. Less prone to angst and soul-searching. Therein lay the difference—malice without unease of conscience is animal savagery.

Adrian unbuckled the coarse straps holding the chest closed and opened the lid. The interior was musty, with lingering smells of oil and old leather. At the top sat his shield. Kite-shaped, painted black with the Maltese cross in white, it bore the scars of many battles, their names and dates painstakingly etched into the reverse side. A summary of the better part of his life.

He placed the shield aside and dug the rest of the armor out, each piece wrapped in wine-colored felt. Then, his longsword, lying at the bottom. It just fit into the chest when placed at an angle from corner to corner. Unlike the surgical rapier he carried when not at war, the longsword was a butcher's tool, a cleaver of human flesh.

How many had died by this? How many would die today? Past the very first, the original victim, did it make any difference? If the Turks harmed Mariel and Sabine, the streets of this heathen quarter would be stained with the blood of their own women and children.

A Hospitaler's armor was his most valuable possession. Received from a retiring or fallen knight, the new owner was merely a caretaker, using the valuable pieces in defense of the faith and preserving them for the man who would take up the duty after him. The practice was more than a ritual. The armor, made from salvaged titanium alloys and unnaturally hard ceramics produced before the Advent, was impossible to replace.

The first layer was a close-fitting arming doublet of lightly padded silk worn like a tunic. It covered his arms and torso from his shoulders down to mid-thigh, softening incoming blows and distributing the force of impact. Despite being cleaned often, the doublet carried permanent stains left by the endless sweat it absorbed.

Sweat—the smell of full and righteous exertion, the signature smell of battle, more so than even blood.

Adrian stood and dropped the next layer over his head. The first layer of real armor, his hauberk consisted of a fine mail of interlocking titanium rings, each one individually riveted shut in a process that took a craftsman hundreds of hours to complete. Chausses of similar manufacture protected his legs.

Next came boots, then an assortment of metal and ceramic plates that supplemented the mail. For the upper body, a cuirass encased his chest and back. Pauldrons guarded his shoulders, rerebraces and vambraces wrapped each arm, then gauntlets. For the lower, greaves on the legs and sabatons for the feet.

Each piece heightened the feeling of invincibility while it choked off the inner voice that preached the virtue of caution.

The plates gleamed. The exotic material wouldn't rust or patina, but the marks of combat were there. Nicks and scratches from glancing scimitars, a deep gouge in the cuirass from an arrow that hit with such force that the shaft splintered and disintegrated on impact. And, all over, the little pits and scoring from wind-blown dirt and sand on the unfinished fringe worlds.

The art of dressing was easier with a squire to help, but he slowly managed it alone. His tabard went over the top of it all, knee-length black linen with the cross sewn large on the chest. Finally, he wrapped a thick leather belt around his waist to secure and carry the scabbard and longsword.

If those who died fighting the heathens were guaranteed salvation, why not fight? What reason to tarry in this universe when the gates of the Kingdom of Heaven were thrown open? The idea had motivated him for years, driven him in the absence of any other cause. Until he picked Mariel up from the concrete and held her in his arms the first time.

He unsheathed the sword and knelt behind it.

"God, allow me to…" he began, as always. Bloody hell. Who was he begging for strength when the only source was within him? "*I'll* save Mariel and Sabine, and seize with my own hands the honor of slaughtering those who offend me. If death comes, it will befall me only after I have killed such a host of villains that Hell would not have enough fire to incinerate them all."

The fleeting images of his fellow knights surrounded him, kneeling as they had done before every battle of the past war.

He stood, and with his helm under his arm, left the room.

Adrian looked down Ayla's slender arm, wrapped in gold bands and bracelets, as she pointed to a cluster of three thick buildings. They formed a little fort near the center of the Muslim district, with gates at the three corners enclosing a secluded triangular courtyard.

"Selim Bey's offices are in the north building," she said. "The south-west building is the Janissary barracks—there are twenty-one of them."

Clouds had moved in over the city. The midday sky was overcast and grey.

"Less a few who recently departed," Adrian said.

"There is a common basement. All three buildings connect to it. This is where they have your women."

"You're certain?"

"I'm certain they are in the compound. I assume they are in the basement."

"Are your boys ready?" he asked.

"They await my signal. Are you sure you don't want some men to accompany you?" she asked, putting her hand on his arm. "I can call on good fighters."

The hint of concern in her voice struck him as surreal. He couldn't feel her hand through the armored vambrace, but the warm tone of her flesh made a sharp contrast with the cool titanium plate. "No. I don't want the trouble of picking out friend from foe."

"And we all look the same to you."

"Not true," he said in passable Turkish. "I lived among Ottoman refugees on Acre long enough to discard the myth of a monolithic enemy. Then there's the fact that you're helping me so readily. That makes you…different." And quite beautiful. How could she be related to Mustafa?

"Every man in there is a traitor to his God-anointed sovereign—my uncle. I help you strike at my enemies, and you take the responsibility, and the blame. It is as if the Almighty himself dropped you in my lap." She gave a satisfied little laugh.

"Sadly, I've no time to lie in your lap. Signal the boys when I'm in position." He stood and walked down the alley, taking place in a shadowy alcove. Once stationed, he put his helm on, narrowing his vision to a thin strip in front of him.

A throng of rowdy young boys approached the compound. They struck up a mad cacophony of hollering and banged their hands on the gate.

"Come quickly! Come quickly!" the boys yelled in their native tongue.

A narrow window slid open, and a dark face with small eyes glanced around.

"What is the meaning of this?" the man shouted over the boy's din. Receiving no intelligible answer, he slammed the window closed and opened the gate.

Adrian left the doorway and strode across the street. Four long steps.

The boys scattered.

Adrian's armored boot crashed into the Turk's gut.

The man's little eyes opened wide. He staggered, and fell to his back with a gasp.

Adrian thrust the longsword down into his chest before stepping over him into the courtyard.

A handful of Janissaries sat cross-legged under a yellow awning, smoking and laughing. There was an awkward moment as first one, then the rest, became aware of his approach.

Time skipped and lagged as Adrian's mind separated the critical from the irrelevant. The only sound was that of his steady breathing inside the helm. He crossed the stone-paved courtyard and was among them.

The longsword fell hard, cleaving through a skull, lopping off a hemisphere that slid from the rest of the head. As one man fell, the blade turned on another and pierced his chest, blood oozing from the deep groove running the length of the steel. The sword pulled back, raised high, and with a final, brutal hack cut deep down into the shoulder of a third man.

The world returned to normal speed. The remaining Turk fled and raised the first alarm.

"*Hristiyanlar!*" the Turk shouted as he scrambled into the barracks. He used the plural, warning his fellows of approaching Christians.

The longsword turned like a divining rod to point in the direction of the heathens. Caution is a virtue when choosing the time and place to give battle, a vice once battle is joined. The attack must be pressed fanatically to tear victory from the body of the enemy.

Hastily armed men poured from the barracks, some with scimitars, some with short blades.

Adrian met the first man in a crash of swords. With a practiced movement, the longsword beat aside the scimitar, thrust, and killed. Finesse, geometry, and timing were not the keys to this style of combat. Strength was.

He felt blades hit hard on his shoulder and back, but the sizzling sound of steel as it skittered and skipped off the armor plate was the only result of the counter attack.

A Janissary slashed at Adrian's chest and connected with the curved scimitar blade. He had no more success than his comrades, and the attack only served to open him to a brutal stabbing as the longsword ran him through.

As Adrian withdrew the red metal, a crushing impact to his neck stunned him. One of his assailants had connected in the narrow gap between the breastplate and helm. The mail scoffed at the blade, but the thin padding of the arming doublet underneath could do little against the blunt trauma of the impact.

Lucky that wasn't in the throat.

Adrian balled his fist and swung the gauntlet like a ram at the man's head. He drew his hand back with chunks of seeping, hairy flesh lodged in the sharp finger joints. The Turk fell.

The final Janissary went down with a hack to his shoulder, snapping the collarbone, and opening a furrow down into the chest.

They should have had time to pull themselves together by now, to mount a defense. He felt the increased humidity inside the helm, and forced his breathing to a slow, steady pace.

The door to the barracks stood open, and he looked into the darkness. He tensed the muscles of his chest in expectation of the next assault.

A click and a low twang sounded from inside. The first bolt whistled at him, striking him square in the chest. There was a loud ping as the projectile struck and deflected.

Soft broadheads. Though it had been most unlikely, Adrian relaxed when the Turks failed to use exotic, armor-penetrating bolts—hardened titanium bodkins were the most dangerous. He slowly approached the door, sword held in a low guard.

Two more bolts came at him. One bounced harmlessly off the breastplate, but the other struck painfully in a gap between his cuirass and shoulder pauldron. The bolt didn't penetrate the fine mail, but the hammer-blow stung.

He stopped in the doorway.

A swarm of light infantry posed the biggest threat to an armored warrior on the battlefield. If brought to the ground, a blade through his helm's eye-slit would be the last thing a knight saw. Achieving the feat was an act of considerable bravery for the skirmishers as a man's natural inclination is to flee from an apparently unstoppable foe.

Standing in the doorway gave him a moment to survey the room without being surrounded.

Half a dozen more Turks assembled inside. Two stood directly opposite Adrian, reloading crossbows. Four more waited in hastily-donned mail, swords in hand.

The next seconds passed in whirlwind of steel and blood.

The crossbowmen again fired, and again their bolts shattered on Adrian's breastplate. In a state of near panic, torn between martyrdom and execution at the hands of their officers, they chose to die for their version of God.

When the clattering, grunting, and screaming ended, Adrian walked over the weeping corpses of the six Janissaries, to the basement stairs.

The trapdoor in the floor stood open, and he descended, aided by a string of tiny diode lights hung on the angled ceiling.

Underground, the air hung still and damp.

Adrian felt the sweat oozing from his skin, soaking the padded under-layer of the armor. The salty smell rose up into his helm and mingled with his heavy breath, thick and stifling.

His sight limited to a narrow rectangular strip, he watched the stone basement come into view as he reached the bottom of the stairs.

"You've fought hard to die here, infidel." A man's loud voice. Words spoke in English and bent by a heavy accent. His tone full of spite and acid.

"Adrian!" Two voices. Women. Mariel and Sabine!

Thank God. At the sound of their voices, he felt a jolt of adrenaline.

"Now you greasy pigs'll die," Mariel shouted.

Adrian heard the sharp crack of a palm on a face, followed by an admonishment in Turkish.

"Arsehole," Mariel muttered.

Lit by weak diodes on the ceiling, it took Adrian's eyes a second to adjust. Arrayed in front of him, three soldiers, with two more men behind, standing next to the women who were tied to rings in the wall. The room was rather large, with cells on one side and implements of interrogation on the other.

"Kill the infidel!" the Turk ordered. He then pushed the other man to a set of stairs on the far side of the room.

The three warriors advanced, scimitars drawn. Wary, they were clad in mail and wore small bucklers on their left arms.

Silahtars. The word translated to 'weapon masters.' The Sultan's House Guards. Unlike Janissaries, these heavy cavalrymen were freeborn, elite troops. The only way for a man to join their ranks was to earn the privilege on the battlefield.

Adrian held the advantage in armor, they in weight of numbers and the killing power of their *kilij* scimitars. He briefly regretted his decision to go without shield. The increased mobility was advantageous, especially indoors, but the *kilij* was a dangerous weapon even to a fully armored knight. Of moderate length, their blades began with a slight curve, which kinked strongly at the midpoint, flaring into a wide, heavy point. In the hands of a strong, skilled warrior, the *kilij* could crack weaker armors and, more dangerously, break mail and splinter the bones underneath.

This plan might have been o'er ambitious.

The *Silahtars* sent one man forward while the other two flanked, limiting Adrian's movement to either side. This would be a savage chess match.

Adrian stepped to the right. The move limited his exposure to the third man but, in exchange, forced him to deal with the remaining two head-on.

The Turks attacked.

Adrian offered his left side as sacrifice, using gauntlet, vambrace, and pauldron as impromptu shields against the first Turk's onslaught while he fought the second.

Kill quickly. He had to dispatch one within the first few seconds, before the third could work his way behind. Failure would be death.

One Turk's *kilij* battered his left arm and shoulder as he fought the other.

A shattering pain hit him just below the elbow when the *kilij* found the gap between armor plates. Broken?

Adrian screamed and thrust at the other Turk's throat. Again, his accuracy and feel for geometry made the difference. The tip of his longsword did not penetrate the Turk's mail, but its massive force of impact, concentrated on the Adam's apple, crushed the airway, and sent the man staggering back.

He felt a tug at his foot.

The other Turk hooked Adrian's boot with the back edge of the *kilij* and pulled hard.

Before he could shift his weight, he was on his back, staring at the wooden beams of the ceiling.

Through the narrow eye slit, the Turk came into view and Adrian saw the sword thrusting down at his face.

Hell.

He closed his eyes as the point came down and jammed into the helm.

Then...he was still alive. He felt the Turk wrenching the sword, twisting his head along with it. Opening his eyes, his lashes brushed metal and he realized the blade, too wide to pass through the slit, had lodged itself with the tip just millimeters from his eye.

Christ.

He reached up and gripped the blade with both mailed hands, dislodging it from the helm and pulling it from the Turk's hand simultaneously. He grabbed the nearest ankle and pulled, bringing the man crashing down next to him.

Sensing the third Turk's presence, he rolled just in time to avoid a blade hammering down from above, and pushed himself back onto his feet.

Now holding a *kilij* in place of his dropped longsword, Adrian swung the heavy blade with all his strength into the side of the standing Turk's head. The sword split the thin steel of the helmet and smashed against the mail underneath. He felt and heard the skull crack.

One more.

The final *Silahtar* returned to his feet, disarmed.

Adrian charged, pushing the tip of the *kilij* into his opponent's gut and shoving him across the room, into the wall where he drove the blade through the mail. Fluids ran from the wound, and the Turk screamed his last.

"Over here!" Mariel shouted.

Adrian turned and found the other Turks gone. He pulled his helm off and drew in a deep, satisfying breath as he ran to the corner where the women—*his* women—were sitting on the floor, hands and feet tied. His dagger quickly sliced through the bonds.

"Are you all right?" he asked, looking them both over. They didn't appear to be injured, but…

"We're okay," Mariel said.

He pulled her to him with his left arm, maybe too hard, and she slammed against the cuirass.

From his right, Sabine threw her arms around his neck and kissed him.

"Nobody kills like you, Adrian," she said.

"What the hell does that mean?" He put an arm around her and pressed her body to his.

"You do it with such confidence."

"He's a Knight of Saint John," Mariel said. "Of course he kills well."

"If only my confidence could've prevented Selim Bey's escape."

"Do not worry." A woman's voice called from the stairs.

Ayla.

Selim Bey and Serhan walked back into the room, hands in the air. Ayla appeared behind them, the tip of a sword pressed to the ambassador's back. A trio of armed men backed her, followed by Mustafa of all people.

"The rat is caught," Ayla said.

Adrian put the point of his dagger over the Ambassador's heart.

"Adrian," Sabine started.

"You're a liar, Selim Bey. You won't live to make a fool of me twice—"

"Adrian!" Sabine shouted. "Don't!"

"You won't be safe until he's dead."

"It wasn't him. It was Serhan."

"She's right, Adrian," Mariel said. "The fancy one was furious when the greasy one brought him down to show us off. They were about to draw steel on each other when you arrived."

Adrian's blade remained poised to kill the Ambassador. "Explain yourself."

"What the girl said is true. I did not order this, but I remain responsible for my lieutenant's actions. I promised neither I nor my men would harm Miss Adler, and I have been proven a liar." He glared at Serhan with murder in his eyes.

"Thankfully." Sabine looked at Mariel. "They hadn't gotten around to harming us, though Serhan had evil designs."

"Who is this filth?" Adrian asked Sabine.

"Serhan Kaş. You may not know his name, but you'll remember the massacre he oversaw at Jedra."

"Indeed." Jedra was perhaps the worst atrocity perpetrated by either side in the last war. A mob of *bashi-bazouk*—irregular troops recruited from Ottoman prisons—descended on the town in a three-day orgy of murder, rape, and looting that left over one thousand dead.

"You *Hrystianlar* are dogs and your women whores. I spit on all—" Serhan began.

Adrian plunged his dagger into Serhan's neck in one stroke, up to the hilt, the tip exiting the opposite side dripping red.

There was a gurgling scream as the Turk grasped at his throat, fell to his knees, and died choking on his own blood.

"He will not be mourned," Selim Bey said. He stood straight, facing Adrian. "I surrender to you, knight."

"Why? Mariel and Sabine say you had no part in this. That's enough for me."

"Unfortunately for me, Miss Adler's killing of Reymont Lucas and your dispatching of my Janissary guards will see me recalled by the Sultan, no doubt to be executed."

Sabine pushed herself in front of Adrian. "You're a Goddamned fool, Selim Bey." She grabbed the man by his coat and shook him violently. "I did not kill Lucas."

"Who did, then?" the Ambassador asked calmly.

"I don't know," she said, letting go of him. "I think it was someone in the Holy See who wanted to kill your port deal."

"Hmm." Selim Bey thought about it. "I request to be taken prisoner by the of the Order of Saint John. In your custody, I'll be as safe from Osman's wrath as possible."

"I'm sorry, but I can't offer that. I'm not acting for the Order in this."

"A pity," Selim Bey said with a resigned frown.

Adrian looked at Ayla.

"Maybe you should rethink your allegiance," he said to the Ambassador. "You and these Corsairs share a common enemy now, don't you?"

Selim Bey nodded and laughed. "Quite right. If Ayla Hatun agrees, perhaps we can talk."

"We do need more competent men," Ayla said.

"Oh yes," Mustafa said, looking the Ambassador up and down. "That we do, and this little coup might turn Ferah's attention away from me."

CHAPTER 23

In one of Ayla's rooms behind the rug shop, Adrian watched Mariel run a cloth over his longsword, mopping up the sticky blood. When the blade gleamed again, she oiled it and returned it to the bottom of the trunk, ready for the next battle.

She was unusually quiet, and he realized how much he missed her stream of banter and probing questions.

"Shall I help you out of your armor?" she asked.

He had no shame, but the last thing he wanted to do was undress in front of her.

"I have a more important job for you." He put his hand on her shoulder. "I want you to see to it that Mustafa makes it back to the ship without being distracted by man or boy, and that he remains there."

"When will you be back?"

"Soon. We're almost done here."

"Adrian?"

"Yes?"

"I was never scared. The whole time those bastards had us. I just knew that any moment you'd be there, and you were."

"A father never abandons his daughter. At least, this one doesn't."

"Nor a daughter her father. I just—" she put her arms around him. "I'm sorry. I need to act like a woman. I'll take Mustafa back to the ship now."

As she left, he had the impression she was trying not to cry.

"Mariel."

She turned.

"Stop trying so damned hard to be a woman. Be yourself and let the rest come as it will."

She smiled before darting out the door.

He sat on an old iron bed and enjoyed a precious moment of solitude. The room was warm with a faint odor of cedar instead of the cold, recirculated air of the ship, and completely silent. No machines hummed in the background.

Mariel.

What had he done? Made a mistake of legendary proportions. He'd encouraged her impossible feelings. Given her some sort of false hope that the nature of their life together could change.

On top of it all, he'd soon have to tell her that she wasn't the woman she thought she was. He couldn't let her meet the nun unprepared for...for what? Shock? How would she take it?

The doctrine was clear: only God could Create a soul. Mariel wasn't a Creation of God; therefore, she couldn't have a soul.

Bullshit.

She had a beautiful soul befitting a pure young woman. Courteous and loyal. Loving, even if it were misdirected. She was courageous and devoted to her duty as a squire. An anonymous verse came to him: Her soul doth magnify the Lord. Or it would, if he existed—what was once a certainty became unimaginable.

If the doctrine were so laughably wrong about her, then what other mistakes, misinterpretations, and lies masqueraded as facts?

Had Bernt been right all along?

What about Sabine and her reformists?

A long line of dominoes toppled in his mind. Had he been killing men for all these years for no good reason?

No.

The Order protected Christendom from the chaos of invasion, ensuring that Christ's words remained sacred. The knights couldn't protect Christians from getting it wrong, but they did preserve hope that things could change for the better.

Maybe Sabine was right—maybe he was a reformist or something even more heretical. How long had he been thinking this way?

A knock at the door roused him.

"Come in."

Sabine entered, closing the door behind her. She stood there, silent, looking at him.

He rose to his feet.

She dropped the wooden bar in place, securing the door.

There was a light in her eyes as she crossed the short distance to stand in front of him. She took his forearm and, without a word, began to unbuckle the vambrace.

"Bine?" he asked.

She dropped the piece of armor to the floor and started work on the rerebrace protecting his upper arm.

Finally, she broke her silence. "I once told Henry that men would do nothing for the women who are close to them."

He considered it, conceding to himself that there was some truth in the statement.

"You prove me wrong. Not only by the way you raise your daughter; you saved me from Dietrich, from the Janissaries, and now from that scum Serhan Kaş." His right arm free, she began to remove the plates from his left.

More armor fell to the floor.

"You aren't indebted to me," he said. "I'd save you from a thousand Saracens and consider myself well rewarded just to look at you."

She laughed and patted her hand on his breastplate. "If anyone else said that...but I believe you. That's why I'm giving you my heart."

His cuirass came off, and to his great relief he stripped off the mail hauberk and arming doublet.

"You are?" he asked.

She pushed herself up onto the tips of her toes and whispered in his ear. "I am. If you'll have it."

"Your heart...is the only thing in this universe I despair for lack of."

She ran her hands through the hair on his chest. "I wish you could ask me to marry you. I'd say yes."

"Marry me, Sabine."

"You're in the clergy, Adrian."

"Reformists believe in clerical marriage, I've heard."

"We do, but..."

"So we need one of *your* priests. It'll have to remain between us for now." He smiled. "Which is just as well, because I don't have a name to give you."

"Yes. Yes! I'll marry you."

He took her in his arms, stared into her vivid blue eyes, and kissed his future wife. His hand on her side, he felt the linen of her blouse glide over the warm, smooth silk underneath.

"I love you," he said.

She slipped out of his embrace to recline enticingly on the bed. "Prove it. Again."

Adrian studied Mariel's room. "You really are the Lady of the Manor."

She had hung some patterned silk on the walls, organized her small collection of books, and decorated the empty spaces on her shelves with brass animals of Turkish make.

"Mustafa gave me some things."

"I see old Geoff is still hanging around." He nodded at the lion, sitting on the fold-down bedside table, under her reading light.

The silence stung. "May I?" he nodded at the fold-down seat built into the bulkhead.

"Yes." She sat on her bed, cross-legged.

"We need to talk."

"Adrian, we don't need to talk about what happened." Her voice carried a hint of a plea. "I don't want to talk at all."

He hung his head, then held his chin up, looking her in the eyes. "We'll make the best of that, love. I've come about something else."

"Oh?"

"We're going to have another guest on board when we leave tonight."

"Who is it?"

"A woman," he said. "She's a nun. Her name's Mary Frances."

"Why are we bringing a nun?"

"She knows the coordinates for the planet we need to visit, and she'll only give them to us if we take her." Out with it. "When you see her, you'll recognize her because she looks like you, only a few years older."

Her eyes widened. "Are you saying that I have a sister?"

Oh God. "No, love. No."

"What is it, then?"

"I've told you about how I found you on New Golan."

"With some heretics."

"Exactly. Those experiments involved creating children using machines." He couldn't have said it worse, but he didn't know how to say it any better. "Normally, a man and a woman—"

"I know how it works, Adrian."

"Oh."

She waited for him to continue.

"Well, they figured out how to take the cells from a man and woman and create the embryo without the...interaction...of the man and woman. They could do this over and over, and each child would be more or less the same."

She nodded slowly. Her eyes were so bright and alive, even in the midst of such a miserable revelation. "I thought I didn't have a family, but now you say I could have an infinite number of sisters I've never met. A real family."

Anxiety twisted his guts. Where was she going? "You have a family, right here. Sabine and I are—"

Mariel's eyes narrowed. "What does this have to do with *her*?"

He sat up straight. "Before we left, Sabine and I were married."

Her eyelids trembled, and her brow furrowed under tension. "You...you married her...in a church? How?"

"Not in a church. By a Reformist preacher. Anyway, it doesn't matter. I'm not concerned with God anymore, I'm concerned with people. You. Her. Everyone on this ship."

One tear ran down her soft face. She spoke quietly. "How could you do this to me? You truly are a heartless and faithless bastard."

He shot to his feet. "Goddamnit, Mariel. What the hell is wrong with you? Has your mind finally cracked?"

She broke down into tears.

The sight of it hit him like a clenched fist.

"You bastard," she said. "Get out!"

She couldn't have been more right.

"I'm sorry, love. Look, we're so close to fixing that now—"

"Get out! I don't want to see your face."

He looked at the floor, shook his head, then slid the door open and stepped out.

Word spread quickly, and at sunset the entire crew was standing at the bottom of the cargo ramp waiting for their passenger to arrive.

Mariel, normally close by Adrian's side, stood apart, refusing to make eye contact. He wrestled with the abhorrent fact that he didn't know how to pull her back.

"Is she really a nun?" Gilly asked.

"She is," Adrian replied.

"Why does a nun want to travel with us?" Nezumi asked.

"You'll have to ask her yourself," Adrian said, "all I know is that she has the coordinates we need."

Two cloaked figures approached the ship. One carried a small bag, the other walked with a limp favoring her left foot.

"Greetings, Knight-Commander," Mary Frances said, pulling her hood back.

For the first time, the rest of the crew saw her. Some took longer than others to comprehend it, but eventually they all looked from the nun, to Mariel, and back.

Mariel stepped into the awkward silence. "We're cousins," she told the crew, before walking up to the nun. "I'm Mariel… of Tarsus."

"Indeed." The nun looked her over slowly and carefully, reached out as if to touch her face, then drew her hand back. "And I am Mary Frances."

There was a round of stiff introductions, during which Anne Kresimir walked up to Adrian and stood very close.

"If anything happens to her, I'll hunt you down, knight. Betray the Holy Father's trust at your peril."

Adrian looked her in the eyes, and pivoted his foot to cover hers. He pressed his boot down on her wounded toe.

She winced, set her jaw and stood tall.

He pushed down harder.

Defiant, she grabbed one of the buckles holding his jerkin closed and squeezed so hard her arm shook, never breaking eye-contact.

"Anne?" Mary Frances called.

Anne pushed Adrian back and pulled her foot from under his.

Mary Frances took Anne's hand and walked her away as the *Miranda's* crew began to climb aboard. She said something to Anne, who looked back at Adrian with a wicked smile, then the two nuns kissed, sharing more than their love for Christ.

Adrian went aboard.

Soon the *Miranda's* engines were turning up, and within minutes the ship lifted off. Nezumi easily achieved orbit, and the crew and passenger unstrapped from the flight deck chairs.

The trip out of the star system took two days, during which very little was heard from Mary Frances. She cloistered herself away in Bernt's old cabin and refused even to take meals with the crew.

Adrian couldn't care less, happy to have one less complication to deal with.

"Where to, chief?" Nezumi asked from the pilot's seat. The *Miranda* sat motionless at the initial navigation point, on the far edge of Bethany's star system.

Mustafa looked to Mary Frances.

"Do you want to use the nav computer?" Nezumi asked her, pointing at the console.

"No. I have the planet's last known coordinates and velocity vectors." She closed her eyes.

Adrian watched as the nun seemed to relax. She always appeared agitated, and her quick transformation to a sort of airy serenity was remarkable.

"9,455 billion kilometers…" Mary Frances whispered.

Adrian and Sabine exchanged curious looks.

"Vectors of 4.15…6.971…21.6…"

Seconds later, Mary Frances walked to the computer and entered three coordinates. "There."

Adrian watched her eyes narrow slightly, and her face harden after she finished. Back to normal.

The nun left the flight deck.

Nezumi looked at Mustafa, waiting for instructions.

The Turk shrugged.

"It would have taken Bernt a lot longer than that," the pilot said, "even with the computer doing the math."

"I doubt she's suicidal, so the coordinates must be good?" Mustafa wondered aloud.

"Don't count on the former," Adrian said, "but I think she wants to get to this planet as much as we do."

"Her coordinates are valid," Nezumi said. "The computer accepted them and plotted the arrival point. It's out in the Gap beyond Acre."

Mustafa hesitated.

"Go," Adrian said.

The Turk nodded.

Nezumi opened the safety cover and pressed the ALC button. The familiar sphere of brilliant starlight formed around the ship, then shifted to red and blue and the *Miranda* began her journey. "Now we wait," he said. He looked over the instruments again, then left.

Mustafa followed.

Sabine sat down at the engineer's station. Being the most experienced with *Machina*, she had agreed to look after the ship's systems on this trip. Lying in Mariel's old bed or drinking coffee in the galley, she had spent hours reading Bernt's operations manuals on the trip out.

"Are you ready to join the Hanseatic League?" he asked.

"Are you ready to step out the airlock?"

He moved behind her, put his hands on her shoulders, and began to knead on her with his thumbs, right over the trapezius. All the tension in her muscles disappeared.

"You have so many practical talents, Adrian. I shall require this more often."

"As you wish, m'lady."

"Is Mariel all right?" she asked.

Adrian continued to work the muscles of her shoulders with his hands. "I wish I knew. Every time I allow myself to hope that her feelings are thawing, she freezes up again."

"You never told me what happened on Bethany."

"I know. I don't want to embarrass her by airing her deepest feelings. It's something like accepting a confession."

"May I give you some advice, husband?"

"Always."

"Strong, bewildering love is normal for a young woman, and this may take a long time to pass. It may never completely fade."

"Love is the finest thing there is, truly. I only wish she hadn't aimed hers at me."

"Accept that she has, so that the fact doesn't push you apart. And remember that, someday, after you're gone, she'll look back on this and the memory of her youthful passion will warm her heart. Take comfort in the fact that you'll be with her forever."

CHAPTER 24

From orbit, Anance bore a resemblance to the blue and green planet seen in pictures of Earth. There were differences. It seemed to be covered with a thick layer of moss cut and pocked with dark blue. There were neither ice caps nor deserts, and the two bodies of water that might be oceans were more properly described as huge lakes.

After landing, the crew packed the flight deck, looking out at the verdant world with much curiosity. Seen from the surface, it was a forbidding subtropical forest.

Adrian watched Sabine at the engineer's console as she studied the readout from the external sensors. She excelled in the role, not least because of her keen ability to assess the multitude of alerts and errors generated by the systems and pick the important information from the chaff.

"Is it safe?" Mustafa asked.

"Perfectly," Sabine said. "The atmospheric oxygen level is high. Temperature is on the warm side and there's high humidity, but the barometer is rock-steady and radiation is negligible."

Nezumi had brought the ship to the single navigation beacon, the only sign the lonely system had ever been visited. The powerful transmitter lay somewhere under the thick canopy, so the pilot spiraled out, finding a suitably large and flat landing site some eight kilometers away. Sabine checked the solidity of the ground with a special radar, then cleared Nezumi to land.

Their clearing was surrounded by a wall of giant trees whose trunks combined with grasses and scrub to form a living rampart.

"Thirty-two degrees." Nezumi said. "With that kind of humidity? Forget it, that's well outside my standard for personal comfort."

Mustafa shook his head. "You know my rule about the pilot leaving the ship."

"You're staying, too," Adrian told the Turk.

"What? Of course I'm going."

"You're hopelessly unfit, and we'll have to hack through that jungle to reach the beacon."

Mustafa sputtered and started to protest.

"Thirty-two is damned hot."

"Fine. Have it your way."

Adrian looked at the faces around him. Gilly was too timid to trust, Tomas injured, and Lars was the oldest. "Mariel, how do you feel?"

"Fine."

Was her tone a bit milder today, or was it wishful thinking? "I need my squire, if she's up to it."

"I'm going, too," Mary Frances said from the back of the crowd.

The hair on Adrian's neck stood up at the sound of her voice.

"As am I," Sabine said.

"Right. Meet at the airlock in half an hour."

The crew filed out.

He turned to Mariel. "Dress cool and bring water."

The crew airlock was a cramped space with two pressure-sealed doors. While capable of opening into a vacuum, its more practical use allowed ingress and egress without adjusting the ship's internal atmosphere.

Mary Frances arrived, with Mustafa on her heels. Sabine and Mariel were already there.

"Ready?" Adrian asked.

"Ready," came the unified response.

The four entered the airlock, equalized the atmosphere, and opened the outer door.

Hot, wet air filled Adrian's lungs. Pungent. Full of organic zest to stimulate the nose. It was a vegetable smell, and harsh, but not as unpleasant as the animal filth of Gereon.

All around, the grey-noise chirping and buzzing of insects.

The ground was firm under his boot as he stepped off the boarding ladder. Bright light from the yellow star in a powder blue sky combined with the warmth and scent to give the clearing the impression of a garden at the height of summer.

Sabine held a glass pad tuned to the navigation beacon. She pointed to the northwest. "That way, Commander."

The ground sloped easily up and down in low waves until they reached the edge of the forest. Resistance to their progress would come from the thick vegetation, and resist it did, a natural pike wall. The only thing for it was to hack through step by broiling step. Adrian used a short, wide blade for the task—two strokes and he could creep forward a couple of meters and do it again, time after time.

The noise startled small animals and large insects in the undergrowth, but the grass, brush, and vine was too thick to allow a good look at the fauna.

Sweat ran off him. He worked slow and steady, taking water at measured intervals. No breeze penetrated the interior of the primeval wilderness, and he estimated they had traveled less than a kilometer when he struggled to coax the last drops of water from his bottle. The short march burned him, the exertion equal to that of a daylong battle.

"You need to let us help," Mariel said. She carried his satchel and rapier over her shoulders.

"You can run back to the ship and get more water," he said, catching his breath against a smooth trunk. The ringing of odd insect sounds surrounded him. But another sound crept in, too…

"Adrian, you've got to let us help or you'll kill yourself," Sabine said.

The new sound, underneath that of the forest life, was light and effervescent.

"Adrian?"

He held up a hand. "Listen."

A few meters beyond he chopped through the brush into the path of a clear stream running quick over smooth stones.

"It flows roughly along the path we need to follow," Sabine said.

"Thank God for that." He scooped up water in his hands and splashed it on his face and head.

The easy walk alongside the stream cooled him and brought his heart rate back to normal. They covered several kilometers over the next hours.

The stream attracted all sorts of life. They saw familiar snakes and lizards, bats, and even a stealthy black shadow in the trees that Adrian took for a panther. None of the creatures were alien. This was a terraformed world, just like every other that sustained life.

Pushing on, he didn't stop until they came to the bright edge of another clearing.

Out under the sunlight were the remains of wooden structures; the old, grey posts and beams standing up through waist-high grass like the desiccated ribcage of a fallen giant. There was no noise, no movement, nor any other signs of human activity.

"How far to the beacon?" he asked Sabine.

"We're close. Less than a kilometer in that direction." She pointed to the north, past the wooden skeleton.

They entered the clearing, walking among the old timbers and remnants of mud-brick walls, all overgrown with grass and vine.

"It's an old village," Mariel said, ducking in and out of the carcasses of little houses. "Who lived here?"

"I don't know," Adrian said. "I was expecting to find Apex technology, not huts."

"There's more here than meets the eye." Mary Frances' voice was startling, having been silent for most of the long walk.

"Indeed," Sabine said. "Look at this."

She stood among the crumbling walls of a dwelling just a few meters square. On the stone floor, cracked and crisscrossed by crawling vines, a skeleton.

A pile of bone, brown and marbled, the flesh long since rotted away or eaten by scavengers.

No one spoke. What could be said for a long-dead person never known to the universe?

Sabine crouched down and took the skull in her hands, prying it out of the dirt, untangling it from vines. "Look here."

Behind where the ear would have been, embedded in the mastoid, a metal object.

"This person had a neural interface," Sabine said. "Why would someone with an implant live in a hut?"

"Let's find the beacon," Adrian said. "Then we'll find some answers."

There were no electronics. A system of massive deadbolts held the door closed, operated by a hand-crank. Reduction gears allowed the crank to turn with little more than the weight of a finger.

The door swung outward with barely any effort, its immense weight precisely balanced on its hinges. Attached to a low, thickly built blockhouse with sloping walls, it was the only visible evidence of a more advanced presence.

Diodes lit up the interior in flat white. The only feature was a square opening in the floor, four meters to a side and covered by grating, with a control panel mounted on a nearby pedestal.

Sabine examined the controls. She pressed a button.

A whirring drifted up the shaft, slowly growing louder, until the grating opened upward and a steel floor, complete with yellow-striped safety rails to waist height, filled the hole.

Adrian stepped aboard. The lift felt solid.

The women followed him, and they descended at the touch of another button.

Faintly lit, the shaft's steel walls soon transitioned to solid stone. The hot, moist air became cooler and dryer as they went. He estimated they had traveled forty meters or more straight down when the lift came to a smooth stop.

Stone surrounded them on three sides, but, on the fourth, there was only a wall of darkness.

One after another, red diodes on the ceiling flickered on, illuminating a tunnel carved from the rock.

Straight and short, the passage bored into the rock for no more than a hundred meters. It ended at a monolithic blast door.

Adrian stood in front of the portal, reached out, and put his hand on it. Smooth and cold, it was impossibly solid. He smacked it with the bottom of his fist. No give, no echo. He moved to the left side, inspecting a thin seam running vertically up from the floor.

A panel embedded in the metal came to life and a rectangular section receded a few millimeters into the wall. A similar panel awoke on the right side of the door.

A voice spoke from somewhere above them. A woman's voice. "Access to this Earth Union facility is restricted. Please proceed with biometric authentication."

"You need to use the scanners simultaneously," Sabine said to Mariel and the nun.

"Try your hand at it," Adrian said to Mariel with a smile.

"That's not even funny, Adrian."

After taking up positions, they pressed their hands to the metal. Both panels blinked.

The door began to raise up.

"That's surprising," Sabine said. "For all their security procedures, the system allowed the same person to authenticate on both panels."

"We aren't the same," Mariel said.

"Far from it." Mary Frances smiled at Mariel.

"Of course not. My apologies."

The door stopped moving after only a few centimeters.

There was a flash of light.

Adrian's hand went to his sword instinctively.

The glowing, holographic image of a woman flickered into their midst. "What are you doing?" she asked. Her voice was frantic. "You've got to get out of there, *now!*"

"Who the hell are you?" Adrian stayed his hand. He couldn't locate the source of the projection.

The image looked like Mariel, but wore spectacles, and was much older. Her clothes were of an ancient style, tight and edgy.

"You don't have time. She'll know you're here any second. Get out! Run!"

Back down the tunnel, the lift engaged and began its trip to the surface.

"Damn!" the holo shouted. She looked at Adrian. "Quickly, what's your name?"

"Adrian. Who are—"

"Adrian, please don't hurt them—they can't resist her. She won't kill you here—I'll help you later, if I can."

"Who the hell are you?"

The holo vanished.

CHAPTER 25

Adrian stared at the rigid formation in front of him. Was this phalanx of uniform, unvarying women the remains of the ASCNT Program? Each one looked like a severe, aboriginal version of Mariel. The sight forced bile up his throat.

Lean and hard, their skin was tanned, stretched over sinewy muscle, and they all stood in the exact same loose and ready pose, right foot forward, knees slightly bent. Their eyes told more of the story—sunk deep in their sockets, they were hazy, with the vacancy he'd often seen in the stare of dying soldiers.

They wore simple robes of raw, uncolored silk tied at the waist with wide sashes. Their hair was pulled back and tied—each identically. On their feet, simple slippers with wooden soles.

Each carried an ash spear of moderate length, with a long, narrow head of hand-forged steel. Tucked into their sashes, knives in leather sheaths.

The elevator had deposited the company and returned to the surface amid the whine of electric motors. The women formed a wall of muscle and bone, and behind him was the immovable blast door.

He faced two dozen of them, Mariel at his side with her sword in hand, Sabine and the nun behind them.

"Release your weapons. Sara commands," a woman in the front rank said, loud, but without conviction.

"Who is Sara?" Adrian asked. He held his sword at guard, working on the geometry of who to kill, and in what order. There was no good solution.

Assume they were competent in hand-to-hand combat. Assume Sabine and the nun were not. Unable to maneuver in their tight confines, Adrian visualized himself and Mariel cutting through six, seven, eight of them before being swamped by weight of numbers and impaled. Against an ideological enemy such a final stand would be honorable, but these weren't Saracens.

"Sara is root."

Sara is root? The hologram said they couldn't resist her.

The womens' bodies and stance betrayed nothing, no mental state whatsoever, but there was fear in their eyes. Adrian saw in them a desire to run away screaming like raw conscripts at their first sighting of the enemy, but they didn't. They couldn't?

"Will you take us to Sara?" Mary Frances asked.

"Yes," the anonymous woman replied.

"That's good, very good," the nun said. "Commander, let's not die at the hands of the auxiliaries."

He wouldn't kill them if he could avoid it, and with martyrdom off the table there were no tactical options. He sheathed his rapier, and unhooked it from his belt.

One of the native women grabbed it.

He turned over his dagger, and watched Mariel do the same with her sword.

"Turn. Hands behind backs."

He looked at Mariel and nodded. All four of them complied with the order.

Their hands were bound with dry, scratchy vine. Once secured, the door raised up and they were herded inside.

A stainless steel cathedral of eternal proportions lay ahead of them. A grand, airy nave with large transepts on either side. High-density diode displays stood in for stained glass, and brightly polished aluminum for gilding on fixtures and furniture. The blue and white flags and seals of the Earth Union replaced the cross.

It was all untouched.

"This is a chrome palace," Sabine said. Her eyes darted to and from the myriad relics, gleaming and blinking.

"Who is this Sara?" Adrian asked as they walked.

No answer.

He halted and turned, facing one of their captors. "Who is Sara?"

"Sara is root. Turn. Walk again." She pointed forward.

It was like talking to one of the idiotic *Machina* that attempted to mimic human conversation. The drink dispenser Mustafa had once installed in the galley came to mind. If you put your cup under the damn thing and said 'water,' you were as likely to get engine coolant or septic bilge. Either way it politely encouraged you to 'enjoy your beverage.'

Two of the women prodded him tentatively with their spears. "Turn. Walk again," they said in unison.

He turned and walked again.

They were led down a wide staircase to an assembly hall. The ceiling at the front was ten meters high, and the floor sloped up to the rear, with row after row of seats. Thousands of empty seats. The walls on either side were painted with murals depicting smiling people engaged in myriad forms of work, from farming to cobbling, and, above them all, the flag of the Earth Union.

They were marched down to the front and lined up before a podium.

One of the natives stepped forward and stood at the pulpit. "Identify yourselves," she said. When the women had spoken before, their tone was hollow. The one at the podium now—seemingly no different from the others—suddenly projected authority, filling the room with her voice.

"Adrian of Tarsus."

"Sabine Adler."

"Mariel of—"

"Silence," the woman said to Mariel. "You and the other rogue are program participants. Your aliases are irrelevant. You will participate."

The guards split into groups, one surrounding Adrian and Sabine, the other pushing Mariel and the nun out of the room.

"Adrian!" Mariel cried.

He started towards her, but the women instantly grabbed him by the arms, their grip firm. "Where are you taking her?" he demanded.

"You are not participants. Explain your function."

"What?" Adrian asked. "Where the hell are you taking them?"

His confiscated dagger was raised to his throat by a woman behind him. Mariel and Mary Frances disappeared through the door.

"Declare your function."

"Are you Sara?" Sabine asked.

"I am Sara. I am root. Declare your function."

"We need to use the medical facilities here," Sabine said, "to help Mariel, the girl you took. We have a field retrofit we believe needs to be used."

There was a pause. The speaking woman stood still, her face a blank. "Access denied. The participant's GENIE version thirteen point eight point one is sufficient to fulfill her function until end of life. Declare your next function."

"Go to Hell," Adrian said.

A longer pause.

"Error. Unknown location."

Adrian and Sabine's footsteps echoed down the cold corridor. Their captors clopped along behind.

The woman behind Adrian prodded him with the tip of his own rapier. She'd once spoken as Sara, but now acted like just another husk. Two others held the daggers taken from Sabine and Mariel.

"You weren't very diplomatic," Sabine said.

"It really isn't what I do, Bine."

"Ooh." She struggled against her bonds.

They marched up to a door labeled 'Life Cycle' which opened automatically. The room lights flickered on, revealing floors and walls of spotless white tile. A waist-high dais accented with chrome stood alone in the center of the room, surrounded by rows of chairs in a horseshoe configuration.

What the hell kind of execution was this? He needed to find a distraction. Could these things even be distracted?

The natives prodded him into the room.

"Welcome to Life Regeneration." It was the hologram they'd met at the entrance, now standing in front of the dais.

"Please enter and take your places," the holo said in a subdued, commiserative tone. "Services will begin promptly when all guests are seated. Would you like to hear an overview of the program?" The hologram looked at Adrian and nodded.

"Yes." Adrian felt the sword in his back.

The room lights lowered, becoming soft and warm. The white tile took on a golden hue.

He watched the hologram, locking eyes with it.

"This is a remembrance ceremony for two participants recently departed from the community. They should ignore me if I stay on script. Upon completion of the ceremony, the deceased will be removed to donate their remaining useful biological material back to the colony."

"How does it work?" Adrian asked.

"The first stage, carried out in the automated facility beneath us, involves a radiological cleansing of the corpse." The holo looked at Adrian intently. "Please ensure that all electronic devices are turned off during this phase, any failure of the room shielding could have adverse effects."

"On their implants," Sabine whispered.

He nodded. Their captors seemed to take no notice of their conversation with the holo.

"After sterilization, any useful organs will be reclaimed by surgical robots and used to extend the lives of other participants. Shall we begin?"

Adrian looked at the holo, then Sabine. "Fine," he said, preparing to clamber onto the dais.

"The female is first on the schedule," the holo said.

Two of the native women crowded Sabine, pressing her towards the dais.

"It's all right," she said, nodding at Adrian. "I understand the process." She sat on the platform, swung her legs up onto it and lay down on her side, her hands still tied behind her.

Music began to play, light and annoying. It was up-tempo and silly for a funeral, and devoid of emotion. The platform lowered Sabine down into the floor. She disappeared into darkness.

A panel began to close over the rectangular opening, sealing her inside.

Adrian looked to the holo, which seemed to be concentrating intensely on something he couldn't see.

A second later, the panel halted half-closed with a metal clank and the thrashing of gears. A bright flash of violet light crackled from within.

Their captors convulsed and exhaled sharply, dropping their weapons as they fell to their knees.

Adrian dropped to the floor and rolled on top of a dagger. He grasped the handle of the blade, turned it up and sliced through the bindings. Hands free, he snatched up his sword and the other dagger.

The natives groaned and cradled their heads, rubbing at the spot behind their ears where the implants were installed.

Adrian leapt for the half open hole in the floor. The panel snapped shut as he fell onto it.

"Not so fast," the holo said.

"Open the damned door!"

The native women continued to writhe.

Adrian glanced around. No choice now but to eliminate them. He raised his sword over the nearest head.

"No!" the holo shouted. "Do it and I'll kill the blonde!"

He stayed his arm.

"I have her strapped to a robotic operating table right now, ready to cut out her organs. Now, who are you?"

"I told you, Adrian of Tarsus."

"Tarsus? What are you doing here?"

The native women were still dazed, but they were shaking it off.

"My daughter. Mariel—the younger girl that Sara took. I'm here to save her."

"The two participants you brought with you," the holo said, more to her self than to Adrian. "One of them is your daughter? How can that be?"

One of the natives looked at Adrian and began to push herself onto her feet.

"Look," Adrian said, "I don't want to kill anyone I don't have to. Open the hatch."

The rest of the natives began to stand up.

"Fine." The door slid open.

Adrian grabbed the edge and dropped into the unlit room below. The hatch closed behind him.

"Sabine?" he called out.

"I'm here!"

Red lights came on. It was a tight space, full of equipment and robotics, with only narrow walkways to move in.

Sabine lay strapped to a perforated steel table under an octopoid array of mechanical arms wielding serrated blades, clamps, and other tools of dismemberment.

He reached to free her.

The holo reappeared, and a shining blade at the end of a thin robot arm flashed at Sabine's throat, stopping just short of killing her.

"Don't move!" the holo said.

A second arm dropped from the wicked ceiling fixture, and tentatively held Adrian at bay with a grooved sectioning knife.

"Who the hell are you?" Adrian asked.

"Doctor Roxanne Wallace, chief scientist for the ASCNT Program."

"You're a hologram," he said.

"Really?" She rolled her eyes. "I'm not letting you loose until I know who you are."

The sectioning knife poked at Adrian.

"I told you, I'm Adrian of Tarsus, Knight-Commander of the Order of Saint John. She's Sabine Adler…my wife."

"Don't kill us," Sabine said.

"Why shouldn't I?"

"All we want," Adrian said, "is to use the medical facilities here. Nothing else."

"How do I know I can trust you?" Wallace asked.

"You don't."

"You can! You can!" Sabine shouted, glaring at Adrian.

Wallace paused, semi-transparent eyes turned up at the ceiling.

The blade-wielding arms pulled back from Sabine's throat and Adrian's chest.

"Very well," Wallace said. "Between you and Sara, I'll gamble on you."

Adrian freed Sabine and helped her off the table.

"There wasn't much more I could do up there," Wallace said. "I'm stuck in one of the standby nodes and only have access to a few secondary systems. Luckily, I've annoyed Sara so much over the years that she filters me out unless I do or say something very unusual."

"Where's Mariel?" Adrian asked.

"In the surgical bay. You'd best move along now. Sara is occupied with your friends at the moment, but she'll receive an interrupt with news of this very soon if she hasn't already."

"Surgical bay? What the hell for?" Adrian started down the tight corridor, Sabine behind him. They ducked under power conduits and squeezed around fiber-optic cable trunks.

"Sara recognizes them as program participants. She's installing neural implants as we speak, to integrate them with the community."

"Like hell she will. Take us there."

"No."

"What?" Adrian stopped.

"It's too late to stop the procedure, but their odds of surviving implantation are very high. Listen to me, Adrian, you're the only chance I may ever have to save this colony from that bitch. I need you to—"

"I don't give a damn about this colony. Take me to Mariel, *now*." He shouted, slamming his fist into a status display, smashing it. He pushed on through the passage.

"You said you're a Knight of the Order of Saint John, Adrian?"

"I am. What of it?" he asked, searching for an exit.

"Also known as the Knights Hospitaler, if memory serves. I'd love to know how that organization came to be resurrected, but for now just answer this: is your order true to its Earthly roots?"

The place was an interminable maze, and even if he made it out, he had no idea where to find Mariel. He stopped and slammed his palm into the wall. "Yes, damn it. We protect the faithful, heal the sick, give of ourselves to the less fortunate."

"There are dozens of people on the surface just like those poor women back there. They're implanted at birth, and live their entire, wretched lives under Sara's control."

"Why don't they live in here, inside?" Sabine asked. "It's an incredible place."

Wallace wouldn't look Sabine in the face. She stared at the floor. "That was the plan, but I allowed errors to creep into the project specifications. Those errors cascaded into a spectacular failure of the Semi-Autonomous Recovery Agent, SARA, once she was activated."

"Recovery agent?" Sabine asked.

"There really isn't time to explain, just know that there are tens of thousands of participant embryos stored here. Sara can perpetuate this gulag almost indefinitely. There are real people living in those bodies, Sabine. They see, hear, and feel, but they have no control from the moment they're born until the moment Sara euthanizes them."

"These participants are all clones?" Adrian asked.

"We don't use that term," Wallace said, snappish. "They're participants in the ASCNT Program. Please see reason. In the time it would take to reach the surgical suite, the implantation will have been completed, and Sara will have deployed more participants to recapture you. The best course now is to get to the core and help me terminate her, freeing everyone, including your Mariel."

Adrian looked at Sabine.

"This place will be swarming with participants in a matter of minutes. Will you help me?" Wallace begged.

She made sense, and her appearance made it seem as though Mariel herself was pleading with him. He set his jaw and clenched his fist tight. "Which way do we go?"

For all the bunker's size, the maintenance pathways were claustrophobic and full of sharp edges, strobing status lights, and burning heat-sinks.

The Wallace hologram guided Adrian and Sabine through the maze.

"The main shaft is just ahead," Wallace said. "We're in the exact center of the facility."

"Here it is," Sabine said.

Metal rungs were mounted on the wall, with retracting hatches above and below.

Sabine hit the foot-switch to open the lower hatch. Nothing happened.

"These hatches don't lock," Wallace said. "Sara must be using the motors to force them closed."

Sabine knelt next to the hatch and opened an access panel. "'Motor, electric, general-purpose, model AN5-37.' I love how you people labeled everything so clearly, Roxanne."

"Standard practice," Wallace said. "And you can call me Roxie."

Adrian shook his head. A hologram named Roxie?

Sabine pulled a cable out of the open panel. "That should take power off it."

Adrian slid the hatch back into its recess. "No mere publican," he said.

"Thank you, Commander."

They slipped down into the room below.

"How many floors down do we have to go?" Adrian asked.

"Three more, to level eight."

Sabine began the process to open the hatch.

"Adrian?" Wallace asked.

"What?"

"What caused the recovery protocol here to activate?"

"Recovery protocol?"

"The RP was set to activate if a control signal from Earth was lost for three-hundred and sixty-five consecutive days. It started a series of processes to recover the human species on this planet. That's what all of this was built for."

"Earth is gone," he said as Sabine got the next hatch open.

"Gone? What do you mean, gone? What does that mean?"

"It means it's gone. We call it the Second Coming, or the Advent."

They dropped down another floor. Wallace reappeared beside Adrian.

"Oh, Christ," Wallace said.

"Exactly."

The holo disappeared.

"Bloody hell," Sabine said. "Where did she go?"

Adrian shrugged. "Should a hologram be emotional?"

"I don't think so."

They sprang the next hatch, and the next, dropping down into the level eight maintenance hub.

There was one door, and Adrian opened it a hair and looked out into an empty corridor. He stepped through, Sabine following close.

Diode panels lined the hallway, filling most of the wall space from floor to ceiling with a dizzying animated rendering of scrolling, flowing, and cascading data. Graphs, timers, alerts, and status reports competed for attention, all of it meaningless to Adrian who focused on a set of double doors at the end of the hall carrying the label: Logic Core.

"Amazing," Sabine said, staring in wonder at the displays. "Look at all the data. This is the most complex thing I've ever seen."

"Let's get this done," he said.

The whirring sound of an elevator filled the hall, followed by a happy tone from a hidden speaker.

"Quick," he pushed Sabine back into the maintenance room and pulled the door almost closed.

The soft clapping of wood-shod feet could be heard outside. He took a careful look. A squad of natives formed a bristling phalanx.

"Damn, there's twenty—no, thirty of them at least. Sara doesn't want us in there."

Wallace's hologram flashed on. "Adrian!"

"Shh," Adrian and Sabine admonished.

"Sorry," Roxie whispered. Her image darkened. "There's something strange happening. There's lots of movement in and around the bunker. More than just a hunt for you."

"Sara's brought in reinforcements down here," Adrian said. "At least thirty. Is there another way in?"

"No, this is the only true class-four security zone in the facility."

"We're going to have to distract them," he said.

"Sara has them scripted to ignore me, but I might be able to trigger an interrupt if I do something odd."

"You have to go in with Bine to shut her down. I'll be the distraction."

"Right," Roxie said. "You can lead them off down the hallway, then circle the outer ring. We'll need a few minutes, but once we terminate Sara, they should become disoriented and give up pursuing you."

"We'll see." He opened the door slowly.

"I don't really know what they'll do once they're free. They don't know what a man is, so they may be frightened or their instinct to mate may kick in. With a vengeance."

"Wonderful."

Before Adrian could leave, the chaotic sound of hand-to-hand combat erupted down the corridor.

"Christ, now what?" Sabine asked, ducking under Adrian's arm to get a look.

"Roxie?" Adrian asked.

"Yes?"

"Why are the participants fighting each other?"

"What?" She blinked out, returning a moment later. "They have no concept of hostility, Adrian. Sara is making them do this. Or..."

"Or what?"

"Sara's corrupt logic could be cascading again. The results are impossible to predict."

He stepped out and looked down the hall at the battle raging between the native women. "Well, we have our distraction now, at least."

"Please hurry," Roxie said, "before they kill themselves."

They approached the melee, Adrian with sword drawn.

The women stabbed and sliced at each other in an oddly mechanical display of brutality. Two bodies already lay on the ground bleeding out, with several more injured. None of the combatants seemed to notice them as they slipped by, hugging the wall, and slid up to the doors of the Logic Core.

"Biometric scanner," Sabine said. "How are we going to get past?"

"Okay," Roxie said. "We need to take power off the panel, then restart it with fingers pressed to the upper left and lower right corners; this will bring the glass up in supervisor mode. From there, we can edit the boot script to force the panel into EPRM maintenance mode—"

Adrian dashed into the middle of the fight, dodging spear tips and female talons. He grabbed one of the fallen bodies and dragged it back to the door.

He pressed the limp hand to the scanner.

The door opened.

"Or you can do that," Roxie said.

"I understand now," Adrian said. "These clones are copies of you."

"Then you can imagine what it's been like watching them be bred, enslaved, and slaughtered again and again for more than a thousand years. Sara dies *now*."

A hologram out for the blood of a computer program? Was this the first fully-electric vendetta?

The doors closed behind them, blocking the sound of the struggle.

Adrian's expectation of a huge, glowing God-machine with thousands of pulsing status lights and miles of wiring didn't materialize. The room was small, with several terminals, but no great Core of computing power.

"This is all of it?" he asked.

"Not quite," Roxie answered. "Look."

The wall at the back of the room was glass, from floor to ceiling. Opaque when they entered, it faded at Roxie's command, becoming transparent.

Adrian and Sabine stared out.

Pure white light bathed a chamber so vast the *Miranda* could alight in it with room to spare.

They looked down from above, onto a farm of computers laid out in a perfect sixteen by sixteen grid. Each node was a gleaming white tower three meters square and thrice as tall, pillars in a heathen temple.

"That's Nebula." Roxie said, reverent. "Bioelectric, Y-scale, self-repairing, and massively redundant. The hardest, fastest cloud ever designed."

"Sara is running on that thing?" Sabine asked.

"Yes. Sara is a relatively crude program designed to manage resources and bootstrap other processes—a bureaucrat if you will—but Nebula gives her immense power. She exceeds her parameters the same way a person of average intellect stumbles into authority then wields it like *homo erectus* with a wooden club."

"Let's end her," Adrian said.

Sabine sat at console and Roxie gave her a set of credentials to log in.

"Type *PS* and hit enter," Roxie said. "There, the SARA process with Process ID seventy-two. Now enter this command: *kill space dash-nine space seventy-two.*"

"Done," Sabine said. She entered *PS* again, displaying the list of running processes. "PID seventy-two is still running, Roxie."

"Kill dash-nine should kill anything. Let me see. Type *TOP* and hit enter."

A list of running processes and statistics filled the screen.

The door slid open.

Adrian turned to face two native women with short spears. The battle still raged outside, but one faction had formed a human wall around the Logic Core.

"Ladies," Adrian said, looking back at Sabine and Roxie, "Sara's sniffed out your assassination plot."

"Hold them off!" Sabine said.

"Don't kill them!" Roxie added.

Don't kill them. Damn it. He drew on the two natives, who approached with caution.

"She's blocking us in the kernel with an uninterruptible system call," Roxie said.

Adrian tuned it out.

The first native lunged with her spear.

He parried it under his left arm, then grabbed hold of the shaft. The woman wrenched and twisted it, trying to pull it free, while the other attacked. He foiled her assaults while the first native continued to tug to release her spear.

"Whenever you're ready," he said over his shoulder.

"Almost," Roxie said.

The participants weren't creative—couldn't adapt. The first one continued to try and free her weapon from his grasp, despite the futility of it.

He parried and blocked the other. The woman was fast and precise, but too predictable to gain an advantage, despite Adrian's handicap holding onto the other spear. "Take your time," he called back as the two natives strained and grunted.

Then, everything flickered. The lights, the computer screens—even the two participants Adrian held at bay twitched and fell back.

"Is that it?" Adrian asked.

"That's it." Roxie said. "After thirteen-hundred years...she's finally gone! When I get back into the primary node, I'm going to overwrite the bitch with a billion zeroes." She tried to throw her spectral arms around Adrian with predictable results.

"Where's Mariel?"

"Probably still in medical. I'll take a look."

Roxie blinked out.

Adrian put his hands on Sabine's shoulders. "How does it feel to be in command of the most powerful *Machina* ever built?"

"If we didn't have to find Mariel, Commander, I'd show you just how arousing all this is."

Roxie returned, holographic face somehow pale. "Adrian?"

"What is it?"

"We might have made a mistake."

CHAPTER 26

"Thank you, Knight-Commander," Mary Frances said over the intercom. "I now have complete control of this facility." The Nebula terminals flickered.

"I've been logged out," Sabine said. She tried to sign in again, and was rejected.

"She must be pushing back through the implant," Roxie said. "I can't imagine anyone overpowering all the input, though. The amount of raw data—it'd be like swimming up a waterfall."

"Where is she? Is Mariel still with her?"

"Yes, they're in the operations center."

Adrian keyed the intercom. "Mariel, are you all right?"

"Yes," Mary Frances said. "Your beautiful, sweet young lady is with me. Join us in operations."

Adrian turned the intercom off.

"What's she going to do?" Roxie asked.

"I've no idea," Adrian said, "but I assure you it won't be good. She's an agent of the Inquisition, and likely mad. Those women are under her control now?"

"Inquisition? What, are you people living in some sort of medieval theme-park?"

"Theme-park?" Adrian asked.

"Never mind. Yes, she's redeploying the participants through-out the site, to what end I don't know."

"Bine?" Adrian pulled the retrofit pad from his satchel. "This thing can communicate with the neural implant, right?"

"Right."

"Can we turn it to our advantage somehow?"

"Where did you get that?" Roxie asked.

"It's a long story. It took me years to find it for Mariel."

"She's a Mark Two, then. They were the first we considered viable for ASCNT, but, as you've no doubt discovered, there were flaws."

"It's a near-field device," Sabine said. "Its range is only a few meters."

"Better than nothing."

Sabine looked at Roxie. "We'll need to change the code to something that'll disable them without killing them."

"Hmm." The holo thought about it. "We could modify it to send the hibernate command. It'll put them into an unconscious mode we intended for medical procedures or long-distance space travel. It won't hurt them."

"Do it." Adrian handed the glass to Sabine.

The steel and glass door to the operations center slid open at their approach.

The corridor was lined on each side with clones standing in perfectly ordered rows, precisely positioned. A strangely pathetic honor guard for no one.

Adrian's eyes shot around the circular room full of status displays and computer terminals, falling on Mariel.

"Knight-Commander. Miss Adler. Please join me—we must celebrate." Mary Frances reclined in a large, swiveling chair at the center of the room.

Mariel stood beside the nun, a blank stare on her face.

"What are we celebrating?" Adrian asked as he made his way to Mariel.

"Why, the liberation of this facility from itself, Commander. You played an important part in it, surely you're pleased?"

He ignored her. "Mariel, are you all right?" He held her chin up with his finger and looked into her eyes. She was in there, somewhere, but like the other clones she couldn't break free from the implant.

"Release her, *now.*"

"Of course, Commander. I was only keeping her safe while you were away."

Mariel shook her head, and life returned to her honey eyes. "Oh, Adrian, they put this thing in my head and it tells me what to do and I can't stop it."

"I'm here now, love."

"How sweet," Mary Frances said. "You enjoy being a father don't you, Commander."

"Sometimes. Then there are the times when your child's in pain and you can't stop it. That's an aspect of Hell."

"You'll want to apply the GENIE upgrade to her. Based on the specifications I'm accessing now, it should be quite effective. I'd suggest taking her to medical for the procedure."

"Soon," Adrian said. "What about you?"

"I'm consolidating control of this site. It's a lot to wrap one's mind around. I feel like I'm learning to walk and talk again."

"Consolidating control to what end?"

"I thought we might talk about that later, privately."

"Now is as good a time as any."

"Very well." She stood. "I've learned much in the past few minutes. The ultimate goal of the ASCNT Program was to, shall we say, reboot the human race in the event of a large-scale catastrophe."

"Like the Advent."

"Just so, and I think it would have succeeded. Using the technology here to get a running start, the population could have approached Apex levels within a few hundred years."

Roxie spoke up. "That's true. We built anti-inbreeding controls into the participants to ensure rapid population growth."

"So what went wrong?" Adrian asked.

Mary Frances laughed. "You won't believe what they did, Commander. Doctor Wallace? Why don't you tell everyone how you buggered the whole thing?"

Roxie glared at the nun. "We gave SARA, the Recovery Agent, an insoluble problem."

Mary Frances clapped her hands. "Nicely understated. Here's what they did, Commander. They created a hierarchy of goals for SARA with survival of the species at the top. Then, they started adding qualifications to it. Protect the planet. Enforce equality. Level outcomes. Impose peace. There were over a thousand restrictions and secondary goals. One of them even states that if religion develops spontaneously, the infected participants are to be euthanized."

Adrian looked to Wallace, who stared at the floor.

"Another goes on at length about 'interdependent and over-lapping systems of discrimination or advantage,' which sounds more like rough sex than philosophy to me. Well," Mary Frances continued, "SARA loaded her instructions and within a few milliseconds determined that the greatest threat to the survival of the species must be the species itself. A quick analysis told her that the only way to meet all of her objectives was to keep the human population small, homogenized, and completely subjugated—in other words, prevent them from being human. Her most glorious decision was to birth only females. She thought it would promote tranquility! Tranquility among women! Lord Christ, I could not make this up."

"That's fascinating," Sabine said, "but what are your intentions?"

"There are over forty thousand embryos here; each will produce an untouched, uncorrupted mind." The nun turned to Adrian. "They're ours, Commander. Ours to shape, to teach, to indoctrinate in the faith. Ours, if you'll join me and our Holy Father. Imagine! An army—each soldier with the unshakable faith of an Inquisitor and the iron fist of a Knight. First we'll burn the reformist heresy out of Christendom, then, united under the Holy Father once again, we'll smash the Saracens and banish the heathens into the dark depths of space!"

Forty-thousand. In the last war, there were only a few battles that engaged so many men, counting both sides. The Order numbered less than three thousand—squires, sergeants, knights and all. As preposterous as it sounded, the opportunity was golden. With unity came strength and with strength, victory. Outcomes Christendom hadn't known in recent times.

"I can tell from the look on your face that you see the beauty of it, Commander."

"You aren't seriously considering this, are you?" Sabine asked.

Unity begets strength, begets victory. No one ever had a real choice, and to pretend that any of these people could have an open future was absurd. There'd been no choice when they took him from his detestable mother and turned him over to the Order. Forced or not, becoming a knight was an honor accorded to few, and the opportunity to fight for his people was a privilege he relished.

"I'm curious," he said. "What makes you think I'd find that appealing? That I'd join you?"

"I know about you, Adrian of Tarsus," Mary Frances said, smiling. "Born to a prostitute and cruelly used until the Inquisition exposed the vermin, saved you and turned you over to the Order. Now you have the opportunity to do the same—for thousands. The Holy Father has prayed at length over the matter, and God has told him that it was His design that a man like you should became involved in this."

His eyes met Mariel's.

She watched him, waiting.

He felt her questioning him without saying a word.

Never mind *them*, the anonymous forty-thousand, what did he want for *her*? Some semblance of a choice? The chance to nudge her life in the direction she chose, no matter how limited the options?

If he demanded that for her, he couldn't deny it to the others.

"No," he said. "We won't use this place to grow an army of slaves."

"Slaves?" Mary Frances shouted. "Slaves? To serve the Holy Father is an honor, not a yoke. You of all people should know that. They took you away and made you a warrior, made you fight. Do you consider yourself a slave?"

"This isn't about me. This is about the tens of thousands of people whose fates neither you nor I will dictate."

"Their futures are already dictated! What good is a choice between life as a serving wench or a whore, between shoveling manure or sucking off dustmen in a dark alley? It's all the same!"

"That choice—whether to shovel shit or to lie down and die—is what separates a free man from a slave. I'll be damned if they don't get to exercise what little sovereignty they have coming to them." He looked at Sabine. "And you'd be shocked what a mere serving girl can do when she ignores the limits imposed by her station."

Adrian took two steps towards the nun. His hand went to his rapier's grip. "Get out of that computer and free these people, now."

"You are a tedious, ungrateful man." Mary Frances laughed as she returned to her chair. "I gave you credit for intellect and devotion that you obviously do not possess. So be it. None shall stand in my way, least of all you."

Adrian whipped his blade from its scabbard, crisp and fast, taking up guard against the nun.

"Before you die," Mary Frances said, "I'm going to prove just how wrong you are about the efficacy of choice by giving you one."

He heard the rasp of a blade leaving its scabbard.

Behind him.

He pivoted.

He came face to face with Mariel, sword drawn and on guard, terror in her eyes.

"Adrian!" Sabine called out. A pair of clones pressed steel to her, pinning her against the wall.

"Your choices, Adrian? Kill the girl and I'll let the woman live, or, if you prefer, I'll run Miss Adler through and Mariel will live on. Either will become my servant, of course, but it's better than death, wouldn't you agree?"

"Let them both go," Adrian said, "or I'll kill you where you sit."

"Ha!" Mary Frances clapped her hands. "My clones can kill Miss Adler at the speed of thought, so please, do come at me." She leaned back in the chair, grinning, beckoning him forward with her fingers.

He reached for his satchel, finding the flap with the tips of his fingers—

Mariel lunged and thrust.

Steel blocked steel with a stinging chime, her blade meeting his parry and passing close by his side.

Mariel pressed the attack.

Under the nun's control his daughter's movements were fast but twitchy, like an old holo with missing frames. She bore down on him hard, saving nothing for defense, leaving herself open to deadly counter-attacks he couldn't launch.

Repelling the onslaught required a hand to parry and one to balance. The neural tool in his satchel was useless—a thousand kilometers away.

"Do you know what's in her mind, Adrian?" Mary Frances asked as the fight swirled. "Fear. She's terrified, as if you were Satan himself."

Adrian fought on the defensive, parrying, dodging, retreating. Warding off one assault after another.

"Yes, fear, but what else lurks in her?" The nun taunted him. "It's lust! She longs to be your whore, for you to take and deflower and use her like a Saracen slave-girl! Ha!"

His blood caught fire. He turned to the offense, ripping the initiative from her and pushing Mariel back.

"Come on, knight! It's one or the other!" Mary Frances shouted. "Dragging it out will only make it worse."

Mariel counter-attacked. She was relentless. Her sword an ethereal razor slashing, feinting, chopping at him.

"Adri—" Mariel said, voice agonized.

"She's strong! She's fighting me!" Mary Frances shouted. "I do hope you'll let me keep her!"

"—can't—"

"I'm sorry, love."

Mary Frances stood, fists clenched. "Do it!"

Mariel swung wide, crossing Adrian's body.

He leaned back, avoiding her stroke by a hair.

The nun's aggressive abandon left Mariel open to all manner of bloody reprisals.

He brought his blade down on hers with crippling force. Striking mid-blade, he pushed through, leveraging to warp and wind her wrist, wrenching the sword from her grasp, her fingers caught in the guard. Her wrist twisted, hideous and unnatural.

He knew the pain of such a knavish ambush, and he prayed her wrist wasn't forever mangled.

She looked up at him, her face stoic, but agony dripping from her eyes.

His left fist hooked round at her, its unyielding muscle and bone striking and sending her sprawling to the floor, mercifully unconscious.

He pulled the devil's hand back. Having brutalized her so horribly, it felt detached, not his own. It fell to the satchel as his eyes rose to meet Mary Frances'.

"As I suspected," the nun said.

Adrian pulled the glass out, activating it with his thumb as he kneeled and flicked it over the metal floor to Sabine.

The muscles in the clone's arms flexed. Blades, one at Sabine's throat and one above her stomach, moved to kill, slicing the skin and drawing blood as they sunk in.

The clones twitched and froze.

Dropping their weapons, they went limp and fell to the floor.

"Bine! The door!" he shouted.

He could only hope that the tool had penetrated through to disable the clones lining the hallway.

A long second passed.

Sabine's hand went to her throat, felt blood, but discovered only a shallow cut.

Adrian watched her regain herself.

She dove for the access panel beside the door, flicked open the clamp holding it, reached in, and ripped a handful of wiring out. A trail of sparks followed.

Mary Frances stood. "Fool. You can't change the outcome. I control this facility, this world, and you along with it. When I'm done with you, I'll have your young whore kill the elder one!"

Hate filled his veins—the kind of acid that burned a man's soul right out of him, leaving only a shell behind.

The struggle became an exorcism.

He advanced.

Mary Frances broke into a fit of laughter at his approach, waving a sword in the air. "You are truly a fool, knight. A stupid little puppy of an apostate barking and chasing your tail, skittering across the floor, falling on your face. A hard kick and you'll squeal, tuck that tail, and run until I catch and skin you."

Completely mad. The acid in his blood faded, replaced by the cold fire of a motivated warrior.

"Shut up and fight, bitch."

Her face twisted with black fury, and she brought her sword to guard. He couldn't read her. Her mind was too far gone to betray her. But, when her arm snapped her blade into position, it was with precision. And lightning-fast.

Attack!

He thrust.

Blade aimed at her heart.

Before his steel came close to touching her, she parried and offered a riposte so quick he could barely defend it. His own parry deflected the blade past his right shoulder. She missed by only a hair.

Her speed allowed her to take the initiative, and he found himself beating aside a series of strikes that seemed to come from random quarters. Not much power behind them, but neither was there any rhythm or pacing to make them predictable.

She didn't move at all like Mariel.

A searing pain lit up his left bicep as she struck a glancing blow, opening up a long, shallow gash.

"Adrian!" Sabine shouted, running towards him.

"Stay back!" he said.

"That's one," Mary Frances said, licking her lips. She didn't press the attack.

She had a right to be confident.

They took up guards again, and with shouts the clash resumed.

Immediately she was on offense, her sword coming at him in a continuous blur.

She tossed the blade to her offhand, changing the geometry of the fight. Before he could react, she bit at his left arm again, opening another, deep, painful cut to the ligament inside his elbow.

"Two," she said. Her voice pitched high.

Again she let him recover.

Adrian drew his dagger—a parrying tool to guard against another such trick.

He counter-attacked with his full strength.

If any of his blows were to hit her, it would surely sever a limb or pierce her thin body, but he couldn't touch her for her damnable speed.

They threw attacks and counter attacks at each other. She was like a dragonfly, moving effortlessly in any random direction she chose. Blood dripped from the wounds on his arm, slicking his hand and dagger, spattering on the floor.

Again she struck him. This time near the wrist. The dagger fell from his grip.

His left arm was shredded.

"Three. Don't worry little knight, it's almost over."

He would die.

He was stronger, but she was young, and held the advantage in speed, with an almost prescient ability to anticipate his movements and counter. At this extreme tempo he could only match her pace for a little longer.

He had to get his hands on her, if not his blade. She had to be close.

That would only happen when she put steel through him.

He fought off every instinct as they railed against the idea. It was either this or be slaughtered. He might not have her speed, but his precision remained unmatched, and he would need every bit of it to live.

They fought on, a whir of reflected light and piercing rasps of steel. He maneuvered, working against her frenzied assault until he created an almost imperceptible opening for her, offering the high inside line for a thrust while his own weapon lingered slightly above, ready to parry.

As he hoped, she seized on the invitation.

Her point came straight in like a long lance. Unchecked, it would enter between his fourth and fifth ribs, opening up his lung.

He twisted his wrist, bringing his blade down on hers.

Instead of beating her attack aside, he carefully guided her stroke down and to his left, deftly inserting her sword between his eighth and ninth ribs.

Oddly, he felt only the impact, as if a mailed fist had struck him hard. Her blade slid into him, and only as it exited his back did the thundering pain catch up with the lightning. He screamed under the agony, and she drove the blade in further, malice in her eyes, until the pommel was flush against him. He dropped his sword and struggled to keep his eyes locked on her.

She smiled broadly, exultant in her victory, lingering and savoring it.

Then, her smile fled.

His bloody left hand seized her wrist, closing around it and crushing it unmercifully. Blood oozed from the wounds on his arm as his muscles contracted.

She lost hold of her sword.

His right hand, now empty, shot up and closed around her slender neck, encircling it almost completely. Stepping close, he lifted her up, feet kicking and her free arm furiously thrashing at him.

In vain.

His grasp tightened. He felt her tendons failing under the constriction. Some part of his mind connected the nun's face with Mariel, and screamed to let go.

It wasn't Mariel.

She clawed at his hand, the vise around her throat, kicking at him wildly.

Odd snapping and popping sounds emanated from her neck.

Not Mariel.

She struggled like an animal in a trap as he throttled the demon out of her.

Mariel.

The pressure cut off her arteries. He heard the tiny wisp of her last breath as her brain starved for air.

Then she went limp.

He held her aloft and choked her for a long time to be certain, then dropped her into the blood pooling at his feet.

The pain crippled him. He could hardly breathe, but it seemed that he had missed his lung and probably liver.

He exhaled and tried to relax the muscles of his chest, then quickly pulled the blade out, hand over hand until it fell to the floor.

He followed it, going down on his knees next to the dead nun, all senses smothered.

CHAPTER 27

Wave after wave rolled in, spreading out into a sparkling glass sheet with veins of white froth before gliding down the sand to churn into the next swell with a roar.

Adrian lay somewhere between the sea and shore, listening to the hypnotic, chaotic noise rising and falling, over and over.

A gull called from above him, lost in the sun, and a fine spray brought salt to his lips, stinging his tongue.

At the same time, he tasted blood.

"Adrian?"

Sabine? Where was she? He looked around, surrounded by waves on all sides. The sun faded, and a frigid mist enveloped him.

"Adrian, can you hear me?"

"Bine. It's cold."

"Can you open your eyes?" she asked.

Open his eyes? They were already open, though heavy fog obscured his sight and the din of the waves grew angry.

"He's coming around," Wallace said.

"Adrian?" Sabine repeated.

"Bine." He opened his eyes tentatively. The light from the ceiling diodes was blinding.

She stood over him, blonde hair illuminated like a halo.

He laughed.

"What's so funny, Commander?" Sabine asked.

"Everything." No, not everything. "Where's Mariel? Is she all right?" He tried to sit up.

"Yes, yes. She's fine. Lie back now." Sabine pushed him down gently. "Doctor Wallace is taking good care of her."

Thank God. "I hit her. Hard."

"You had to. You knocked her out so that *thing* couldn't control her. It probably saved her life."

"Tell me I didn't hurt her badly."

"You made rubbish of her wrist," Wallace said, "but the surgical robotics here are the best. I estimate she'll retain ninety-five percent range of motion, maybe more—she's young, and a Mark Two."

"She's not a fucking Mark Two. She's Mariel of Tarsus."

"Of course," Wallace said. "You must understand, though, that her genetic engineering gives her advantages. Among them, rate and completeness of healing."

He felt the bed moving, raising him to an upright position. Eyes better adjusted, he looked around. There were others in the room, beyond Sabine and Wallace. Two clone women, now dressed in one-piece blue coveralls with the Earth Union seal on the back.

"What other advantages does it give her?" he asked.

"Strength and agility slightly better than average, and a predisposition to intellect," Wallace explained. "Most important, she's immune or resistant to many diseases, which will allow her to live fifteen to twenty percent longer than was average in my time."

The anesthesia he'd been under was rapidly wearing off. He felt first soreness, then searing pain in his left side.

An instrument next to the bed buzzed softly.

"How do you feel?" Wallace asked.

"Like I've been run through."

"Rate the pain on a scale of one to ten."

"Six…eight."

"That's a good sign. You'll be fine, but I'm going to give you some dihydrodone to keep you comfortable."

"What's that?"

"A potent synthetic opioid. Enjoy."

"We have to do something." Adrian twisted in his chair to shift his weight off his left side. The swelling was down, and the pain much reduced. He sat at a stainless steel table in the bunker's long cafeteria with Sabine, Mustafa, and the Wallace hologram.

"It's simple enough," Mustafa said. "They can be Muslim or Christian. Nothing else is realistic. Are there even forty-thousand Jews in the whole universe?"

Adrian stared at Mustafa, but said nothing.

"What?" the Turk asked.

"There's more than that. There has to be."

"I don't know of anything else. Maybe some Eastern rubbish about staring into a star?"

"Neither do I."

A silence followed, finally broken by Sabine. "If you're so disillusioned, Adrian, why do you still wear your Crusader's cross?"

"I'd be a fool to burn my own house down," he said. "And then there are some things in it worth holding onto."

"Torture and murder?" Roxie asked.

He turned his head face her. "Fellowship and a common purpose."

"I'll destroy them," Roxie said. "I'll turn off the cryogenics."

"I thought you loved them?" Adrian asked.

"These embryos are cells, Adrian, they haven't developed consciousness yet. They aren't human beings. There's nothing there to love."

Not human? "If you harm those women—"

"Please don't turn off the cryogenics, Roxie," Sabine said. "We'd rather not do that."

"Then leave them in storage until circumstances are more favorable," Roxie offered.

"That seems eminently reasonable," Mustafa said.

"Not here." Adrian said. "They know the location of this planet. When they figure out that Mary Frances isn't coming back, they'll send someone else." The worst part was not knowing exactly who 'they' were.

"So move them," Roxie said. "The freezers themselves aren't enormous, and their cryogenic systems are closed-circuit. As long as you provide reliable power, they'll be fine."

"To where, though?" Mustafa asked.

"Maybe Valetta," Adrian said, weighing the option. "I believe the Grand Master would see things my way, but…there'd be pressure, and someday a new Grand Master. No, it's too great a responsibility, maybe Roxy is right."

"Oh, do you think?" the hologram asked.

"Straight to hell with that nonsense." Sabine stood. "Over my dead body, *husband*."

"What's this?" Mustafa sat up straight. He pointed to Adrian, then Sabine. "Husband, and…"

"Wife," Adrian finished the observation in terse tone of a bark. "Right, then. Does *Miranda* have enough power to take them with us?"

Sabine sat. "What's the power load, Roxie?"

"One point seven kilowatts per unit. Times four."

"Yes," Sabine said, rolling her eyes up as she calculated. "Adrian, it should work."

"Good," he said. "We'll figure out what to do with them later." He couldn't imagine a scenario in which he'd let them sit forever frozen in a machine.

"How's that new brain working?" Adrian asked.

"It's not a new brain, Adrian," Mariel said.

Roxie's hologram moved to the bedside. "You may feel a bit disoriented for the first few days. The upgraded neural pathways take time to build out fully. Once we're sure everything's good, we'll have that implant out of you."

"I told you we'd fix you up." Adrian sat on the edge of the bed and tousled her hair.

Roxie smiled and blinked out.

"I knew you would, it was only a matter of time, but, Adrian?"

"Love?"

"About what Mary Frances said—"

"We don't have to talk about that," Adrian said, holding up a hand. "She was mad."

"I want you to know that I'm not afraid of you, and I never will be."

"I'm glad of it, squire." It was good that she wasn't afraid of him, but what about the rest of it? Didn't she want to clarify that, too? If she would just tell him that the rest of it was a lie, a demented taunt from a madwoman...

"I'm too old to be a squire."

"Too old? Truly?"

"I want to go to Valetta."

"What the hell for?" Was she going to say the one thing he couldn't stand to hear? Christ—she was.

"I'm going to join the Order. I mean really join—take vows."

A cold shiver came over him. "That's not what I wanted for you."

"Why not?" She sat up straight.

"You can do better. You're smart and strong. You could apprentice for a trade. Hell, Sabine would probably teach you the dark art of running a public house."

"Yes, because smart and strong people serve drinks or count money." She raised her voice. "I know full well what smart, strong people do, Adrian, because I've watched you do it for ten years, and I'll thank you not to try to deceive me."

"You have a choice, Mariel. I didn't." He stood and turned away from her.

"Don't turn your back on me! Don't you see you've succeeded? You've given me the opportunity to make this choice, at this moment, and I'm making it."

Succeeded? Hardly. "What are you going to do in the Order?"

"I'm going to become a knight, like you."

He crossed his arms and looked at the floor. "You understand that what you've seen on the *Miranda* isn't the typical life of a knight, don't you? I had to call in every favor I could claim to get this post, all so I could find this thing you needed."

"I'm not stupid, Adrian."

"I know, love." He shook his head. "I am. I'm the stupid one. Somehow, I got it in my mind that we were a family, and that we would be together. That we'd someday get past all this and find our own way."

"We are a family, and we always will be, but as you say, I need to find my own way. I have to do something on my own. I have to prove that I can. You have to let go."

Let go? How could a man just let go and send his little girl alone into a universe of malice? He'd failed, utterly and completely. She'd slip away now, into danger from which he couldn't protect her.

All because she had a choice, and made the wrong one. Or maybe it was worse—maybe she was doing this to spite him. A knife in the back because he couldn't love her the way she wanted?

Why couldn't he just say no? Put an end to the idea and refuse to hear of it again? Of all the things he was capable of, that wasn't among them. It never had been.

"Fine, then. I'll see to it that you get there." He turned and left her.

CHAPTER 28

Adrian awoke before dawn. He stared at the wooden beams of his ceiling, and then turned his head to look at Sabine, lying next to him, breathing soft through slightly parted lips.

As usual, she'd become entangled in the sheets during the night, leaving him uncovered—a pleasure in the cool morning air. He rolled out of bed, careful not to disturb her, and threw a long, loose shirt over his head. In the next room, he passed the table with the holo-projector. Its status lights were blinking, meaning Roxie was up to something. He stepped out the front door, closing it quietly behind him.

He'd found the town of Bursa, on a planet contested by the Corsairs, exactly as Mustafa described it. Incredibly, the Turk had neither lied about nor embellished his description of the little paradise. They'd set themselves up about a hundred kilometers to the south, on a sheltered bay ringed by waves of fertile hills under a sky presenting infinite shades of brilliant blue.

Equipment scavenged from Anance allowed them to build out their little village quickly, and he found himself living among one-hundred and nineteen women—counting Roxie—most of whom he couldn't tell apart. Thank God Sabine was blonde.

The situation wasn't as idyllic as some men might suppose. One-hundred and nineteen highly intelligent, headstrong women could, at times, push at the limit of his patience. He was happy, though, and busy, but also restless. If pressed, he might admit to being bored.

And Mariel was on Valetta, the home of the Order. The separation was as doleful today as it was more than a year ago.

Adrian's habit saw him at the beach at first light, walking naked out into the rising tide and swimming to one of the sandy islands a kilometer from shore. He would lie out for a while, until the sun was fully up, before swimming back to find Sabine awake and planning his day.

Today, as he returned to shore, he noticed two figures standing by the flat stone where he left his shirt.

He emerged from the ocean and was surprised to see that the pair were strangers. A man and a woman.

He stopped in his tracks, suddenly aware of his nakedness—the woman was no stranger.

It was Mariel.

She stood there looking like a knight, in leather and a lightweight chain hauberk covered by a white tabard. Her hair was shorter, but her eyes were just as bright and alive as always. At her side, a rapier, not unlike his own—plain, unadorned.

There was less girl and more woman in her bearing. Taller. Leaner, if that were possible, a bit more muscular, and with some swagger in the way she stood smiling with her hand on her hip. This wasn't a woman whose will had been crushed.

Perhaps he hadn't failed after all? What he saw in front of him was a miracle in progress. Maybe the act of volition itself was ennobling, above and apart from the object of one's will? Regardless, she was magnificent.

She averted her eyes.

He grabbed up his shirt and threw it on.

"How are you, love?" he asked.

Without a word she threw her arms around him, kissed his cheek, and then stole a quick, light kiss on the lips.

He shook his head, but closed his own arms around her and held her tight.

"I couldn't be happier. How's my fuzzy lion?"

"He's well enough, if restive. You're thin, have they been feeding you?"

The stranger's mouth hung open as he watched the reunion. "Fuzzy lion? Knight-Commander?" he asked.

"Who asks?"

"My name is Lucas, Brother Marc Lucas."

"Lucas? By chance from Civitate Dei?"

The young man hesitated. "Yes, sir. Originally."

"What do you want, Brother?"

"Grand Master Lazcaris sent me. And Sister Mariel."

Sister Mariel. She was a comrade in arms now, not just a daughter.

"Why?" he asked.

"I have orders for you." Lucas handed over a sealed letter. "I'm your new Lieutenant, and Sister Mariel is to be your Lance-Bearer."

"Why does a retired man need a Lieutenant and a Lance-Bearer?" The latter was the final step in a prospective knight's training—more than a squire, a social equal learning to lead rather than follow.

"The Grand Master's assessment of your status differs from your own, Commander," Mariel said. "I'm to remind you of the responsibility that comes with your rank, and to tell you—and these are his words, sir—that your little sabbatical is fucking over and that you are to extract your head from your arsehole and return to duty at once."

"That sounds like Guy Lazcaris." Adrian broke the seal and read the letter. "This is insane," he said after digesting it.

Lucas shook his head and pointed at the paper. "The Grand Master didn't tell me anything."

Adrian grinned and cleared his throat. "'The Order of Saint John requires you to—'" He stopped, looked at Mariel and Lucas, and refolded the letter. "The Order requires you come to breakfast with me. You've met my daughter already. Follow me and I'll introduce you to my wife."

"Wife and daughter, sir?" Lucas looked at Mariel. "Knight-Aspirant Mariel is your daughter? How—"

"That's right." Adrian cut him off short. "I'm a reform-minded man, Lucas."

"As am I, sir, though I'd not have said it so direct." Lucas walked alongside Adrian for a few steps, shaking his head. "In truth, I believed they sent me out here as punishment for being *too* reform-minded, but now I don't know what to think."

Adrian looked at his new Lieutenant through narrowed eyes. What mischief now?

The three crested a dune, feet digging into the fine white sand. What they saw on the other side stopped them cold.

A woman in black leather astride a muscular dapple-grey stallion, leading a score of armed men.

Anne Kresimir.

The rugged soldiers behind her wore mail over bright blue and gold-striped uniforms. Swiss mercenaries, sharpened by the incessant wars between the cantons. Serious opponents with pike, halberd, or, in this case, sword and buckler.

The horse reared up tall and snorted like a demon trying to break free from Hell.

With tight reign and pressure from her thighs, Anne brought the beast under a semblance of control.

So much for boredom.

"I said I'd hunt you down, knight!" Anne shouted from the saddle. "I knew your little girl would eventually lead me to you."

"Bloody hell. Who's that?" Lucas looked to Adrian.

"A malignant nun," Mariel said, nonchalant.

"Lend me a blade, will you love?" Adrian reached out and took the offered stiletto.

The light of the new sunrise flickered across the steel.

Far from **THE END**

ABOUT THE AUTHOR

I am a computer geek, history nut, aviation enthusiast, and very efficient procrastinator. I play tabletop role-playing games (Dungeons & Dragons, Shadowrun, White Wolf, etc.) like it's 1989. I like to listen to Bach, Van Halen, and Snoop Dogg in that order. I loves dogs. All of them. Since 2013 I've been working hard on this, *The White Light of Tomorrow*, my first novel, which draws on my interest in science fiction and my love of history and technology.

WEBSITE
DPIERCEWILLIAMS.COM

GOODREADS
GOODREADS.COM/DPIERCEWILLIAMS

MINDS.COM
MINDS.COM/DPIERCEWILLIAMS

FACEBOOK
FB.COM/DPIERCEWILLIAMS

TWITTER
TWITTER.COM/DPierceWilliams

PINTEREST
PINTEREST.COM/DPIERCEWILLIAMS